"The girl! Guard the girl!" screamed Revelation.

Cormac swung his eyes from Revelation's battle with the two demons to see Anduine being dragged from the altar by two men. He leapt forward, and the first of the men ran at him. As his mouth opened to reveal long curved fangs, fear struck Cormac like a physical blow and his pace faltered. But just as the creature bore down on him with terrifying speed, the boy's courage flared. The sword flashed up and then down, cleaving the demon's collarbone and exiting through the belly. With a hideous scream the beast died. Cormac hurdled the body, and the creature holding Anduine threw her to one side and drew a gray sword.

"Your blood is mine," it hissed, baring its fangs.

Their swords met in flashing arcs, and Cormac was forced back across the circle in a desperate effort to ward off the demonic attack. Within seconds he knew he was hopelessly outclassed...

By David Gemmell
Published by Ballantine Books:

LION OF MACEDON
DARK PRINCE

KNIGHTS OF DARK RENOWN

MORNINGSTAR

The Drenai Saga
      LEGEND
      THE KING BEYOND THE GATE
      QUEST FOR LOST HEROES
      WAYLANDER

The Stones of Power Cycle
      GHOST KING
      LAST SWORD OF POWER
      WOLF IN SHADOW
      THE LAST GUARDIAN*
      BLOODSTONE*

*Forthcoming

LAST SWORD OF POWER

The Stones of Power
Book Two

David Gemmell

A Del Rey® Book
BALLANTINE BOOKS • NEW YORK

A Del Rey® Book
Published by Ballantine Books
Copyright © 1988 by David A. Gemmell

All rights reserved under International and Pan-American Copyright Conventions. Published in the United States by Ballantine Books, a division of Random House, Inc., New York. Originally published in Great Britain in 1988 by Century Hutchinson Ltd.

http://www.randomhouse.com

ISBN: 0-345-41684-8

Manufactured in the United States of America

First American Edition: September 1996
Second Ballantine Books Edition: June 1997

10 9 8 7 6 5 4 3 2 1

Dedication

This novel is dedicated with great affection to the many people who have made my trips to Birmingham full of enchantment. To Rog Peyton, Dave Holmes, and Rod Milner of *Andromeda* for the fun and the liquor; to Bernie Evans and the Brum Group for the magic of *Novacon*; to Chris and Pauline Morgan for the mysteries of the "Chinese"; and to the staff of the Royal Angus Hotel for smiling in the face of sheer lunacy.

Acknowledgments

Last Sword of Power, as with all my other novels, is the result of many months of hard work from a gifted team. Without them my poor spelling, lousy punctuation, and talent for split infinitives would be far more widely known. To my editor, Liza Reeves, and my copy editor, Jean Maund, many thanks. I am also more than grateful to my "readers" Edith Graham and Tom Taylor and my proofreader Stella Graham. Thanks also to my father-in-law, Denis Ballard, for supplying the research on Roman Britain.

Prologue

REVELATION STOOD WITH his back to the door, his broad hands resting on the stone sill of the narrow window, his eyes scanning the forests below as he watched a hunting hawk circling beneath the bunching clouds.

"It has begun, my lord," said the elderly messenger, bowing to the tall man in the monk's robes of brown wool.

Revelation turned slowly, his smoke-gray eyes fastening on the man, who looked away, unable to bear the intensity of the gaze.

"Tell it all," said Revelation, slumping in an ivory-inlaid chair before his oak desk and gazing absently at the parchment on which he had been working.

"May I sit, my lord?" the messenger asked softly, and Revelation looked up and smiled.

"My dear Cotta, of course you may. Forgive my melancholy. I had hoped to spend the remaining days of my life here in Tingis. The African weather suits me, the people are friendly, and with the exception of Berber raids, the country is restful. And I have almost completed my book . . . but then, such ventures will always take second place to living history."

Cotta sank gratefully into a high-backed chair, his bald

head gleaming with sweat, his dark eyes showing his fatigue. He had come straight from the ship, eager to unburden himself of the bad news he carried yet loath to load the weight on the man before him.

"There are many stories of how it began. All are contradictory or else extravagantly embroidered. But as you suspected, the Goths have a new leader of uncanny powers. His armies are certainly invincible, and he is cutting a bloody path through the northern kingdoms. The Sicambrians and the Norse have yet to find him opposing them, but their turn will come."

Revelation nodded. "What of the sorcery?"

"The agents of the Bishop of Rome all testify that Wotan is a skilled nigromancer. He has sacrificed young girls, launching his new ships across their spread-eagled bodies. It is vile . . . all of it. And he claims to be a god!"

"How do the man's powers manifest themselves?" asked the abbot.

"He is invincible in battle. No sword can touch him. But it is said he makes the dead walk—and more than walk. One survivor of the battle in Raetia swears that at the end of the day the dead Goths rose in the midst of the enemy, cutting and killing. Needless to add, the opposition crumbled. I have only the one man's word for this tale, but I think he was speaking the truth."

"And what is the talk among the Goths?"

"They say that Wotan plans a great invasion of Britannia, where the magic is strongest. Wotan says the home of the Old Gods is Britannia and the gateway to Valhalla is at Sorviodunum, near the Great Circle."

"Indeed it is," whispered Revelation.

"What, my lord abbot?" asked Cotta, his eyes widening.

"I am sorry, Cotta, I was thinking aloud. The Great Circle has always been considered a place of magic by the Druids—and others before them. And Wotan is right. It is a gateway of sorts, and he must not be allowed to pass through it."

"I cannot think there is a single army to oppose him, except the Blood King, and our reports say he is sorely beset by rebellion and invasion in his own land. Saxons, Jutes, Angles, and even British tribes rise against him regularly. How would he fare against twenty thousand Gothic warriors led by a sorcerer who cannot be bested?"

Revelation smiled broadly, his woodsmoke eyes twinkling with sudden humor. "Uther can never be underestimated, my friend. He, too, has never known defeat . . . and he carries the Sword of Power, Cunobelin's blade."

"But he is an old man now," said Cotta. "Twenty-five years of warfare must have taken their toll. And the Great Betrayal . . ."

"I know the history," Revelation snapped. "Pour us some wine while I think."

The abbot watched as the older man filled two copper goblets with deep red wine, accepting one of them with a smile to offset the harshness of his last response.

"Is it true that Wotan's messengers seek out maidens with special talents?"

"Yes. Spirit seers, healers, speakers in tongues . . . it is said he weds them all."

"He kills them," said Revelation. "It is where his power lies."

The abbot rose and moved to the window, watching the sun sink in fire. Behind him Cotta lit four candles, then waited in silence for several minutes. At last he spoke. "Might I ask, my lord, why you are so concerned about events across the world? There have always been wars. It is the curse of man that he must kill his brothers, and some argue that God himself made this the punishment for Eden."

Revelation turned from the glory of the sunset and went back to his chair.

"All life, Cotta, is balanced. Light and dark, weak and strong, good and evil. The harmony of nature. In perpetual darkness all plants would die. In perpetual sunlight they would wither and burn. The balance is everything. Wotan must be opposed lest he become a god—a dark and malicious god, a blood drinker, a soul stealer."

"And you will oppose him, my lord?"

"I will oppose him."

"But you have no army. You are not a king or a warlord."

"You do not know what I am, old friend. Come, refill the goblets, and we will see what the graal shows."

Revelation moved to an oak chest and poured water from a clay jug into a shallow silver bowl, carrying it carefully to the desk. He waited until the ripples had died and then lifted a golden stone above the water, slowly circling it. The candle flames guttered and died without a hint of breeze, and Cotta found himself leaning forward, staring into the velvet-dark water of the bowl.

The first image that appeared was that of a young boy, red-haired and wild-eyed, thrusting at the air with a wooden sword. Nearby sat an older warrior, a leather cup strapped over the stump where his right hand should have been. Revelation watched them closely, then passed his hand over the surface. Now the watchers could see blue sky and a young girl in a pale green dress sitting beside a lake.

"Those are the mountains of Raetia," whispered Cotta. The girl was slowly plaiting her dark hair into a single braid.

"She is blind," said Revelation. "See how her eyes face the sun unblinking."

Suddenly the girl's face turned toward them. "Good morning," she said, the words forming without sound in both men's minds.

"Who are you?" asked Revelation softly.

"How strange," she replied. "Your voice whispers like the morning breeze and seems so far away."

"I am far away, child. Who are you?"

"I am Anduine."

"And where do you live?"

"In Cisastra with my father, Ongist. And you?"

"I am Revelation."

"Are you a friend?"

"I am indeed."

"I thought so. Who is that with you?"

"How do you know there is someone with me?"

"It is a gift I have, Master Revelation. Who is he?"

"He is Cotta, a monk of the White Christ. You will meet him soon; he also is a friend."

"This I knew. I can feel his kindness."

Once more Revelation moved his hand across the water. Now he saw a young man with long, raven-dark hair leading a fine herd of Sicambrian horses in the vales beyond Londinium. The man was handsome, with a finely boned face framed by a strong, clean-shaven jaw. Revelation studied the rider intently.

This time the water shimmered of its own accord, a dark storm cloud hurling silent spears of jagged lightning streaming across a night sky. From within the cloud came a flying creature with leather wings and a long wedge-shaped head. On its back sat a yellow-bearded warrior; his hand rose, and lightning flashed toward the watchers. Revelation's arm shot forward just as the water parted; white light speared up into his hand, and the stench of burning flesh filled the room. The water steamed and bubbled, vanishing in a cloud of vapor. The silver bowl sagged and flowed down onto the table, a hissing black and silver stream that caused the wood to blaze. Cotta recoiled as he saw Revelation's blackened hand. The abbot lifted the golden stone and touched it to the seared flesh. It healed instantly, but even the magic could not take away the memory of the pain, and Revelation sagged back into his chair, his heart pounding and cold sweat on his face. He took a deep breath and stared at the smoldering wood. The flames died, the smoke disappearing as around them the candles flared into life.

"He knows of me, Cotta. But because he attacked me, I learned of him. He is not quite ready to plunge the world into darkness; he needs one more sacrifice."

"For what?" whispered the old man.

"In the language of this world? He seeks to open the gates of hell."

"Can he be stopped?"

Revelation shrugged. "We will see, my friend. You must take ship for Raetia and find Anduine. From there take her to Britannia, to Noviomagus. I will meet you in three months. Once there you will find an inn in the southern quarter, called, I believe, the Sign of the Bull. Come every day at noon and wait one hour. I shall join you when I can."

"The blind girl is the sacrifice?"

"Yes."

"And what of the red-haired boy and the rider?"

"As yet I do not know. Friends or enemies . . . only time will tell. The boy looked familiar, but I cannot place him. He was wearing Saxon garb, and I have never journeyed among the Saxons. As for the rider, I know him; his name is Ursus, and he is of the House of Merovee. He has a brother, I think, and he yearns to be rich."

"And the man on the dragon?" Cotta asked softly.

"The enemy from beyond the Mist."

"And is he truly Wotan, the gray god?"

Revelation sipped his wine. "Wotan? He has had many names. To some he was Odin the One-Eyed, to others Loki. In the east they called him Purgamesh, or Molech, or even Baal. Yes, Cotta, he is divine—immortal if you will. And where he walks, chaos follows."

"You speak as if you knew him."

"I know him. I fought him once before."

"What happened?"

"I killed him, Cotta," answered the abbot.

◊ 1 ◊

GRYSSTHA WATCHED AS the boy twirled the wooden sword, lunging and thrusting at the air around him. "Feet, boy; think about your feet!"

The old man hawked and spit on the grass, then scratched at the itching stump of his right wrist. "A swordsman must learn balance. It is not enough to have a quick eye and a good arm—to fall is to die, boy."

The youngster thrust the wooden blade into the ground and sat beside the old warrior. Sweat gleamed on his brow, and his sky-blue eyes sparkled.

"But I am improving, yes?"

"Of course you are improving, Cormac. Only a fool could not."

The boy pulled clear the weapon, brushing dirt from the whittled blade. "Why is it so short? Why must I practice with a Roman blade?"

"Know your enemy. Never care about his weaknesses; you will find those if your mind has skill. Know his strengths. They conquered the world, boy, with just such swords. You know why?"

"No."

Grysstha smiled. "Gather me some sticks, Cormac. Gather me sticks you could break easily with finger and thumb." As the boy grinned and moved off to the trees, Grysstha watched him, allowing the pride to shine now that the boy could not see him closely.

Why were there so many fools in the world? he thought as pride gave way to anger. How could they not see the potential in the lad? How could they hate him for a fault that was not his?

"Will these do?" asked Cormac, dropping twenty finger-thin sticks at Grysstha's feet.

"Take one and break it."

"Easily done," said Cormac, snapping a stick.

"Keep going, boy. Break them all."

When the youngster had done so, Grysstha pulled a length of twine from his belt. "Now gather ten of them and bind them together with this."

"Like a beacon brand, you mean?"

"Exactly. Tie them tight."

Cormac made a noose of the twine, gathered ten sticks, and bound them tightly together. He offered the four-inch-thick brand to Grysstha, but the old man shook his head.

"Break it," he ordered.

"It is too thick."

"Try."

The boy strained at the brand, his face reddening and the muscles of his arms and shoulders writhing under his red woolen shirt.

"A few moments ago you snapped twenty of these sticks, but now you cannot break ten."

"But they are bound together, Grysstha. Even Calder could not break them."

"That is the secret the Romans carried in their short swords. The Saxon fights with a long blade, swinging it wide. His comrades cannot fight close to him, for they might be struck by his slashing sword, so each man fights alone, though there are ten thousand in the fray. But the Roman, with his gladius—he locks shields with his comrades, and his blade stabs like a viper bite. Their legions were like that brand, bound together."

"And how did they fail if they were so invincible?"

"An army is as good as its general, and the general is only a reflection of the emperor who appoints him. Rome has had her day. Maggots crawl in the body of Rome, worms writhe in the brain, rats gnaw at the sinews."

The old man hawked and spit once more, his pale blue eyes gleaming.

"You fought them, did you not?" said Cormac. "In Gallia and Italia?"

"I fought them. I watched their legions fold and run before the dripping blades of the Goths and the Saxons. I could have wept then for the souls of the Romans that once were. Seven legions we crushed until we found an enemy worth fighting: Afrianus and the Sixteenth. Ah, Cormac, what a day! Twenty thousand lusty warriors, drunk with victory, facing one legion of five thousand men. I stood on a hill and looked down upon them, their bronze shields gleaming. At the center, on a pale stallion, sat Afrianus himself. Sixty years old and, unlike his fellows, bearded like a Saxon. We hurled ourselves upon them, but it was like water falling on a stone. Their line held. Then they advanced and cut us apart. Fewer than two thousand of us escaped into the forests. What a man! I swear there was Saxon blood in him."

"What happened to him?"

"The emperor recalled him to Rome, and he was assassinated." Grysstha chuckled. "Worms in the brain, Cormac."

"Why?" queried the boy. "Why kill an able general?"

"Think on it, boy."

"I can make no sense of it."

"That is the mystery, Cormac. Do not seek for sense in the tale. Seek for the hearts of men. Now, leave me to watch these goats swell their bellies and get back to your duties."

The boy's face fell. "I like to be here with you, Grysstha. I . . . I feel at peace here."

"That is what friendship is, Cormac Daemonsson. Take strength from it, for the world does not understand the likes of you and me."

"Why are you my friend, Grysstha?"

"Why does the eagle fly? Why is the sky blue? Go now. Be strong."

Grysstha watched as the lad wandered disconsolately from the high meadow toward the huts below. Then the old warrior swung his gaze up to the horizon and the low, scudding clouds. His stump ached, and he pulled the leather cap from his wrist, rubbing at the scarred skin. Reaching out, he tugged the wooden blade from the ground, remembering the days when his own sword had had a name and a history and, more, a future.

But that had been before the day fifteen years ago when the Blood King had cleaved the South Saxon, butchering and burning, tearing the heart from the people and holding it above their heads in his mailed fist. He should have killed them all, but he did not. He made them swear an oath of allegiance and lent them coin to rebuild ruined farms and settlements.

Grysstha had come close to killing the Blood King in

the last battle. He had hacked his way into the shield square, cutting a path toward the flame-haired king, when a sword had slashed down across his wrist, almost severing his hand. Then another weapon had hammered into his helm and he had fallen, dazed. He had struggled to rise, but his head was spinning. When at last he regained consciousness, he opened his eyes to find himself gazing at the Blood King, who was kneeling beside him. Grysstha's fingers reached out for the man's throat, but there were no fingers—only a bloody bandage.

"You were a magnificent warrior," said the Blood King. "I salute you!"

"You cut off my hand!"

"It was hanging by a thread. It could not be saved."

Grysstha forced himself to his feet, staggered, then gazed around him. Bodies littered the field, and Saxon women were moving among the corpses, seeking lost loved ones.

"Why did you save me?" snarled Grysstha, rounding on the king.

The man merely smiled and turned on his heel. Flanked by his guards, he strode from the field to a crimson tent by a rippling stream.

"Why?" bellowed Grysstha, falling to his knees.

"I do not think he knows himself," said a voice, and Grysstha looked up.

Leaning on an ornate crutch carved from dark shining wood was a middle-aged Briton with a wispy gray-blond beard over a pointed chin. Grysstha saw that his left leg was twisted and deformed. The man offered the Saxon his hand, but Grysstha ignored it and pushed himself to his feet.

"He sometimes relies on intuition," the man said gently, his pale eyes showing no sign of offense.

"You are of the tribes?" said Grysstha.

"Brigante."

"Then why follow the Roman?"

"Because the land is his and he is the land. My name is Prasamaccus."

"So I live because of the king's whim?"

"Yes. I was beside him when you charged the shield wall; it was a reckless action."

"I am a reckless man. What does he mean to do with us now? Sell us?"

"I think he means to leave you in peace."

"Why would he do anything so foolish?"

Prasamaccus limped to a jutting boulder and sat. "A horse kicked me," he said, "and my leg was not strong before that. How is your hand?"

"It burns like fire," said Grysstha, sitting beside the tribesman, his eyes on the women still searching the field of battle as the crows circled, screeching their hunger.

"He says that you also are of the land," said Prasamaccus. "He has reigned for ten years. He sees Saxons and Jutes and Angles and Goths being born in this Island of Mist. They are no longer invaders."

"Does he think we came here to serve a Roman king?"

"He knows why you came: to plunder and kill and grow rich. But you stayed to farm. How do you feel about the land?"

"I was not born here, Prasamaccus."

The Brigante smiled and held out his left hand. Grysstha looked down at it and then took it in the warrior's grip, wrist to wrist.

"I think that is a good first use of your left hand."

"It will also learn to use a sword. My name is Grysstha."

"I have seen you before. You were at the great battle near Eboracum the day the king came home."

Grysstha nodded. "You have a good eye and a better memory. It was the Day of the Two Suns. I have never seen the like since, nor would I wish to. We fought alongside the Brigante that day, and the coward-king Eldared. Were you with him?"

"No. I stood under the two suns with Uther and the Ninth Legion."

"The Day of the Blood King. Nothing has been right since then. Why can he not be beaten? How does he always know where to strike?"

"He is the land, and the land knows."

Grysstha said nothing. He had not expected the man to betray the king's secret.

Of seven thousand Saxon warriors who had begun the battle, a mere eleven hundred remained. Uther required them to kneel and swear a blood oath never to rise against him again. In return the land would be theirs, as before, but now by right and not by conquest. He also left them their own king, Wulfhere, son of Orsa, son of Hengist. It was a brave move. Grysstha knelt with the others in the dawn light before the king's tent, watching as Uther stood with the boy Wulfhere.

The Saxons smiled even in defeat, for they knew they knelt not before the conqueror but before their own sovereign lord.

The Blood King knew it, too.

"You have my word that our friendship is as strong as this blade," he said, hoisting the Sword of Cunobelin high into the air, where the dawn sun glistened like fire on the steel. "But friendship has a price. This sword will accept no other swords in the hands of the Saxon." An angry murmur rippled among the kneeling men. "Be true to your word and this may change," said the king, "but if you are not true, I shall return, and not one man, not one woman, not one squalling babe will be left alive from Anderida to Venta. The choice is yours."

Within two hours both the king and his army had departed, and the stunned Saxons gathered in the Council of Wotan. Wulfhere was only twelve and could not vote, and Calder was appointed steward to help him govern. The rest of the day was devoted to the election of men to the council. Only two survived out of the original eighteen, but by dusk the positions had been filled once more.

Two hours after dawn the eighteen met, and the real business began. Some were for heading east and linking with Hengist's son, Drada, who was, after all, Wulfhere's uncle and blood kin. Others were for waiting until another army could be gathered. Still more suggested sending for aid across the water, where the Merovingian wars were displacing fighting men.

Two events turned the day. At noon a wagon arrived bearing gifts of gold and silver from the king, to be distributed "as the council sees fit." This gift alone meant that food could be bought for the savage winter ahead, along with blankets and trade goods from the Merovingians in Gallia.

Second, the steward Calder made a speech that would live long in the minds, if not the hearts, of his listeners.

"I fought the Blood King, and my sword dripped red with the blood of his guards. But why did we fight him? Ask yourselves that. I say it was because we felt he could be beaten and there would be plunder from Venta,

Londinium, Dubris, and all the other merchant towns. But now we know. He cannot be beaten . . . not by us . . . perhaps not by Drada. You have seen the wagon—more coin than we could have taken in a campaign. I say we wait and judge his word: return to our farms, make repairs, gather harvests where we can."

"Men without swords, Calder. How, then, shall we reach Valhalla?" shouted a tall warrior.

"I myself follow the White Christ," said Calder, "so I have no interest in Valhalla. But if it worries you, Snorri, then join Drada. Let any man who wishes to fight on do the same. We have been offered friendship, and surely there are worse things in the world to receive from a conqueror than a wagon of gold."

"It is because he fears us," said Snorri, lurching to his feet. "I say we use his gold to buy men and arms and then march on Camulodunum."

"You will perhaps take the barn with you on your campaign," said Calder. Laughter followed his words, for it was well known that Snorri had hidden from the Romans under a blanket in the broad barn, running clear only when the enemy put it to the torch. He had been voted to the council merely on the strength of his landholdings.

"I was cut off, and it was that or die," said Snorri. "I'll take my gold and join Drada."

"No one takes the gold," said Calder. "The gift is to the council, and we will vote on its use."

At the last, Snorri and four other landsmen, with more than two hundred men, joined Drada; the rest remained to build a new life as vassals of the Blood King.

For Grysstha the decision tasted of ashes. But he was Calder's carle and was pledged to obey him, and the decisions of the great rarely concerned him.

That night, as he stood alone on High Hill, Calder came to him.

"You are troubled, my friend?" the steward asked.

"The Days of Blood will come again. I can feel it in the whisper of the wind. The crows know it, too."

"Wise birds, crows. The eyes of Odin."

"I heard you told them you followed the White Christ."

"You think the Blood King had no ears at our meeting? You think Snorri and his men will live to join Drada? Or that any of us would have been left alive had I not spoken as I did? No, Grysstha. I follow the Old Gods who understood the hearts of men."

"And what of the treaty with Uther?"

"We will honor it as long as it suits us, but one day you will be avenged for the loss of your sword arm. I had a dream last night, and I saw the Blood King standing alone on the top of a hill, his men all dead around him and his banner broken. I believe Odin sent that dream; it is a promise for the future."

"It will be many years before we are that strong again."

"I am a patient man, my friend."

The Blood King slowly dismounted, handing the reins of his warhorse to a silent squire. All around him the bodies of the slain lay where they had fallen, under a lowering sky and a dark cloud of storm crows waiting to feast.

Uther removed his bronze helm, allowing the breeze to cool his face. He was tired now, more tired than he would allow any man to see.

"You are wounded, sire," said Victorinus, approaching

through the gloom, his dark eyes narrowed in concern at the sight of blood seeping from the gash in the king's arm.

"It is nothing. How many men did we lose?"

"The stretcher bearers are still out, sire, and the surgeon is too busy to count. I would say around eight hundred, but it might be less."

"Or more?"

"We are harrying the enemy to the coast. Will you change your mind about not burning their ships?"

"No. Without ships they cannot retreat. It would cost nearly a legion to destroy their army utterly, and I do not have five thousand men to spare."

"Let me bind your arm, sire."

"Stop fussing over me, man! The wound is sealed— well, almost. Look at them," said the king, pointing to the field between the stream and the lake and the hundreds of bodies lying twisted in death. "They came for plunder. Now the crows will feast on their eyes. And will the survivors learn? Will they say, 'Avoid the realm of the Blood King'? No, they will return in their thousands. What is it about this land that draws them?"

"I do not know, sire, but as long as they come, we will kill them," said Victorinus.

"Always loyal, my friend. Do you know what today is?"

"Of course, my lord. It is the Day of the Blood King."

Uther chuckled. "The Day of the Two Suns. Had I known then that a quarter century of war would follow . . ." He lapsed into silence.

Victorinus removed his plumed helm, allowing his white hair to flow free in the evening breeze. "But you always conquer, my lord. You are a legend from Camulodunum to Rome, from Tingis to Byzantium: the Blood

King who has never known defeat. Come, your tent is ready. I will pour you some wine."

The king's tent had been pitched on the high ground overlooking the battlefield. Inside a brazier of coals was glowing beside the cot bed. Uther's squire, Baldric, helped him out of his chain mail, his breastplate, and his greaves, and the king sank gratefully to the cot.

"Today I feel my age," he said.

"You should not fight where the battle is thickest. A chance arrow, a lucky blow . . ." Victorinus shrugged. "We . . . Britain . . . could not stand without you." He passed the king a goblet of watered wine, and Uther sat up and drank deeply.

"Baldric!"

"Yes, my lord."

"Clean the sword—and be careful, for it is sharper than sin."

Baldric smiled and lifted the great Sword of Cunobelin, carrying it from the tent. Victorinus waited until the lad had gone, then pulled up a canvas stool and sat beside the monarch.

"You are tired, Uther. Leave the Trinovante uprising to Gwalchmai and me. Now that the Goths have been crushed, the tribes will offer little resistance."

"I will be fine after a night's sleep. You fuss over me like an old woman!"

Victorinus grinned and shook his head, and the king lay back and closed his eyes. The older man sat unmoving, staring at the face of his monarch—the flaming red hair and the silver-blond beard—and remembered the youth who had crossed the borders of hell to rescue his country. The hair was henna-dyed now, and the eyes seemed older than time.

For twenty-five years this man had achieved the impossible, holding back the tide of barbarian invaders threatening to engulf the Land of Mist. Only Uther and the Sword of Power stood between the light of civilization and the darkness of the hordes. Victorinus was a pure-blood Roman, but he had fought alongside Uther for a quarter of a century, putting down rebellions, crushing invading forces of Saxons, Norse, Goths, and Danes. For how much longer could Uther's small army prevail?

For as long as the king lived. This was the great sadness, the bitter truth. Only Uther had the power, the strength, the personal magnetism. When he was gone, the light would go out.

Gwalchmai entered the tent but stood in silence when he saw the king sleeping. Victorinus rose and drew a blanket over the monarch; then, beckoning to the old Cantii warrior, he left the tent.

"He's soul-weary," said Gwalchmai. "Did you ask him?"

"Yes."

"And?"

"What do you think, my friend?"

"If he dies, we are lost," said Gwalchmai. He was a tall man, stern-eyed under bushy gray brows, and his long silver hair was braided after the fashion of his Cantii forebears. "I fear for him. Ever since the betrayal . . ."

"Hush, man!" hissed Victorinus, taking his comrade by the arm and leading him away into the night.

Inside the tent Uther's eyes opened. Throwing off the blanket, he poured himself some more wine and this time added no water.

The Great Betrayal. Still they spoke of it. But whose

was the betrayal? he wondered. He drained the wine and refilled the goblet.

He could see them now on that lonely cliff top . . .

"Sweet Jesus!" he whispered. "Forgive me."

Cormac made his way through the scattered huts to the smithy, where Kern was hammering the blade of a plow. The boy waited until the sweating smith dunked the hot metal into the trough and then approached him.

"You have work for me?" he asked. The bald thickset Kern wiped his hands on his leather apron.

"Not today."

"I could fetch wood."

"I said not today," snapped the smith. "Now begone!"

Cormac swallowed hard. "I could clean the storeroom."

Kern's hand flashed for the boy's head, but Cormac swayed aside, causing the smith to stumble. "I am sorry, Master Kern," he said, standing stock-still for the angry blow that smacked into his ear.

"Get out! And don't come back tomorrow."

Cormac walked stiff-backed from the smithy, and only when out of sight of the building did he spit the blood from his mouth. He was hungry and alone. All around him he could see evidence of families: mothers and toddlers, young children playing with brothers and sisters, fathers teaching sons to ride.

The potter had no work for him, and neither did the baker or the tanner. The widow Althwynne lent him a hatchet, and he chopped wood for most of the afternoon, for which she gave him some pie and a sour apple. But she did not allow him into her home, or smile, or speak more than a few words. In all his fourteen years Cormac Daemonsson had seen the homes of none of the villagers.

He had long grown used to people making the sign of the protective horn when he approached and to the fact that only Grysstha would meet his eyes. But then, Grysstha was different . . . He was a man, a true man who feared no evil. A man who could see a boy and not a demon's son. And Grysstha alone had talked to Cormac of the strange day almost fifteen years before when he and a group of hunters had entered the Cave of Sol Invictus to find a great black hound lying alongside four squealing pups—and beside them a flame-haired babe still wet from birth. The hound attacked the hunters and was slain along with the pups, but no man among the Saxons cared to kill the babe, for they knew he had been sired by a demon and none wanted to earn the hatred of the pit dwellers.

Grysstha had carried the child from the cave and found a milk nurse for him from among the captured British women. But after four months she had suddenly died, and then no one would touch the child. Grysstha had taken him into his own hut and fed him with cow's milk through a needle-pierced leather glove.

The babe had even been the subject of a council meeting, where a vote was taken as to whether he lived or died. Only Calder's vote had saved young Cormac, and that had been given after a special plea from Grysstha.

For seven years the boy lived with the old warrior, but Grysstha's disability meant that he could not earn enough to feed them both, and the child was forced to scavenge in the village for extra food.

At thirteen Cormac realized that his association with the crippled warrior had caused Grysstha to become an outcast, and he built his own hut away from the village. It was a meager dwelling with no furniture but a cot bed, and Cormac spent little time there except in winter, when he shivered despite the fire and dreamed cold dreams.

That night, as always, Gryssstha stopped at his hut and banged on the doorpost. Cormac called him in, offering him a cup of water. The old man accepted graciously, sitting cross-legged on the hard-packed dirt floor.

"You need another shirt, Cormac; you have outgrown that. And those leggings will soon climb to your knees."

"They will last the summer."

"We'll see. Did you eat today?"

"Althwynne gave me some pie—I chopped wood for her."

"I heard Kern cracked your head."

"Yes."

"There was a time when I would have killed him for that. Now, if I struck him, I would only break my good hand."

"It was nothing, Gryssstha. How went your day?"

"The goats and I had a wonderful time. I told them of my campaigns, and they told me of theirs. They became bored long before I did!"

"You are never tiresome," said Cormac. "You are a wonderful storyteller."

"Tell me that when you've listened to another storyteller. It is easy to be the king when no one else lives in your land."

"I heard a saga poet once. I sat outside Calder's hall and listened to Patrisson sing of the Great Betrayal."

"You must not mention that to anyone, Cormac. It is a forbidden song—and death to sing it." The old man leaned back against the wall of the hut and smiled. "But he sang it well, did he not?"

"Did the Blood King really have a grandfather who was a god?"

"All kings are sired by gods, or so they would have us believe. Of Uther I know not. I only know that his wife was caught with her lover, that both fled, and that he hunted them. Whether he found them and cut them to pieces as the song says or whether they escaped, I do not know. I spoke to Patrisson, and he did not know, either. But he did say that the queen ran off with the king's grandfather, which sounds like a merry mismatch."

"Why has the king not taken another wife?"

"I'll ask him the next time he invites me to supper."

"But he has no heir. Will there not be a war if he dies now?"

"There will be a war anyway, Cormac. The king has reigned for twenty-five years and has never known peace . . . uprisings, invasions, betrayals. His wife was not the first to betray him. The Brigantes rose again sixteen years ago, and Uther crushed them at Trimontium. Then the Ordovice swept east, and Uther destroyed their army at Viriconium. Lastly the Jutes, two years ago. They had a treaty like ours, and they broke it; Uther kept his promise and had every man, woman, and child put to death."

"Even children?" whispered Cormac.

"All of them. He is a hard, canny man. Few will rise against him now."

"Would you like some more water?"

"No, I must be getting to my bed. There will be rain tomorrow—I can feel it in my stump—and I'll need my rest if I'm to sit shivering."

"One question, Grysstha."

"Ask it."

"Was I really born to a dog?"

Grysstha swore. "Who said that to you?"

"The tanner."

"I have told you before that I found you in the cave beside the hound. That's all it means. Someone had left you there, and the bitch tried to defend you, as she did her own pups. You had not been born more than two hours, but her pups were days old. Odin's blood! We have men here with brains of pig swill. Understand me, Cormac. You are no demon child; I promise you that. I do not know why you were left in that cave or by whom. But there were six dead men on the path by the cliff, and they were not killed by a demon."

"Who were they?"

"Doughty warriors, judging by their scars. All killed by one man—one fearsome man. The hunters with me were convinced once they saw you that a pit dweller was abroad, but that is because they were young and had never seen a true warrior in action. I tried to explain, but fear has a way of blinding the eyes. I believe that the warrior was your father and that he was wounded unto death. That's why you were left there."

"And what of my mother?"

"I don't know, boy. But the gods know. One day perhaps they'll give you a sign. But until then you are Cormac the man, and you will walk with your back straight. For whoever your father was, he was a man. And you will prove true to him, if not to me."

"I wish you were my father, Grysstha."

"I wish it, too. Good night, boy."

◇ 2 ◇

THE KING, FLANKED by Gwalchmai and Victorinus, walked out into the paddock field to view his new horses. The young man standing beside the crippled Prasamaccus stared intently at the legendary warrior.

"I thought he would be taller," he whispered, and Prasamaccus smiled.

"You thought to see a giant walking head and shoulders above other men. Oh, Ursus, you of all people ought to know the difference between men and myths."

Ursus' pale gray eyes studied the king as he approached. The man was around forty years of age and walked with the confident grace of a warrior who had never met his equal. His hair flowing to his mail-clad shoulders was auburn red, though his thick square-cut beard was more golden in color and was streaked with gray. The two men walking beside him were older, perhaps in their fifties. One was obviously Roman, hawk-nosed and steely-eyed, while the second wore his gray hair braided like a tribesman.

"A fine day," said the king, ignoring the younger man and addressing himself to Prasamaccus.

"It is, my lord, and the horses you bought are as fine."

"They are all here?"

"Thirty-five stallions and sixty mares. May I present Prince Ursus of the House of Merovee?"

The young man bowed. "It is an honor, my lord."

The king gave a tired smile and moved past the young man. He took Prasamaccus by the arm, and the two walked on into the field, stopping by a gray stallion of some seventeen hands.

"The Sicambrians know how to breed horses," said Uther, running his hand over the beast's glistening flank.

"You look weary, Uther."

"It reflects how I feel. The Trinovante are flexing their muscles once more, as are the Saxons in the Middle Land."

"When do you ride?"

"Tomorrow, with four legions. I sent Patreus with the Eighth and the Fifth, but he was routed. Reports say we lost six hundred men."

"Was Patreus among them?" Prasamaccus asked.

"If not, he'll wish he was," snapped the king. "He tried to charge a shield wall up a steep slope."

"As you yourself did only four days ago against the Goths."

"But I won!"

"You always do, my lord."

Uther grinned, and for a moment there was a flash of the lonely youth Prasamaccus had first met a quarter of a century before. But then it was gone, and the mask settled once more.

"Tell me of the Sicambrian," said the king, staring across at the young dark-haired prince clad all in black.

"He knows his horses."

"That was not my meaning, and well you know it."

"I cannot say, Uther. He seems . . . intelligent, knowledgeable."

"You like him?"

"I rather think that I do. He reminds me of you—a long time ago."

"Is that a good thing?"

"It is a compliment."

"Have I changed so much?"

Prasamaccus said nothing. A lifetime earlier Uther had dubbed him Kingsfriend and asked always for his honest council. In those days the young prince had crossed the Mist in search of his father's sword, had fought demons and the Witch Queen, had brought an army of ghosts back to the world of flesh, and had loved the mountain woman Laitha.

The old Brigante shrugged. "We all change, Uther. When my Helga died last year, I felt all beauty pass from the world."

"A man is better off without love. It weakens him," said the king, moving away to examine the horses. "Within a few years we will have a better, faster army. All these mounts are at least two hands taller than our horses, and they are bred for speed and stamina."

"Ursus brought something else you might like to see," said Prasamaccus. "Come, it will interest you." The king seemed doubtful, but he followed the limping Brigante back to the paddock gates. There Ursus bowed once more and led the group to the rear of the herdsmen's living quarters. In the yard behind the buildings a wooden frame had been erected—curved wood attached to a straight spine, representing a horse's back. Over this Ursus draped a stiffened leather cover. A second section was tied to the front of the frame, and the prince secured the hide, then returned to the waiting warriors.

"What in Hades is it?" asked Victorinus. Ursus lifted a short bow and nocked an arrow to the string.

With one smooth motion he let fly. The shaft struck the rear of the "horse" and, failing to penetrate fully, flapped down to point at the ground.

"Give me the bow," said Uther. Drawing back the string as far as the weapon could stand, he loosed the shaft. It cut through the leather and jutted from the hide.

"Now look, sire," said Ursus, stepping forward to the "horse." Uther's arrow had penetrated a mere half inch. "It would prick a good horse, but it would not have disabled him."

"What of the weight?" asked Victorinus.

"A Sicambrian horse could carry it and still work a full day as well as any British warhorse."

Gwalchmai was unimpressed. The old Cantii warrior hawked and spit. "It must cut down on the speed of the charge, and that is what carries us through the enemy. Armored horses? Pah!"

"You would perhaps think of riding into battle without your own armor?" snapped the prince.

"You insolent puppy!" roared Gwalchmai.

"Enough!" ordered the king. "Tell me, Ursus, what of the rains? Would they not soften your leather and add to the weight?"

"Yes, my lord. But each warrior should carry a quantity of oiled beeswax to be rubbed into the cover every day."

"Now we must polish our horses as well as our weapons," Gwalchmai said with a mocking grin.

"Have ten of these . . . horse jerkins . . . made," said Uther. "Then we shall see."

"Thank you, sire."

"Do not thank me until I place an order. This is what you are seeking, yes?"

"Yes, sire."

"Did you devise the armor?"

"Yes, my lord, although my brother Balan overcame the problem of the rain."

"And to him will go the profit for the wax I order?"

"Yes, my lord," said Ursus, smiling.

"And where is he at present?"

"Trying to sell the idea in Rome. It will be difficult, for the emperor still sets great store by the marching legions even though his enemies are mounted."

"Rome is finished," said Uther. "You should sell to the Goths or the Huns."

"I would, my lord, but the Huns do not buy—they take. And the Goths? Their treasury is smaller than my own."

"And your own Merovingian army?"

"My king, long may he reign, is guided in matters military by the mayor of the palace. And he is not a visionary."

"But then, he is not assailed on all sides and from within," said Uther. "Do you fight as well as you talk?"

"Not quite."

Uther grinned. "I have changed my mind. Make thirty-two, and Victorinus will put you in command of one turma. You will join me at Petvaria, and then I will see your horse armor as it needs to be seen—against a real enemy. If it is successful, you will be rich and, as I suspect you desire, all other fighting kings will follow Uther's lead."

"Thank you, sire."

"As I said, do not thank me yet. You have not heard my offer."

With that the king turned and walked away. Prasamaccus draped his arm over Ursus' shoulder.

"I think the king likes you, young man. Do not disappoint him."

"I would lose my order?"

"You would lose your life," Prasamaccus told him.

Long after Grysstha had returned to his own hut in the shadow of the long hall, Cormac, unable to sleep, wandered out into the cool of the night to sit below the stars and watch the bats circle the trees.

All was quiet, and the boy was truly, splendidly, perfectly alone. Here, in the glory of the hunter's moonlight, there was no alienation, no sullen stares, no harsh words. The night breeze ruffled his hair as he gazed up at the cliffs above the woods and thought of his father, the nameless warrior who had fought so well. Grysstha said he had killed six men.

But why had he left the infant Cormac alone in the cave? And where was the woman who bore him? Who would leave a child? Was the man—so brave in battle— so cruel in life?

And what mother could leave her babe to die in a lonely cave?

As always there were no answers, but the questions chained Cormac to this hostile village. He could not leave and make a future for himself, not while the past was such a mystery.

When he was younger, he had believed that his father would one day come to claim him, striding to the long hall with a sword at his side and a burnished helm on his brow. But no longer could the dreams of childhood sustain him. In four days he would be a man . . . and then what? Begging for work at the smithy, or the mill, or the bakery, or the slaughterhouse?

Back in his hut he slept fitfully beneath his threadbare blanket, rising before the dawn and taking his sling to the hills. There he killed three rabbits, skinning them expertly with the small knife Grysstha had given him the year before. He lit a fire in a sheltered hollow and roasted the meat, enjoying the rare sensation of a full belly. But there was little goodness in rabbit meat, and Grysstha had once told him a man could starve to death while feasting on such fare. Cormac licked his fingers and then wiped them on the long grass, remembering the Thunder Feast the previous autumn, where he had tasted beef at the open banquet when King Wulfhere had visited his former steward, Calder. Cormac had been forced to stay back from the throng around the Saxon king but had heard his speech. Meaningless platitudes mostly, coming from a weak man. He looked the part with his mail shirt of iron and his ax-bearing guards, but his face was soft and womanly and his eyes focused on a point above the crowd.

But the beef had been magnificent. Grysstha had brought him three cuts, succulent and rich with the blood of the bull.

"Once," the old man said, between mouthfuls, "we ate like this every day! When we were reavers and our swords were feared. Calder once promised we would do so again. He said we would be revenged on the Blood King, but look at him now—fat and content beside the puppet king."

"The king looks like a woman," said Cormac.

"He lives like one," snapped Grysstha. "And to think his grandfather was Hengist! Would you like more meat?"

And they feasted that night like emperors.

Now Cormac doused his fire and wandered high into the hills, along the cliff tops overlooking the calm sea. The breeze was strong there and cool despite the morning sun, clear in a cloudless sky.

Cormac stopped beneath a spreading oak and leapt to hang from a thick branch. One hundred times he hauled himself up to touch his chin to the wood, feeling the muscles in his arms and shoulders swell and burn. Then he dropped lightly to the ground, sweat gleaming on his face.

"How strong you are, Cormac," said a mocking voice, and he swung around to see Calder's daughter, Alftruda, sitting in the grass with a basket of berries beside her. Cormac blushed and said nothing. He should have walked away, but the sight of her sitting there cross-legged, her woolen skirt pulled up to reveal the milky whiteness of her legs . . . "Are you so shy?" she asked.

"Your brothers will not be pleased with you for speaking to me."

"And you are frightened of them?"

Cormac considered the question. Calder's sons had tormented him for years, but mostly he could outrun them to his hiding places in the woods. Agwaine was the worst, for he enjoyed inflicting pain. Lennox and Barta were less overtly cruel, but they followed Agwaine's lead in everything. But was he frightened?

"Perhaps I am," he said. "But then, such is the law that they are allowed to strike me but it is death if I defend myself."

"That's the price you pay for having a demon for a father, Cormac. Can you work magic?"

"No."

"Not even a little, to please me?"

"Not even a little."

"Would you like some berries?"

"No, thank you. I must be heading back; I have work to do."

"Do I frighten you, Cormac Daemonsson?"

He stopped in midturn, his throat tight. "I am not . . . comfortable. No one speaks to me, but I am used to that. I thank you for your courtesy."

"Do you think I am pretty?"

"I think you are beautiful. Especially here, in the summer sunlight, with the breeze moving your hair. But I do not wish to cause you trouble."

She rose smoothly and moved toward him. He backed away instinctively, but the oak barred his retreat. He felt her body press against his, and his arms moved around her back, drawing her to him.

"Get away from my sister!" roared Agwaine, and Alftruda leapt back with fear in her eyes.

"He cast a spell on me!" she shouted, running to Agwaine.

The tall blond youth hurled her aside and drew a dagger from its sheath. "You will die for this obscenity," he hissed, advancing on Cormac.

Cormac's eyes flickered from the blade to Agwaine's angry face, reading the intent and seeing the blood lust rising. He leapt to his right—to cannon into the huge figure of Lennox, whose brawny arms closed around him. Triumph blazed in Agwaine's eyes, but Cormac hammered his elbow into Lennox's belly and then up in a second strike, smashing the boy's nose. Lennox staggered back, almost blinded. Then Barta ran from the bushes, holding a thick branch above his head like a club. Cormac leapt feetfirst, his heel landing with sickening force against Barta's chin and hurling him unconscious to the ground.

Cormac rolled to his feet, swinging to face Agwaine, his arm blocking the dagger blow aimed at his heart. His fist slammed against Agwaine's cheek, and then his left foot powered into his enemy's groin. Agwaine screamed once and fell to his knees, dropping the dagger. Cormac swept it up, grabbed Agwaine's long blond hair, and hauled back his head, exposing the throat.

"No!" screamed Alftruda.

Cormac blinked and took a deep, calming breath. Then he stood and hurled the dagger far out over the cliff top. "You lying slut!" he said, advancing on Alftruda.

She sank to her knees, her eyes wide and terrorfilled. "Don't hurt me!"

Suddenly he laughed. "Hurt you? I would not *touch* you if my life depended on it. A few moments ago you were beautiful. Now you are ugly and will always be so."

Her hands fled to her face, her fingers touching the skin, questing, seeking her beauty. Cormac shook his head. "I am not talking of a spell," he whispered. "I have no spells."

Turning, he looked at his enemies. Lennox was sitting by the oak with blood streaming from his smashed nose, Barta was still unconscious, and Agwaine was gone.

There was no sense of triumph, no joy in the victory.

For in defeating these boys, Cormac had sentenced himself to death.

* * *

Agwaine returned to the village and reported Cormac's attack to his father, Calder, who summoned the village elders, demanding justice. Only Grysstha spoke up for Cormac.

"You ask for justice. For years your sons have tormented Cormac, and he has had no aid. But he has borne it like a man. Now, when set upon by three bullies, he defends himself and faces execution? Every man here who votes for such a course should be ashamed."

"He assaulted my daughter," said Calder. "Or are you forgetting that?"

"If he did," said Grysstha, rising, "he followed in the tracks of every other able-bodied youth within a day's riding distance!"

"How dare you?" stormed Calder.

"Dare? Do not speak to me of dares, you fat-bellied pig! I have followed you for thirty years, living only on your promises. But now I see you for what you are—a weak, greedy, fawning bootlicker. A pig who sired three toads and a rutting strumpet!"

Calder hurled himself across the circle of men, but Grysstha's fist thundered into his chin, throwing him to the dirt floor. Pandemonium followed, with some of the councillors grabbing Grysstha and others holding the enraged leader. In the silence that followed Calder fought to control his temper, signaling to the men on either side of him to let him go.

"You are no longer welcome here, old cripple," he said. "You will leave this village as a Nithing. I will send word to all villages in the South Saxon, and you will be welcome nowhere. And if I see you after today, I shall take my ax to your neck. Go! Find the dog child and stay with him. I want you there to see him die."

Grysstha shrugged off the arms holding him and stalked from the hall. In his own hut he gathered his meager belongings, pushed his hand ax into his belt, and marched from the village. Evrin the baker moved alongside him, pushing two black loaves into his arms.

"Walk with God," Evrin whispered.

Grysstha nodded and marched on. He should have left a long time ago and taken Cormac with him. But loyalty was stronger than iron rings, and Grysstha was pledged to Calder by blood oath. Now he had broken his word and was Nithing in the eyes of the law. No one would ever trust him again, and his life was worthless.

Yet even so joy began to blossom in the old warrior's heart. The heavy mind-numbing years as a goatherd were behind him now, as was his allegiance to Calder. Grysstha filled his lungs with clean, fresh air and climbed the hills toward the Cave of Sol Invictus.

Cormac was waiting for him there, sitting on the altar stone, the bones of his past scattered at his feet.

"You heard?" said Cormac, making room for the old man to sit beside him on the flat stone. Grysstha tore off a chunk of dark bread and passed it to the boy.

"Word filtered through," he said. Cormac glanced at the blanket sack Grysstha had dumped by the old bones of the warhound.

"Are we leaving?"

"We are, boy. We should have done it years ago. We'll head for Dubris and get some work—enough to earn passage to Gallia. Then I'll show you my old campaign trails."

"They attacked me, Grysstha. After Alftruda put her arms around me."

The old warrior looked into the boy's sad blue eyes.

"One more lesson in life, Cormac: women always bring trouble. Mind you, judging from the way Agwaine was walking, he will not be thinking about girls for some time to come. How did you defeat all three?"

"I don't know; I just did it."

"That's your father's blood. We'll make something of you yet, lad!"

Cormac glanced around the cave. "I have never been here before. I was always afraid. Now I wonder why. Just old bones." He scuffed his feet in the loose dirt and saw a glint of light. Leaning forward, he pressed his fingers into the dust, coming up with a gold chain on which hung a round stone like a golden nugget veined with slender black lines.

"Well, that's a good omen," muttered Grysstha. "We've been free men for only an hour and already you find treasure."

"Could it have been my mother's?"

"All things are possible."

Cormac looped the chain over his head, tucking the golden stone under his shirt. It felt warm against his chest.

"Are you in trouble, too, Grysstha?"

The warrior grinned. "I may have said a word or two too many, but they flew home like arrows!"

"Then they will be hunting us both?"

"Aye, come morning. We'll worry then. Now get some rest, boy."

Cormac moved to the far wall and settled himself down on the dusty floor, his head resting on his arms. Grysstha stretched out on the altar and was asleep within minutes.

The boy lay listening to the warrior's deep heavy snoring, then drifted into a curious dream. It seemed he opened his eyes and sat up. By the altar lay a black warhound and five pups, and beyond her was a young woman with hair of spun gold. A man knelt beside her, cradling her head.

"I am sorry I brought you to this," he said, stroking her hair. His face was strong, his hair dark and shining like raven's wings, his eyes the blue of a winter's sky.

She reached up and touched his cheek, smiling through her pain.

"I love you. I have always loved you . . ."

Outside a bugle call drifted through the morning air, and the man cursed softly and stood, drawing his sword. "They have found us!"

The woman moaned as her labor began. Cormac moved across to her, but she did not see him. He tried to touch her, but his hand passed through her body as if it were smoke.

"Don't leave me!" she begged. The man's face showed his torment, but the bugle sounded once more and he turned and vanished from sight. The woman cried out, and Cormac was forced to watch impotently as she struggled to deliver her child. At last the babe came forth, blood-covered and curiously still.

"Oh, no! Dear sweet Christ!" moaned the woman, lifting the child and slapping its tiny rump. There was not even a flicker of movement. Laying the babe in her lap, she lifted a golden chain from around her neck, closing the child's tiny fingers around the stone at its center. "Live!" she whispered. "Please live!"

But there was no movement . . . no sign of life.

From the sunlit world outside came the sound of blade on blade, the cries of the wounded, the angry shouts of the combatants. Then there was silence, save for the birds singing in the forest trees. A shadow crossed the entrance, and the tall man staggered inside, blood pouring from a wound in his side and a second one in his chest.

"The babe?" he whispered.

"He is dead," said the woman.

Hearing something from beyond the cave, the man turned. "There are more of them. I can see their spears catching the sun. Can you walk?" She struggled to stand but fell back, and he moved to her side, sweeping her into his arms.

"He's alive!" shouted Cormac, tears in his eyes. "*I'm* alive! Don't leave me!"

He followed them out into the sunlight, watching the wounded man struggle to the top of the cliff before sinking to his knees, the woman tumbling from his arms. A horseman galloped into sight, and the warrior drew his sword, but the man hauled on the reins, waiting.

From the woods another man came limping into view, his left leg twisted and deformed. The tall warrior drew back his sword and hurled it into the trees, where it lanced into a thick ivy-covered trunk. Then he lifted the woman once more, turned, and gazed at the sea foaming hundreds of feet below.

"No!" screamed the crippled man. The warrior looked toward the horseman, who sat unmoving, his stern face set, his hands resting on the pommel of his saddle.

The warrior stepped from the cliff and vanished from sight, taking the woman with him.

Cormac watched with tears in his eyes as the cripple fell to earth, but the horseman merely turned his mount and rode away into the trees. Farther down the trail Cormac could see the hunting party approaching the cave. He ran like the wind, arriving to see the stone in the child's hands glow like a burning candle and an aura of white light shine over the infant's skin. Then came the first lusty cry. The hunters entered, and the black warhound leapt at them, only to be cut down by knives and axes.

"Odin's blood!" said one of the men. "The bitch gave birth to a child."

"Kill it!" cried another.

"You fools!" said Grysstha. "You think the dog killed those Romans?"

Cormac could bear to watch no more and shut his eyes as Grysstha reached for the babe . . .

He opened them to see the dawn light creeping back from the cave mouth and Grysstha still asleep on the altar. Rising, he moved to the old man and shook him awake.

"It is dawn," he said, "and I saw my mother and father."

"Give me time, boy," muttered the old warrior. "Let me get some air." He stretched and sat up, rubbing at his eyes and groaning at the stiff, cold muscles of his neck. "Pass me the water sack."

Cormac did so, and Grysstha pulled the stopper and drank deeply. "Now, what is this about your mother?"

The boy told him about the dream, but Grysstha's eyes did not show great interest until he mentioned the crippled man.

"Tell me of his face."

"Light hair, thin beard. Sad eyes."

"And the horseman?"

"A warrior, tall and strong. A cold, hard man with red

hair and beard, wearing a helm of bronze banded by a circle of iron."

"We'd best be going, Cormac," said the old warrior suddenly.

"Was my dream true, do you think?"

"Who knows, boy? We'll talk later."

Grysstha swung his blanket sack to his shoulder and walked from the cave. There he stopped stock-still, dropping the sack.

"What is wrong?" asked Cormac, moving into the sunlight. Grysstha gestured him to silence and scanned the undergrowth beneath the trees.

Cormac could see nothing, but suddenly a man rose from behind a thick bush with an arrow nocked to his bow, the string drawn back. Cormac froze. Grysstha's arm hammered into the boy's chest, hurling him aside just as the archer loosed his shaft. The arrow sliced through Grysstha's jerkin, punching through to pierce his lungs. A second arrow followed. The old man shielded Cormac with his body as blood bubbled from his mouth.

"Run!" he hissed, toppling to the earth.

An arrow flashed by Cormac's face, and he dived to the left as other shafts hissed by him, then rolled and came up running. A great shout went up from the hidden men in the undergrowth, and the sound of pounding feet caused Cormac to increase his speed as he hurdled a fallen tree and sprinted for the cliff tops. Arrows sailed over him, and he dodged to the left and the right, cutting up through the forest path, seeking a hiding place.

There were several hollow trees where he had previously hidden from Agwaine and his brothers. He was feeling more confident now as he increased the distance between himself and his pursuers.

But the baying of the warhounds brought fresh terror. The trees would offer no sanctuary now.

He emerged at the cliff tops and swung, expecting to see the dark hurtling forms of Calder's twin hounds, fangs bared for his throat. But the trail was empty for the moment. He drew his slender skinning knife, eyes scanning the trees.

A huge black hound bounded into sight. As it leapt, Cormac dropped to his knees and rammed the blade into its belly, disemboweling it as the beast sailed above him. The stricken dog landed awkwardly, its paws entangling in its ribboned entrails. Cormac ignored it and ran back to the trees, forsaking the path and forcing his body through the thickest part of the undergrowth.

Suddenly he stopped, for there, embedded in the ivy-covered trunk of a spreading oak, was the sword of his dream. Sheathing his knife, he took hold of the ivory hilt and drew the blade clear. The sword was the length of a man's arm, and not one spot of rust had touched the blade in the fifteen years it had been hidden here.

Cormac closed his eyes. "Thank you, Father," he whispered.

The hilt was long enough for the sword to be wielded double-handed, and the boy swung the blade several times, feeling the balance.

Then he stepped out into the open as the second hound rounded the trail, hurtling at the slim figure before it. The blade lanced its neck, half severing the head. His eyes blazing with an anger he had never experienced before, Cormac loped down the trail toward the following hunters.

Near a stand of elm the sound of their pursuit came to him, and he stepped from the track, hiding himself behind a thick trunk. Four men ran into view—Agwaine in the lead, his brothers following, and bringing up the rear the blacksmith Kern, his bald head shining with sweat.

As they raced past Cormac's hiding place, he took a deep breath, then leapt into the path to face the astonished Kern. The blacksmith was carrying a short double-headed ax but had no time to use it, for Cormac's sword swept up, over, and down to cleave the man's jugular. Kern staggered back, dropping his ax, his fingers scrabbling at the wound as he sought to stem the flooding lifeblood.

Cormac ran back into the trees, following the other three. Agwaine and Lennox had disappeared from sight, but Barta was lumbering far behind them. Darting out behind him, Cormac tapped his shoulder, and the blond youngster turned.

Cormac's blade slid through the youth's woolen jerkin and up into the belly, ripping through lungs and heart. Savagely he twisted the sword to secure its release, then dragged it clear. Barta died without a sound.

Moving like a wraith, Cormac vanished into the shadow-haunted trees, seeking the last of the hunters.

On the cliff top Agwaine had found the butchered hounds. Turning, he ran back to warn his brother that Cormac was now armed; then he and Lennox retreated back along the trail, finding the other bodies.

Together the survivors fled the woods. Cormac emerged from the trees to see them sprinting back into the valley.

At first he thought to chase them to the Great Hall itself, but common sense prevailed, and, his anger ebbing, he returned to the cave. Grysstha had propped himself against the western wall; his white beard was stained with his blood, and his face was pale and gray.

As Cormac knelt beside the old man, taking his hand, Grysstha's eyes opened.

"I can see the Valkyrie, Cormac," he whispered, "but they ignore me, for I have no sword."

"Here," said the boy, pushing the ivory hilt into the warrior's left hand.

"Do not ... do not ... tell anyone ... about your birth." Grysstha slid sideways to the ground, the sword slipping from his fingers.

For a while Cormac sat in silence with the body of his only friend. Then he stood and wandered into the sunlight, staring down at the village far below.

He wanted to scream his anger to the skies, but he did not. One of Grysstha's sayings sprang to his mind: "Revenge is a better meal when served cold."

Sheathing the sword in his belt, he gathered Grysstha's possessions and set off for the east. At the top of the last rise he turned once more.

"I will return," he said softly. "And then you will see the demon. I swear it!"

◊ 3 ◊

PRASAMACCUS STRETCHED OUT his legs before the log fire in the grate and sipped the honeyed wine. His daughter, Adriana, offered a goblet to Ursus, who accepted it with a dazzling smile.

"Do not waste your charm," said Prasamaccus. "Adriana is betrothed to the herdsman's son, Gryll."

"Are they in love?"

"Why ask me? Adriana is standing here."

"Of course. My apologies, my lady."

"You must forgive my father," she said, her voice deep and husky. "He forgets that the customs of his guests are rarely like his own. Are women still bought and sold by the Sicambrians?"

"That is somewhat harsh. Dowries are paid to prospective husbands, but then, that is still the case in Uther's Britain, is it not? And a woman is servant to her husband. All religions agree on this."

"My father told Gryll there would be no dowry. And we will be wed at the Feast of Midwinter."

"And are you in love?"

"Yes, very much."

"But no dowry?"

"I think Father will relent. He has too much money already. And now, if you will excuse me, I am very tired."

Ursus stood and bowed as Adriana kissed Prasamaccus' bearded cheek and left the room.

"She is a good girl, but she must think I'm growing senile! She will slip out through the yard and meet Gryll by the stables. How is your wine?"

"A little sweet for my taste."

Prasamaccus leaned forward, tossing a log to the fire. "Honey aids the mind and clears the stomach. It also wards off evil spirits."

Ursus chuckled. "I thought that was bitter onions."

"Those, too," agreed the Brigante. "And mistletoe and black dogs with white noses."

"I think you have drunk a little too much wine, my friend."

"It is a fault of mine on lonely evenings. You know, I was with the king before he *was* the king—when he was a hunted boy in the mountains and he crossed the Valley of the Dead to another world. I was young then. I watched him become a man, I watched him fall in love, and I watched his great heart slowly die. He was always a man of iron will. But now that is all he has left: the iron. The heart is dead."

"His wife, you mean?"

"The lovely Laitha. Gian Avur, Fawn of the Forest."

"I understand the song is forbidden here. I suppose it is understandable: a king cuckolded by a relative, betrayed by a friend."

"There was more to it than that, Ursus. Far more. There always is. Culain lach Feragh was a warrior without peer and a man of great honor. But his weakness was that he lived without love. Laitha was raised by him, and she had loved him since childhood, but they were doomed."

"You speak as if man had no choices."

"Sometimes he does not. Culain would have died before hurting Uther or Gian, but the king knew that his wife had always loved Culain, and evil thoughts grew in him like a dry grass fire. He was always on some mission of war, and he took to living with the army. He rarely spoke to Gian and appointed Culain as her champion. He forced them together, and finally they gave in to their desires."

"How did he find out?"

"It was an open secret, and the lovers grew careless. They would be seen touching hands, walking arm in arm in the gardens. And Culain often visited the queen's apartments late in the night, emerging at dawn. One night the King's Guards burst into the queen's bedchamber, and Culain was there. They were dragged before the king, who sentenced them both to death. But Culain escaped. Three days later he attacked the party taking the queen to the scaffold, and they got away."

"But that is not the end of the story?"

"No. Would that it were." Prasamaccus lapsed into silence, his head tipping back to rest on the high back of the chair. The goblet slipped from his fingers to the rug, and Ursus scooped it up before the wine could stain the goatskin. Then the prince smiled and stood. There was a blanket draped across a stool by the bedroom door. He took it and covered Prasamaccus, then entered his own room.

Adriana smiled and pulled back the blankets. Slipping from his clothes, he joined her, stroking the golden hair back from her face.

Her arm circled his neck, drawing him down.

* * *

Ursus washed in the barrel of cold water at the back of the lodge, enjoying the crispness of the dawn air on his naked skin. His sleep had been untroubled by dreams, and the future was filled with the promise of gold. If the king of legend adopted his horse armor, all other fighting monarchs would follow and Ursus would retire to a palace in the Great River Valley with a score of concubines.

At twenty Ursus had his future clearly mapped out. Although of the House of Merovee, he and Balan were but distant relatives of Meroveus and had no claim to the crown of the long-haired kings. And the life of a soldier offered no delights to a man who had spent his youth in the pleasure palaces of Tingis.

He scrubbed himself dry with a soft woolen towel and donned a fresh black shirt under his oiled jerkin. From a small leather flask he poured a few drops of perfume onto his palm and spread it through his long dark hair. The stink of the stables was galling, and he wandered to the open fields, enjoying the scent of the wild roses growing by the ancient circle of Standing Stones.

Prasamaccus joined him. The older man seemed nervous.

"What is wrong, my friend?" asked Ursus, sitting on the flat-topped altar stone.

"I drank like an old fool, and now there is a hammer inside my head."

"Too much honey," said Ursus, trying not to smile.

"And too loose a tongue. I should not have spoken so about the king and his business."

"Put your fears at rest, Prasamaccus; I cannot remember any of it. The wine went straight to my head also. As far as I recall, you spoke of Lord Uther as the finest king in Christendom."

Prasamaccus grinned. "Which he is. Thank you, Ursus."

Ursus said nothing. He was staring at the ragged line of armed men cresting the far hills.

"I do hope they are ours," he whispered.

Prasamaccus shielded his eyes, then swore. Pushing himself to his feet, the older man hobbled toward the house, shouting at the top of his voice and pointing to the now-charging line. Herdsmen and horse handlers came running from the stables with bows in hand while the twenty regular legionaries, armed with swords and shields, formed a fighting line in the yard before the house. Ursus sprinted back to his room to gather his own bow and quiver. Adriana was crouching below the main window.

"Who are they?" Ursus asked as the riders neared.

"Trinovante tribesmen," she said.

An arrow flashed through the open window, slamming into the door frame across the room. Ursus stepped back from view, nocking an arrow to his bow.

The horsemen thundered into the yard, leaping from their mounts to engage the legionaries. Outnumbered four to one, the line gave way, the garishly clad tribesmen hacking and cutting a path toward the house.

Ursus risked a glance through the window as a warrior with a braided beard leapt for the opening. Dragging back on the bowstring, he released the shaft to slice into the tribesman's throat, and the man fell back.

"I think we should leave," said Ursus, seizing Adriana by the hand and hauling her to her feet. The door burst inward, and three warriors entered the room, swords red with the blood of the fallen legionaries.

"I hope the thought of ransom has occurred to you," said Ursus, dropping the bow and spreading his arms wide.

"Kill him!" ordered a tall dark-haired warrior with a fading scar on his cheek.

"I am worth quite a lot . . . in gold!" said the prince, backing away.

The warriors advanced. Ursus stepped forward, twisted on the ball of his foot, and leapt, his right heel cracking against a warrior's chin and somersaulting the man into his companion. The prince landed lightly, diving to his right to avoid a slashing cut from Scarface. Then, rolling to his feet, he ducked under a second sweep and drove his fingers up under the tribesman's breastbone. The man gasped, his face turning crimson . . . then he fell. Ursus scooped up the fallen man's sword and plunged it through the chest of the first warrior, who had started to rise. Adriana hit the third man with a stool, knocking him from his feet.

A trumpet blast echoed outside, and the thunder of hooves followed. Ursus ran to the window to see Uther, Victorinus, and a full century of mounted legionaries hammering into the bewildered tribesmen. Many of the Trinovantes threw down their weapons, but they were slain out of hand.

Within a few minutes the battle was over, the bodies being dragged from the yard.

The king entered the house, his pale eyes gleaming, all weariness gone from him.

"Where is Prasamaccus?" he asked, stepping over the bodies. The warrior hit by Adriana groaned and tried to stand. Uther spun, his great sword cleaving the man's neck. The head rolled to rest against the wall, the body slumping to pump blood to the floor. Adriana looked away.

"I said, where is Prasamaccus?"

"Here, my lord," said the cripple, stepping into view from the back room. "I am unharmed."

The king relaxed, grinning boyishly. "I am sorry we were not here sooner." He moved to the window. "Victorinus! There are three more in here!"

A group of legionaries entered the lodge, dragging the bodies out into the sunshine.

Uther sheathed his sword and sat. "You did well, Ursus. You fight as well as you talk."

"Fortune favored me, sire, and Adriana downed one with a stool."

"Hardly surprising; she comes from fine stock."

Adriana curtseyed and then moved to the cupboard, fetching the king a goblet and filling it with apple juice from a stone jug. Uther drank deeply.

"You will be safe now. Gwalchmai has isolated the main band, and by tonight there will not be one rebel Trinovante alive from here to Cumbretovium."

"Are your subjects always this unruly?" asked Ursus, and a flash of annoyance showed on the king's face.

"We British do not make good subjects," said Prasamaccus swiftly. "It is the land, Ursus. All the tribes revere their own kings, their own war leaders and holy men. The Romans destroyed most of the Druids, but now the sect is back, and they do not accept Roman authority."

"But Britannia is no longer ruled by Rome," said the prince. "I do not understand."

"To the tribes Uther is a Roman. They care nothing that Rome is gone."

"I am the high king," said Uther, "by right and by conquest. The tribes accept that, but the Druids do not. Neither do the Saxons, the Jutes, the Angles, or the Goths, and only in recent years have the Sicambrians become friends."

"You suffer no shortage of enemies, Lord Uther. Long may you have strong friends! How will you deal with the problem of the Druids?"

"The way the Romans did, my boy. I crucify them where I find them."

"Why not gather your own?"

"I would as soon take a viper to my bed."

"What do they want, after all, but that which all men want—power, riches, soft women? There must be some among them who can be bought. It would at least sow dissension among your enemies."

"You've a sharp mind, young Ursus."

"And an inquiring one, sire. How was it you knew the attack would come here?"

"The land knew, and I am the land," answered Uther, smiling.

Ursus pushed the question no further.

Cormac ran until his legs burned and his lungs heaved, but he knew he could not outrun the horsemen following on the narrow trail or outfight those who had cut across the stream to his left and were moving to outflank him. He struggled to reach the high ground, where he felt he would be able to kill one, perhaps two, of the hunters. He prayed one of them would be Agwaine.

He tried to leap a rounded boulder in the trail, but his tired legs struck the stone, spilling him to the grass, his sword spinning from his fingers. He scrambled forward to retrieve it just as a hand circled the hilt.

"An interesting blade," said a tall, hooded man, and Cormac dragged his knife clear and prepared to attack. But the stranger reversed the sword, offering the hilt to the startled boy. "Come, follow me."

The hooded man ducked into the undergrowth, pushing aside a thick bush to reveal a shallow cave. Cormac scrambled inside, and the man pulled the bush across the opening. Less than a minute later the Saxon hunters swept past the hiding place. The stranger threw back his hood and ran his hands through the thick black and silver hair that flowed to his broad shoulders. His gray eyes were deep-set, and his beard swept out from his face like a lion's mane. He grinned.

"I'd say you were outnumbered, young man."

"Why did you help me?"

"Are you not one of God's creatures?"

"You are a holy man?"

"I understand the mysteries. What are you called?"

"Cormac. And you?"

"I am Revelation. Are you hungry?"

"They will return. I must go."

"I took you for a bright lad, a boy with wit. If you leave here now, what will happen?"

"I am not a fool, Master Revelation. But what will happen will still happen an hour from now, or a day. I cannot cross the entire South Saxon without being seen. And I do not want you to be slain with me. Thank you for your kindness."

"As you will, but eat! It is the first rule of the soldier."

Cormac settled his back against the wall and accepted the bread and cheese he was offered. The food was welcome, as was the cool water from the man's leather-covered canteen.

"How is it that you, a Saxon, have such a sword?"

"It is mine."

"I am not disputing its ownership. I asked how you came by it."

"It was my father's."

"I see. Obviously a fine warrior. The blade is of a steel that comes only from Hispania."

"He was a great warrior; he killed six men on the day I was born."

"Six? Truly skilled. And he was a Saxon?"

"I do not know. He died that day, and I was raised by . . . by a friend." Grysstha's face leapt to Cormac's mind, and for the first time since his death tears flowed. The boy cleared his throat and turned away. "I am sorry, I . . . I am sorry." Choking sobs fought their way past his defenses; he felt a strong hand on his shoulder.

"In life, if one is lucky, there are many friends. You are lucky, Cormac. For you have found me."

"He's dead. They killed him because he spoke up for me."

The man's hand moved to Cormac's forehead. "Sleep now and we will speak later, when the danger is past."

As Revelation's fingers touched his brow, a great drowsiness flowed over the boy like a warm blanket. He slept without dreams.

He awoke in the night to find himself covered by a thick woolen blanket, his head resting on a folded cloak. Rolling over, he saw Revelation sitting by a small fire, lost in thought.

"Thank you," said Cormac.

"It was my pleasure. How do you feel?"

"Rested. The hunters?"

"They gave up and returned to their homes. I expect

they will come back in the morning with hounds. Are you hungry?" Revelation lifted a copper pot from the fire, stirring the contents with a stick. "I have some broth, fresh rabbit, dried beef, and herbs." He poured a generous portion into a deep wooden bowl and passed it to the boy. Cormac accepted it gratefully.

"Are you on a pilgrimage?" he asked between mouthfuls.

"Of a kind. I am going home."

"You are a Briton?"

"No. How is the broth?"

"Delicious."

"Tell me of Grysstha."

"How do you know the name?"

The bearded man smiled. "You mentioned it in your sleep. He was your friend?"

"Yes. He lost his right hand fighting the Blood King. After that he was a goatherd; he raised me, and I was like his son."

"Then you were his son; there is more to being a parent than the ties of blood. Why do they hate you?"

"I don't know," said Cormac, remembering Grysstha's dying words. "Are you a priest?"

"What makes you think so?"

"I saw a priest of the White Christ once. He wore a habit like yours and sandals. But he had a cross of wood he wore on his neck."

"I am not a priest."

"A warrior, then?" Cormac said doubtfully, for the man carried no weapons except for a long staff that now lay beside him.

"Nor a warrior. Simply a man. Where were you heading?"

"Dubris. I could find work there."

"For what are you trained?"

"I have worked in a smithy, a mill, and a pottery. They would not let me work in the bakery."

"Why?"

"I was not allowed to touch their food, but sometimes the baker would let me clean his rooms. Are you going to Dubris?"

"No. To Noviomagus to the west."

"Oh."

"Why not come with me? It is a pleasant walk, and the company would be fine."

"West is where my enemies are."

"Do not concern yourself with enemies, Cormac. They shall not harm you."

"You do not know them."

"They will not know you. Look!" From his backpack the man pulled a mirror of polished brass. Cormac took it and gasped, for staring back at him was a dark-haired youth, thin-lipped and round of face.

"You are a nigromancer," he whispered, fear rising.

"No," said the man softly. "I am Revelation."

Despite his shock, Cormac struggled to think through the choices facing him. The stranger had not harmed him, had allowed him to keep his sword, and had treated him kindly. But he was a sorcerer, and that alone was enough to strike terror into the boy's heart. Suppose he wanted Cormac for some ghastly blood sacrifice, to feed his heart to a demon? Or as a slave?

And yet if Cormac tried to reach Dubris alone, he would be hunted down and slain like a mad dog.

At least if the sorcerer had evil plans for him, they were not plans for that day.

"I will travel with you to Noviomagus," he stated.

"A wise choice, young Cormac," said Revelation, rising smoothly and gathering his belongings. He scraped the pot and bowl clean with a handful of scrub grass and returned them to his backpack. Then, without a backward glance, he set off in the moonlight toward the west.

Cormac joined him, struggling to match the man's long stride as they walked out of the forested hills and across the dales of the South Saxon. At midnight Revelation stopped in a sheltered hollow and lit a fire, using an ornate tinderbox that fascinated Cormac. Of silver, it was embossed with a fire-breathing dragon. Revelation tossed it to the boy, then added twigs to the tiny blaze, feeding it to greater strength.

"It was made in Tingis, in the north of Africa, by an old Greek named Melchiades. He loves to create works of art around items we use every day. It is an obsession with him, but I love his work." Cormac opened the box carefully. Inside was a sprung lever in the shape of a dragon's head; in the mouth was a sharp-edged flint. When the lever was depressed, the flint ran along a serrated iron grille, causing a shower of sparks.

"It is beautiful."

"Yes. Now make yourself useful and gather some wood." Cormac handed back the box and moved among the trees, gathering windfall fuel. When he returned, Revelation had spread ferns on the ground by the fire for a soft bed. The tall traveler built up the blaze and then lay down under his blanket; he was asleep within seconds. Cormac sat beside him for a while, listening to the sounds of the night.

Then he, too, slept.

Soon after dawn the travelers set off once more, having finished a breakfast of fresh bread and cheese. How the bread could be fresh worried Cormac not at all now that he knew his companion was a man of magic. Anyone who could alter another man's face and hair would have no difficulty creating a tasty loaf!

The riders came into sight just before noon, behind a dog handler with six leashed wolfhounds. As the dogs spotted the two travelers, they bounded forward, baying furiously. Their strength dragged the handler from his feet, and he was forced to release the ropes as they sped onward.

"Stand still," ordered Revelation. He raised his staff and waited as the hounds closed with ferocious speed, fangs bared for the attack.

"Down!" he bellowed, and the hounds ceased their growling and halted before him. "Down, I said!" Obediently the dogs dropped to their haunches as the five horsemen cantered forward. They were led by Agwaine, his brother Lennox behind him. The other three were carles from Calder's hall, grim-eyed men bearing hand axes.

The red-faced, mud-spattered dog handler gathered the trailing leashes and pulled the dogs back into line.

"Good day," said Revelation, leaning forward on his staff. "Hunting?"

Agwaine touched his heels to his horse and rode close to Cormac. "We are seeking a boy around this lad's age, wearing a similar tunic."

"A red-haired lad?"

"You have seen him?"

"Yes. Is he a runaway?"

"What he is is no business of yours," snapped Agwaine.

"Come, boy," Revelation told Cormac, and walked on, threading his way through the riders. Cormac followed swiftly.

"Where do you think you're going?" shouted Agwaine as he hauled on the reins, turning his horse and cantering to block Revelation's path.

"You are beginning to irritate me, young puppy. Move aside."

"Where is the boy?"

Revelation raised his hand suddenly, and Agwaine's horse shied, tipping the youth to the grass. Revelation walked on.

"Take him!" yelled Agwaine, and the three Saxon carles dismounted and ran forward.

Revelation swung to face them, once more leaning on his staff.

The men approached warily. The staff lanced upward to connect with the nearest man's groin, and with a strangled scream he dropped his ax and fell to his knees. Revelation blocked a wild ax blow, and his staff thundered against a bearded chin, poleaxing a second warrior. The third looked to Agwaine for orders.

"I would think twice before hunting the boy," said Revelation. "From what I have seen here, you would have trouble tackling a wounded fawn."

"Ten gold pieces," said Agwaine, lifting a leather pouch from his saddlebag and tipping the coins into his hand.

"Ah, now that is a different matter, young sir. The boy told me he was heading for Dubris. I last saw him yesterday on the high path."

Agwaine dropped the money back into his pouch and rode away.

"No more than I would expect from a Saxon," said Revelation, smiling. He gathered up his pack and strolled toward the west with Cormac running alongside him.

"I thought you said you were no warrior."

"That was yesterday. Who was that young man?"

"Agwaine, son of Calder."

"I dislike him intensely."

"So do I. Had it not been for him, Grysstha would still be alive."

"How so?"

"He has a sister, Alftruda. She put her arms around me, so Agwaine and his brothers attacked me. That's why."

"A childish squabble? How can that cause a man's death?"

"It is the law. I am not allowed to strike any villager, not even to protect myself."

"A strange law, Cormac. Does it apply only to you?"

"Yes. How far is Noviomagus?"

"Three days away. Have you ever seen a Roman town?"

"No. Are there palaces?"

"I think for you there will be. And once there, I can purchase some clothes for you and a scabbard for your father's sword."

Cormac looked up at the gray-haired traveler. "Why are you being so kind to me?"

Revelation grinned. "Perhaps it is because I dislike Agwaine. Then again, perhaps I like you. You choose."

"Will you use me for sorcery? Will you betray me?"

Revelation stopped and laid his hand on Cormac's shoulder.

"In my life there are deeds never to be forgotten or forgiven. I have killed. I have lied. I have cheated. Once I even killed a friend. My word used to be a thing of iron, but I have broken even that. So how can I convince you I mean you no harm?"

"Just tell me," said Cormac simply.

Revelation offered his hand, and Cormac took it. "I shall not betray you, for I am your friend."

"Then that is good enough," said the boy. "When can I look like myself again?"

"As soon as we reach Noviomagus."

"Is that your home?"

"No, but I am meeting someone there. I think you will like her."

"A girl!" exclaimed Cormac, crestfallen.

"I am afraid so. But curb your disappointment until you have met her."

◇ 4 ◇

NOVIOMAGUS WAS A thriving estuary town that was growing rich on trade with the Sicambrians in Gaul, the Berbers of Africa, and the merchants of Italia, Graecia, Thrace, and Cappadocia. A mixture of older well-constructed Roman dwellings and inferior copies built of sandstone blocks and timber, Noviomagus contained more than six thousand inhabitants.

Cormac had never seen so many people gathered in one place as there were when he and Revelation threaded their way through cramped, choked streets, past bazaars and markets, shops, and trading centers. To the lad the people were as splendid as kings in their cloaks of red, green, blue, orange, and yellow. Glorious patterns of checks, stripes, and swirls or pictures of hunting scenes were woven into tunics, shirts, and capes. Cormac was dazzled by the opulence around him.

A full-breasted woman with dyed red hair approached Revelation. "Come and relax with Helcia," she whispered. "Only ten denarii."

"Thank you, I have no time."

"A real man always has time," she said, her smile fading.

"Then find a real man," he told her, moving on.

Three more young women propositioned the travelers, and one even ran her hand down Cormac's tunic, causing him to leap back, red-faced and ashamed.

"Ignore them, Cormac," said Revelation, stepping from the street into an alley so narrow that the two of them could not walk side by side.

"Where are we going?" asked the youth.

"We are here," answered Revelation, pushing open a door and stepping into a long room furnished with a dozen bench tables and chairs.

The air was close, and there were no windows. The two travelers sat down at a corner table, ignoring the other five customers. A thin hatchet-faced man approached, wiping his hands on a greasy rag.

"You want food?"

"Ale," said Revelation, "and some fruit for the boy."

"There are oranges just in, but they are expensive," said the innkeeper. Revelation opened his hand to show a shining silver half piece. "Will that be all? I've got some steak ready."

"Some for my companion, then,"

"What about a woman? We've three here better than anything you've ever seen; they'll make you feel like a king."

"Perhaps later. Now bring the ale and the fruit."

The man returned with a leather-covered tankard and a bowl bearing three fist-sized spheres of yellow gold.

"Rip off the skin and eat the segments inside," advised Revelation.

Cormac did so and almost choked on the sweet, acid juice. He devoured the fruit and licked his fingers.

"Good?"

"Wonderful. Oranges! When I am a man, I shall plant my own and eat them every day."

"Then you will have to live in Africa, across the sea, where the sun burns a man's skin blacker than darkness."

"Would they not grow here?"

"The winter is too cold for them. What do you think of Noviomagus?"

"It's very noisy. I wouldn't like to live here. People keep touching me, and that is rude. And those women— if they are so hungry for love, why don't they marry?"

"A good question, Cormac. Many of them *are* married—and they are not hungry for love; they are hungry for money. In towns like this money is the only god. Without it you are nothing."

The steak was thin and tough, but to Cormac it tasted magnificent, and he finished it at a speed that surprised the innkeeper.

"Was it all right, sir?"

"Wonderful!" Cormac replied.

"Good," said the man, studying Cormac's face for any sign of sarcasm. "Would you like some more fruit?"

"Oranges," Cormac said, nodding.

A second bowl of fruit followed the first. The inn began to fill with customers, and the two travelers sat in silence, listening to the babble of voices around them.

Most conversations concerned the wars and their subsequent—or imagined—effect on trade. Cormac learned that the Northern Trinovantes had rebelled against the high king. In the southeast a force of Jutes had sailed to Londinium, sacking the town before being crushed by Uther's fleet in the Gallic waters. Three ships had been sunk, and two more set ablaze.

"They don't seem to fear an attack here," said Cormac, leaning forward.

Revelation nodded. "That is because of the dark side of business, Cormac. Noviomagus, as I said, treats money like a god. Therefore, they trade with anyone who will pay. They send iron goods from the Anderida mines, swords, axes, spears, and arrowheads to the Goths, the Jutes, and the Angles. The weapons of war are purchased here."

"And the king allows this?"

"There is little he can do to stop it, and they also supply him with weapons and armor. The finest leather breastplates are made in Noviomagus, as well as swords of quality and bronze shields."

"It is not right to trade with your enemies."

"Life is very simple when one is young."

"How does the king survive if even his own people support his enemies?"

"He survives because he is great. But think on this: these merchants supply the Jutes and earn great wealth. The king taxes them, which brings gold to his treasury. With this gold he buys weapons to fight the Jutes. So without the Jutes, Uther would have less gold with which to oppose them."

"But if the Jutes—and the others—didn't attack him, he would not need so much gold," Cormac pointed out.

"Good! There is the seed of a debater within you. But if there were no enemies, he would not need an army, and without an army we would not need a king. So without the Jutes Uther would have no crown."

"You are making my head spin. Can we go now? The air in here is beginning to smell."

"A little while longer. We are meeting someone. You go outside—but do not wander far."

Cormac eased his way out into the alley to see a young girl struggling with a burly warrior wearing a horned helm. On the ground beside them lay an elderly man with blood seeping from a wound to his head. The warrior pulled the struggling girl from her feet, his right hand clamped across her mouth.

"Stop!" shouted Cormac, dragging his sword from his belt. The warrior cursed, flinging the girl to the ground. Cormac rushed forward, and to his surprise and relief, the attacker turned and fled. The lad approached the girl, helping her to her feet. She was slim and dark-haired, her face oval, her skin ivory pale. Cormac swallowed hard and knelt beside the old man; he was clean-shaven and wearing a long blue toga. The boy lifted his wrist, feeling for a pulse.

"I am sorry, my lady, but he is dead."

"Poor Cotta," she whispered.

"Why were you attacked?"

"Is there an inn near here called the Sign of the Bull?" she asked, turning her head toward him. He looked then into her pale gray eyes and saw that she was blind.

"Yes, I will take you there," he said, reaching out his hand. She did not move, so he took her arm.

"We cannot leave him like this," she said. "It is not right."

"I have a friend nearby. He will know what to do."

He led her into the inn, steering her carefully around the tables. The sudden noise of the interior alarmed her, and she gripped his arm, but he patted her hand and led her to Revelation, who stood swiftly.

"Anduine, where is Cotta?"

"Someone killed him, my lord."

Revelation cursed, flicked the silver coin to the waiting innkeeper, and then took the girl by the hand and led her outside. Cormac followed, a curious feeling of emptiness within him now that his charge was no longer in his care.

Outside, Revelation was kneeling by the old man. He closed the dead eyes and then stood. "We must leave him here. Swiftly."

"But Cotta . . ."

"If he could speak, he would insist on it. What did you see, Cormac?"

"A foreign man with a horned helm was pulling her away. I ran at him, and he fled."

"Bravely done, lad," said Revelation. "Thank the Source you had a need for fresh air." Dipping into the pocket of his coarse woolen habit, Revelation produced a small golden stone, which he held over the girl. Her dark hair lightened to corn yellow, and her simple dress of pale green wool became a tunic and trews of rust-brown and beige.

Three men entered the alley. Two wore bronze helms decorated with ravens' wings; the third was clothed all in black and carried no weapons.

"She's gone," said one of the men, running past Cormac. The other two entered the inn. Revelation led Anduine back along the alley as the two Vikings emerged from the building.

"You there! Wait!" came the shout.

Revelation turned. "Put you arms about her and treat her like your lover," he whispered to Cormac. Then he said, "Can I assist you, brothers? I have no money."

"The boy was seen with a girl in a green dress. Where is she?"

"The blind wench? A man came for her. He seemed greatly agitated; I think that is his friend lying dead back there."

Behind them Cormac leaned in to Anduine, resting his arms on her shoulders. He did not know what to do but had seen the village boys with the maidens. Softly he kissed her cheek, shielding her face from the three armed men.

"We are dead men!" hissed one of the warriors.

"Be silent, Atha! Girl, come here," ordered the leader.

Just then a group of militiamen rounded the alley, led by a middle-aged officer.

"What's going on here?" he asked, sending two of his men to check the body.

"The old man was robbed," said Revelation. "A terrible thing in such a civilized town."

"Did you see the attack?"

"No," said Revelation, "I was at the inn having a meal with my son and his wife. Perhaps these fine fellows can help you."

"Are you carrying money?" the officer asked.

"No," said Revelation with a sad smile, opening his arms for the search, which was swift and thorough.

"Do you have friends in Noviomagus?"

"I fear not."

"Work?"

"Not at present, but I am hopeful."

"Melvar!" called the officer, and a young soldier ran up. "Escort these . . . travelers from the town. I am sorry, but no one may stay who does not have means of support."

"I understand," said Revelation, taking Anduine by the

arm and leading her from the alley. She stumbled and almost fell, and the black-clad Viking leader cursed loudly.

"Blind! It's her!" He tried to follow, but the officer barred his way.

"Just a moment, sir. There are a few questions."

"We are merchants from Raetia. I have documents."

"Then let me see them, sir."

Beyond the alley the soldier Melvar led the trio to the western edge of Noviomagus. "You might be able to get work on some of the farms north of here," he said. "Otherwise I'd suggest Venta."

"Thank you," said Revelation. "You have been most kind."

"What is happening?" asked Cormac when the officer had gone. "Who were those warriors?"

"Wotan's hunters, and they are seeking Anduine."

"Why?"

"She is his bride, and he wants her."

"But he is a god . . . isn't he?"

"He is a devil, Cormac, and he must not have her. Now let us begone, for the hunt has just begun."

"Can you not work more magic?"

Revelation smiled. "Yes, but now is not the time. There is a circle of standing stones near here. We must reach them by nightfall and then . . . then you will need more courage than most men possess."

"Why?" asked Cormac.

"The demons are gathering," said Revelation.

The stones formed a circle some sixty feet across around the flat-topped crest of a hill eight miles from Noviomagus. Cormac led the weary Anduine to the center of the hill, where he spread his blanket and sat beside her. The blind girl had borne the journey well, staying close to Cormac, who steered her carefully away from jutting tree roots and rocks.

Revelation had moved ever farther ahead, and when the tired youngsters reached the hill, he was kneeling by an old altar stone, carefully notching his staff. Cormac approached him, but he waved the boy away, then began to measure the distance from the altar to the first standing stone, a massive gray-black monolith twice as tall as himself. Cormac returned to Anduine, gave her some water, and wandered to the other side of the circle. The huge stones were more jagged there, and one of them had fallen, the base cracked like a rotten tooth. Cormac knelt beside it. Carved into the stone was a heart bearing letters in Latin. The boy could not read Latin, but he had seen such inscriptions before. Two lovers had sat here, looking to the future with hope and joy. There were other carvings, some recent, and Cormac wished he could read them.

"Where is Revelation?" asked Anduine.

Cormac rose and, taking her hand, led her to the fallen stone, where they sat in the fading sunshine.

"He is close, marking the ground with chalk and measuring the distance between the stones."

"He is creating a spirit fortress," said Anduine, "sealing the circle."

"Will it keep the demons out?"

"It depends on how much magic he holds. When he came to see me in Austrasie, his power stone was almost finished."

"Power stone?"

"They are called Sipstrassi. All the lords carry them; my grandfather had three."

Cormac said nothing but watched as Revelation continued his esoteric work with the chalk, joining an apparently random series of lines, half circles, and six-sided stars.

"Why are they hunting you?" he asked Anduine. "There must be other brides less troublesome."

She smiled and took his hand. "You were born in a cave, and your life has been very sad. Your great friend was slain, and your sorrow is as deep as the sea. You are strong both in the body and in the soul, and there is a small wound—like a gash—on your right arm, where you fell while being chased by the hunters." Reaching out, she took his right hand, her fingers sliding softly along the skin of his arm until she reached the graze. "And now," she said, "it is gone."

He glanced down. All signs of the tear in the skin had vanished.

"You, too, are a sorceress?"

"And that is why they want me. They killed my father, but Cotta and the Lord Revelation rescued me. They thought I would be safe in Britannia, but there is no safe place. The gates are open."

Revelation joined them, his face streaked with sweat and dust, his gray eyes showing his fatigue. "The power of the stone is used up," he said. "Now we wait."

"Why has Wotan left the Halls of Asgard?" asked Cormac. "Is it Ragnorak? Has the end of the world come?"

Revelation chuckled. "Three fine questions, Cormac! The most important, though, is the last. If we are all alive in the morning, I will answer it for you. But for now let us prepare. Take Anduine to the altar stone and lift her over the chalk marks. None of them must be disturbed."

The youth did as he was bidden, then drew his sword and plunged it in the ground beside him. The sun was dipping over the sea in red fire, and the sky was streaked with glowing clouds.

"Come here," said Revelation, and Cormac squatted down beside him.

"Tonight you will be tested. I want you to understand that it will begin with deceit and they will want you to leave the circle. But you must be strong no matter what happens. Do you understand?"

"Stay within the circle. Yes, I understand."

"If they break through, one of us must kill Anduine."

"No!"

"*Yes.* They must not have her power. There is so much I wish I could explain, Cormac. You asked about Ragnarok. It will come soon if they take her, later if they do not. But believe me, it will be better for her to die at our hands than theirs."

"How can we fight demons?"

"You cannot. I can. But if they fail, they will be followed by men. I wish I knew how many. Then you will fight. I hope Grysstha taught you well."

"He did," said Cormac. "But I am frightened now."

"As am I; there is no shame in that. Fetch your sword."

Cormac turned and rose to see the maid Anduine kneeling by the blade, her hands slowly running down the length of the steel.

"What are you doing?" he asked.

"Nothing that will harm you, Cormac," she replied, pulling the sword clear of the earth and offering it to him hilt first.

The sun sank, the last glimmerings of light fading in the western sky. A cool wind rose, hissing through the long grass. Cormac shivered and took his sword to the waiting Revelation.

"Sit down and gaze upon the blade," said Revelation. "It is a part of you now. Your harmony, your spirit, your life flows through it. These three mysteries a warrior must understand: life, harmony, and spirit. The first is life, sometimes called the Greek gift, for it is taken back day after day. What is it? It is breath, it is laughter, it is joy. It is a candle whose flame falls toward a tomb. The brighter the light, the shorter its existence. But one thing is certain, and this the warrior knows. All lives end. A man can hide in a cave all his days, avoiding war, avoiding pestilence, and still he will one day die. Better the bright flame, the great joy. A man who has never known sorrow can never appreciate joy. So the man who has not faced death can never understand life.

"Harmony, Cormac, is the second mystery. The tree knows harmony, and the breeze and the quiet stars. Man rarely finds it. Find it now, here on this lonely hill. Listen to the beating of your heart, feel the air in your lungs, see the glory of the moon. Be at one with the night. Be at one with these stones. Be at one with your sword and yourself. For in harmony is strength, and in strength there is life.

"Lastly there is spirit. Tonight you will want to run . . . to hide . . . to escape. But spirit will tell you to stand firm. It is a small voice and easy to shut out. But you will listen. For spirit is all a man has against the darkness. And only by following the voice of spirit can a man grow strong. Courage, loyalty, friendship, and love are all gifts of spirit.

"I know you cannot understand now all that I am saying, but soak the words into your soul. For tonight you will see evil and know despair."

"I will not run. I will not hide," said the boy.

Revelation placed his hand on Cormac's shoulder. "I know that."

A swirling mist rose up around them like the smoke of a great fire, rolling tendrils questing across the circle and recoiling as they touched the chalk lines. Higher and higher it rose, closing over their heads in a gray dome. Cormac's mouth was dry, but sweat dripped into his eyes. He wiped it clear and stood with his sword at the ready.

"Be calm," Revelation said softly.

A sibilant whispering began within the mist, and Cormac heard his name being called over and over. Then the gray wall parted, and he saw Grysstha kneeling at the edge of the circle, the two arrows still jutting from his chest.

"Help me, boy," groaned the old man.

"Grysstha!" yelled Cormac, moving toward him, but Revelation's hand gripped his arm.

"It is a lie, Cormac. That is not your friend."

"It is! I know him."

"Then how is he here, forty miles from where his body lay? No, it is a deceit."

"Help me, Cormac. Why won't you help me? I spent my years helping you."

"Be strong, boy," whispered Revelation, "and think on this: If he loved you, why would he call you to be slain by demons? It is *not* him."

Cormac swallowed hard, tearing his eyes from the kneeling man. Then the figure rose, the flesh stripping away like the skin of a snake. It swelled and curved, dark horns sprouting from its brow, long gleaming fangs rimming its mouth.

"I see you!" it hissed, pointing a taloned finger at Revelation. "I know you!"

A black sword appeared in its hand, and it rushed at the slender chalk line. White fire blossomed, scorching its skin. It fell back, screaming, then attacked once more. Other bestial figures appeared behind it, screeching and calling. Cormac hefted his sword, the blade gleaming white as captured moonlight. The mass beyond the circle charged, and a thunderous explosion roared from the ground. Many of the demonic beasts fell back, writhing and covered in flames, but three entered the circle. Revelation raised his staff over his head and was instantly clothed in black and silver armor, the staff now a silver lance that split into two swords of dazzling brightness. He leapt to meet the attackers, and with a wild scream Cormac rushed to aid him.

A demon with the face of a lion lunged at him with a dark sword. Cormac blocked the blow, rolled his wrists, and sent his own blade hissing into the creature's neck. Green gore fountained into the air, and the beast fell dying.

"The girl! Guard the girl!" screamed Revelation.

Cormac swung his eyes from Revelation's battle with the two demons to see Anduine being dragged from the altar by two men. Without pause for thought, he leapt forward. The first of the men ran at him, and the boy saw that his attacker's eyes were as red as blood. As the man's mouth opened to reveal long curved fangs, fear struck Cormac like a physical blow and his pace faltered. But just as the creature bore down on him with terrifying speed, the boy's courage flared. The sword flashed up to block a blow from a slender dagger and then down, cleaving the demon's collarbone and exiting through the belly. With a hideous scream the beast died. Cormac hurdled the body, and the creature holding Anduine threw her to one side and drew a gray sword.

"Your blood is mine," it hissed, baring its fangs.

Their swords met in flashing arcs, and Cormac was forced back across the circle in a desperate effort to ward off the demonic attack. Within seconds he knew he was hopelessly outclassed. Three times his enemy's sword was blocked within inches of his throat, and every counter of his own was turned aside with contemptuous ease. Suddenly he tripped over a jutting rock, tumbling to his back. The demon leapt for him, the sword slashing down . . . only to be blocked by the blade of Revelation. The silver-armored warrior brushed aside a second blow, spun on his heel, and beheaded his opponent.

As suddenly as it had come, the mist disappeared, the stars and moon shining with pure light on the stones.

"Are we safe?" whispered Cormac as Revelation pulled him to his feet. Beyond the circle stood seven Viking warriors.

"Not yet," said Revelation.

The black-clad man they had seen in Noviomagus stepped forward. "Release the girl and you will live."

"Come and take her," offered Revelation, and the warriors advanced in a grim line, some holding swords and others holding axes. Cormac stood rooted to the spot, waiting for Revelation to signal a move. When it came, it surprised the Vikings as much as it astonished Cormac.

Revelation charged.

His swords slashed down at the first men in the line, and two were dead in that instant. In the chaotic melee that followed Cormac screamed a wild battle cry and launched himself at the Vikings to Revelation's right, his sword hammering into a man's arm and half severing it. The attacker yelled in pain and leapt to his left, blocking his comrades' attack on Cormac. The boy lunged his sword into the man's suddenly unprotected belly, then shoulder charged his way through them.

A sword sliced into his shoulder, but diving to the ground, he rolled under a swinging ax, crashing into the axman's legs. The Viking tumbled to the ground, and Cormac swung his sword viciously into his neck. Bright blood spurted over the blade. Rising to his feet, he saw that Revelation had killed the last of the warriors; the black-clad leader was sprinting away across the circle. Revelation swept up a fallen ax and hurled it with terrifying force to take the leader in the back of the neck, almost severing the head. Cormac glanced around the circle, but no fresh enemies could be seen. Then he looked toward Revelation and froze, his sword dropping from his fingers.

Gone was the beard and the lion's mane of silver hair. Instead, standing before him was the dark-haired warrior of his dream, the man who had leapt from the cliff on the day Cormac was born.

"What is the matter, boy? Is my real face so terrible?"

"It is to me," said Cormac. "Tell me your name, your true name."

"I am Culain lach Feragh, once called the Lance Lord."

"The Great Betrayer."

Culain's gray eyes locked onto Cormac's. "I have been called that—and not without justification. But what is it to you?"

"I am the babe you left in the cave, the son you left to rot."

Culain's eyes closed, and he turned away momentarily. Then, taking a deep breath, he turned to Cormac.

"Can you prove this?"

"I don't have to. I know who I am. Grysstha found me the day you . . . I was going to say died, but that is obviously not true. You helped my mother to the Cave of Sol Invictus. You told her you were sorry you had led her to this. Then you killed those men and went to the cliff top. There you threw the sword into a tree while the horseman and the cripple watched."

"Even if you were the babe, you were too young to see all that," said Culain.

Cormac lifted the stone from around his neck and tossed it to the warrior. "I didn't know any of it until the day I ran away, when I slept in the cave and saw a vision. But I was found in that cave, beside the warhound and her pups, and for all my life men have called me 'demon's son.' Had it not been for Grysstha, I would have been slain then."

"We thought you dead," whispered Culain.

"For years I dreamed you would come for me . . . it gave me hope and strength. But you never did. Why did you not come back—even to bury your son?"

"You are not my son, Cormac. Would that you were!"

"But you were with her!"

"I loved her, but I am not your father. That honor goes to her husband, Uther, high king of Britain."

Cormac stared at the strong, square face of the warrior who had been Revelation and searched in his own heart for hatred. There was nothing. In that moment of recognition something had died within the boy, and its passing

had been masked by his instant anger. Now that anger
was gone, and Cormac was more truly alone than he had
ever been.

"I am sorry, boy," said Culain. "Pick up your sword.
We must go."

"Go?" whispered Cormac. "I'll not go with you."

He retrieved his blade, turned his back on Culain and
Anduine, and began to walk toward the south and Noviomagus. But just before he reached the edge of the circle a
blinding flash of light reared up before him, and his vision swam. As swiftly as it had come, the brightness was
gone, and Cormac blinked.

Ahead of him was not the scene of recent memory, the
sea glistening darkly beyond the white walls of Noviomagus. Instead, mountains reared against the horizon,
snow-capped and majestic, cloaked in forests of pine and
rowan.

"We need to speak," said Culain. "And you are safer
here."

Suddenly Cormac's anger flared once more, this time
as a berserk fury. Without a word he leapt at Culain,
sword flashing for the man's head. Culain blocked the
blow with dazzling speed but was forced back by the ferocious double-handed assault. Time and again Cormac
came within scant inches of delivering the death blow,
but each attack was countered with astonishing skill. In
the background, unable to see what was happening,
Anduine stumbled forward with arms outstretched, calling their names. In his rage Cormac did not notice the
blind girl, and his sword slashed in a wide arc, missing
Culain and slicing toward the girl. Culain leapt feetfirst at
the boy, catapulting him from his feet, the swinging
sword catching Anduine high in the shoulder. Blood

spurted from the scored flesh and Anduine screamed, but Culain ran to her, holding Cormac's stone against the wound, which sealed instantly.

From the ground Cormac viewed the scene with horror and deep shame. He sat up and, leaving his sword where it lay, approached the others.

"I am sorry, Anduine. I did not see you."

She reached out, and he took her hand. Her smile was as welcome as sunshine after a storm.

"Are we all friends again?" she asked. Cormac could not reply, and from Culain there was a grim silence. "How sad," said Anduine, her smile fading.

"I will find some wood for a fire," said Culain. "We will camp here tonight, and tomorrow we will journey into the mountains. I used to have a home here; it will afford us safety for a while at least."

He stood and wandered from the circle. Under the bright moonlight Cormac sat with Anduine, unable to find the words to approach her. But he held to her hand as if it were a talisman.

She shivered. "You are cold?"

"A little."

Reluctantly he released her hand and fetched the blanket, which he wrapped around her slender frame. During the battle with the Vikings the spell of changing had vanished, and now she was as Cormac had first seen her: dark-haired and possessed of a fragile beauty. She held the blanket to her with both hands, and Cormac felt the absence of her touch.

"Has your anger gone?" she asked.

"No, it is waiting deep inside me. I feel it like the winter chill. I wish I did not."

"Revelation is not your enemy."

"I know. But he betrayed me, he left me."

"He thought you dead."

"But I wasn't! All the years of my life have been filled with pain. Had it not been for Grysstha, I would have died. And no one would have cared. I never knew my mother; I never felt her touch or her love. And why? Because Culain stole her from her husband. From my father! It was wrong!"

"The story of the betrayal is well known," she whispered. "Perhaps too well known. But there is nothing base about Revelation. I know. I think you should wait until you can speak with him. Hold your anger."

"He was the king's closest friend," said Cormac. "The queen's champion. What can he say to lessen his shame? If he needed to rut like a bull, why did he not choose one of a thousand other women? Why my mother?"

"I cannot answer these questions. But he can."

"That, at least, is true enough," said Culain, dropping the bundle of dry wood to the grass. Once more he wore the brown woolen habit and carried the wooden staff of Revelation, though this time there was no beard, no lion's mane of gray hair.

"What happened to my mother?" Cormac asked once the fire was lit.

"She died in Sicambria two years ago."

"Were you with her?"

"No; I was in Tingis."

"If you were so in love, why did you leave her?"

Revelation did not reply but lay back, his eyes fixed to the stars.

"This is not the time," said Anduine softly, laying her hand on Cormac's arm.

"There will never be a time," hissed the boy, "for there

are no answers. Only excuses! I do not know if Uther loved her, but she was his wife. The betrayer knew that and should never have touched her."

"Cormac! Cormac!" said Anduine. "You speak as if she were an object like a cloak. She was not—she was a woman and a strong one. She traveled with the Blood King across the Mist and fought the Witch Queen alongside him. Once, when he was a hunted child, she saved him by killing an assassin. Did she not have a choice?"

Revelation sat up and added wood to the fire. "Do not seek to defend me, Anduine, for the boy is right. There are no answers, only excuses. That is all there is to be said. I wish it were different. Here, Cormac, this is yours." He tossed the stone and the chain across the fire. "I gave it to your mother a year before you were born; it was what saved you in the cave. It is Sipstrassi, the stone from heaven."

"I do not want it," said Cormac, letting it fall to the ground. He watched with satisfaction as the anger flared in Revelation's eyes and then saw the iron control with which the warrior quelled it.

"Your anger I can understand, Cormac, but your stupidity galls me," said Revelation, lying down and turning his back to the fire.

◊ 5 ◊

THE FOLLOWING MORNING the trio made their way deep into the Caledones mountains, far to the north of the Wall of Hadrian, arriving at a ruined cabin just after noon. The roof had given way, and a family of pack rats nested by the stone hearth. Revelation and Cormac spent several hours repairing the building and cleaning the dust of many years from the floors of the three-roomed dwelling.

"Could you not use magic?" asked Cormac, wiping sweat and dirt from his face as Revelation packed the roof with turf.

"Some things are better done with hands and heart," Revelation answered.

These were the first words spoken by the two men since the clash in the circle, and once more an uncomfortable silence settled. Anduine was sitting beside the nearby stream, scrubbing rusted pots and carefully removing fungi from the wooden platters Cormac had found in a rotting cupboard. Late in the afternoon Revelation set traps in the hills above the cabin, and after a cool uncomfortable night on the floor of the main room, they breakfasted on roast rabbit and wild onions.

"To the north of here is a second cabin," said Revelation, "and close by you will find apple and pear trees. The game is also plentiful higher in the mountains—deer and mountain sheep, rabbits and pigeon. Can you use a bow?"

"I can learn," said Cormac, "but I am expert with the sling."

Revelation nodded. "It is wise also to learn what plants give nourishment. The leaves of marigold contain goodness, as do nettles, and you will find onions and turnips in profusion in the western valley."

"You sound as if you were going away," said Anduine.

"I must. I need to find a new stone, for I have little magic left."

"How long will you be away?" she asked, and Cormac hated the edge of fear in her voice.

"Less than a week if all goes well. But I will remain here for a while. There is much to be done."

"We do not need you," said Cormac. "Go when you please."

Revelation ignored him but later, as Anduine stripped and dressed the rest of the meat, took him out into the open ground before the cabin.

"She is in great danger, Cormac, and if you are to protect her, you must make yourself stronger, faster, more deadly than you are now. As matters stand, an old milkmaid could take her from you."

Cormac sneered and was about to reply when Revelation's fist hammered into his chin. The youth hit the ground hard, his head spinning.

"The Romans call it boxing," said Revelation, "but it was refined by a Greek called Carpophorus. Stand up."

Cormac pushed himself to his feet, then dived at the taller man. Revelation swayed back, lifting his knee into Cormac's face, and the ground came up at him once more. Blood oozed from his nose, and he had difficulty keeping Revelation in focus. Still he rose and charged, but this time a fist crashed into his belly and he doubled over, all air smashed from his lungs, and lay on the ground battling for breath. After several minutes he struggled to his knees. Revelation was sitting on a fallen log.

"Here, in these high lonely mountains, I trained your father—and your mother. Here the Witch Queen sent her killers, and from here Uther set out to recapture his father's kingdom. He did not whine or complain; he did not sneer when he should have been learning. He merely set his sights on a goal and achieved it. You have two choices, child: leave or learn. Which do you make?"

"I hate you," whispered Cormac.

"That is immaterial. Choose!"

Cormac looked up into the cold gray eyes and bit back the angry words crowding for release. "I will learn."

"Your first lesson is obedience, and it is vital. In order to be stronger you must push yourself to the edge of your endurance. I shall ask you to do more than is necessary, though at times you will feel I am being needlessly cruel. But you must obey. Do you understand, child?"

"I am not a child," snapped Cormac.

"Understand this, *child*. I was born when the sun shone on Atlantis. I fought with the Israelites in the land of Canaan, and I was a god to the Greeks and a king among the tribes of Britannia. My days are numbered in tens of thousands. And what are you? You are the leaf that spans a season, and I am the oak that weathers the centuries. You are a child. Uther is a child. The oldest man in the world is a child to me. Now, if you must hate me—and I fear you must—at least hate me like a man and not like some petulant babe. I am stronger than you, more skilled than you. I can destroy you with or without weapons. So learn, and one day you may beat me . . . though I doubt it."

"One day I will kill you," said Cormac.

"Then prepare yourself." Revelation thrust a long stick into the ground, then a second a foot to the left. "You see that stand of pine on the mountain?"

"Yes."

"Run to it and return here before the shadow touches the second stick."

"Why?"

"Do it or leave this mountain," said Revelation, standing and wandering away toward the cabin.

Cormac took a deep breath, wiped the clotting blood from his nose, and set off at an easy lope, the clean mountain air filling his lungs, his legs driving him easily up the mountain trail. Once he was among the trees, he could not see the stand of pine, and he increased his pace. His calves began to burn, but he pushed himself. As the gradient grew ever more steep, his breathing grew faster. He emerged from the trees still a half mile short of the target and staggered to a walk, sucking in great gulps of air. He was tempted to sit and recover his strength or even to return to Revelation and tell him that he had reached the pine. But he did not. He struggled on and up. Sweat drenched his face and tunic, and his legs felt as if candle flames had been lit inside them when at last he staggered into the grove. Hanging from a branch was a clay jug of water. He drank deeply and set off for the cabin. On the downhill run his tired legs betrayed him. Missing his footing, he stumbled, fell, and rolled down the slope, coming up hard against a tree root, which gouged his side. Up once more, he continued his halting run until he came into the clearing before the cabin.

"Not good," said Revelation, staring coolly at the red-faced youth. "It is only two miles, Cormac. You will do it again this evening and tomorrow. Look at your mark."

The shadow was three finger breadths past the stick.

"Your arms and shoulders are strong, but it is strength without speed. How did you build them?"

Cormac, at last able to excel, moved to a tree and leapt to grab an overhanging branch. Swiftly he raised himself to touch his chin to the branch over and over with smooth, rhythmic movements.

"Keep going," said Revelation.

At the count of one hundred Cormac dropped to the ground, the muscles of his arms burning, his eyes gleaming with triumph.

"That builds strength but not speed," said Revelation. "It is worthwhile, but it must be complemented with other work. You are powerful for your age, but you are not supple. A swordsman must be lightning-swift." He took a long whittled stick and held it horizontally between his fingers. "Place your hand over the top of the stick, fingers straight, and when I release it, catch it."

"Simple," said Cormac, holding his hand over the wood and tensing for the strike. Revelation released the stick, and Cormac's hand swept down, clutching at air.

"Simple?" echoed Revelation.

Three times more Cormac attempted to catch the stick and once almost made it, his fingers striking the wood and accelerating its fall.

"You are too stiff in the hips, and the muscles of your shoulders are tense and therefore immobile."

"It is not possible," said Cormac.

"Then you hold the stick." The boy did so, and as his fingers parted, Revelation's hand dropped like a striking snake when the stick had fallen less than a foot. "Speed, Cormac. Action without thought. Do not concern yourself about catching the stick, merely do it. Empty your mind, loosen your limbs."

After some thirty attempts Cormac succeeded. There followed another ten failures. It was galling for the boy, but his will to succeed carried him on. Before the morning was spent he had caught the wood seven times with his right hand and three times with his left.

Revelation lifted his hand to his face, and his image shifted and blurred, becoming once more Culain of the Silver Lance.

For an hour more Culain and the tiring youth practiced with swords. Cormac almost forgot his hatred of the tall warrior as he marveled at the man's natural grace and superb reflexes. Time and again he would roll his wrists, his blade skimming over Cormac's to hiss to a halt touching the skin of the boy's neck, arm, or chest.

Culain lach Feragh was more than a warrior, Cormac realized; he was a prince among warriors.

But as soon as the session was over Cormac's hostility returned. Culain read it in his eyes and sheathed his sword, creating once more the silver lance.

"Take Anduine up into the hills," he said. "Help her identify the paths." Turning on his heel, the warrior strode into the cabin, bringing the girl out into the sunlight.

Cormac took her arm and led her into the trees.

"Where is the sun?" she asked. "I cannot feel her heat."

"Above the woods, shielded by the leaves."

"Tell me about the leaves."

Bending, he lifted a fallen leaf from the ground and pressed it into her hand. Her fingers fluttered over the surface. "Oak?"

"Yes. A huge, hoary oak, as old as time."

"Is it a handsome tree?"

"Like a strong old man, grim and unyielding."

"And the sky?"

"Blue and clear."

"Describe blue—as you see it," she said.

He stopped and thought for a moment. "Have you ever felt silk?"

"Yes. I had a dress of silk for my last birthday."

"Grysstha once had a small piece of silk, and it was wondrous soft and smooth. Blue is like that. Just to look upon it fills the heart with joy."

"A sky of silk," she whispered. "How pretty it must be! And the clouds. How do you see the clouds?"

"There are few clouds today, and they float like white honey cakes, far away and yet so clear that you feel you could reach out and touch them."

"A silk and honey cake sky," she said. "Oh, Cormac, it is so beautiful. I cannot see it, but I can feel it deep in my heart."

"I would cut off my arm to let you see it," he said.

"Don't say that," she said. "Don't ever think that I am unhappy because I cannot share your visions. Take me farther up the mountain. Show me flowers that I can touch and smell and describe them to me in silks and honey cakes."

Each morning, when his arduous training was completed, Cormac would take Anduine walking through the woods—into hidden glens and hollows and often to a small lake, cool and clear beneath the towering mountains. He would marvel at her memory, for once having walked a path and found landmarks she could touch—a rounded boulder with a cleft at the center, a tree with a huge knot on the bark, a V-shaped root—she would walk it unerringly from then on. Sometimes she could judge the trails by the gradients or, knowing the hour, by the position of the sun as it warmed her face. Once she even challenged Cormac to a race and all but beat him to the cabin, tripping at the last over a jutting root.

The youth came to love those walks and their conversations. He took joy in describing the flying geese, the hunting fox, the proud longhorn cattle, the regal stags. She in turn enjoyed his company, the warmth of his voice, and the touch of his hand.

Only on the days when he had failed in tasks set him by Revelation did she find his presence unsettling, feeling his anger and hatred charging the air around her with a tension she had no desire to share.

"He does it only so that you will improve," she said one damp morning as they sat beneath an oak, waiting for a shower to pass.

"He wants to see me fail."

"Not so, Cormac, and you know it. He trained your father here, and I would imagine he felt as you do."

Cormac was silent for a time, and she felt his emotions soften. His fingers slid across her hand, squeezing it gently. She smiled. "Are you feeling yourself again?"

"Yes. But I do not understand the man. In the circle he told me to kill you should the demons break through. They did so, but he did not try to kill you. Then he brought us here in a flash of light. Why did he not do it at the start? Then we would not have had to fight the demons at all."

"For me that is what makes him great," said Anduine, leaning in to Cormac and resting her head on his shoulder.

"He was right. It would be better for me to die than to aid Wotan with my soul. But that is the *strategist* speaking. When it came to the battle, it was the *man* who fought it, and he would give the last drop of his blood before taking mine. As to coming here, he could not while the demons lived. All the enemies had to be slain so that none could mark our passing. Had we run here at the start, then they would have followed. As it is, Cormac, one day they will find us."

He put his arm around her, drawing her to him. "I, too, would die before allowing them to harm you."

"Why?" she whispered.

He cleared his throat and stood. "The rain is stopping. Let us find the orchard."

They discovered the lake on Midsummer Day, disturbing a family of swans, and Cormac splashed into the water, hurling his tunic and leggings to a rock by the waterside. He swam for some minutes, while Anduine sat patiently beneath a towering growth of honeysuckle. Then he waded ashore and sat beside her, reveling in the warmth of the sun on his naked body.

"Do you swim?" he asked.

"No."

"Would you like to learn?"

She nodded and stood, untying the neck of her pale green dress and slipping it over her shoulders. As it fell to the ground, Cormac swallowed hard and looked away. Her body was ivory-pale, her breasts full, her waist tiny, her hips . . .

"Follow me into the lake," he said, clearing his throat and turning from her. She laughed as she felt the cool water on her feet and ankles, then waded farther.

"Where are you?" she called.

"I am here," he answered, taking her hand. "Turn to face the shore and lean back into my arms."

"The water will go over my head."

"I will support you. Trust me."

She fell back into his arms, kicking out her legs and floating on the surface of the lake. "Oh, it is beautiful," she said. "What must I do?"

Remembering the teachings of Grysstha in the river of the South Saxon, he said, "Your lungs will keep you afloat as long as there is air in them. Breathe in deeply, spread your arms, and kick out with your feet." His arms slid under her body, and he found himself gazing down at her breasts, her white belly, and the triangle of dark hair pointing like an arrow to her thighs. Swinging his head, he fixed his gaze on her face. "Take a deep breath and hold it," he said. Gently he lowered his hands. For several seconds she floated, and then, as if realizing she was unsupported, she dropped her hips and her head dipped below the sparkling water. Swiftly he raised her as she flung her arms around his neck, coughing and sputtering.

"Are you all right?"

"You let me go," she accused him.

"I was here. You were safe." Leaning down, he kissed her brow, pushing the dark, wet hair back from her face. She laughed and returned the kiss, biting his lip.

"Why?" she asked him, her voice husky.

"Why what?"

"Why would you die for me?"

"Because you are in my care. Because . . . you are my friend."

"Your friend?"

He was silent for a moment, savoring the touch of her body against his. "Because I love you," he said at last.

"Do you love me enough to give me your eyes?"

"My eyes?"

"Do you?"

"I do not understand you."

"If you say yes, you will be blind but I will be able to see. Do you love me that much?"

"Yes. I love you more than life." Her hands swept up, touching both sides of his face, her thumbs resting on his eyelids. Darkness enveloped him, a terrible, sickening emptiness. He cried out, and she led him to the shoreline, where he stubbed his toe on a rock. She helped him sit, and fear swept over him. What had he *done*?

"Oh, Cormac, so that is the sky. How wonderful! And the trees, just as you described them. And you, Cormac, so handsome, so strong. Do you regret your gift?"

"No," he lied, his pride overcoming his terror.

Her hands touched his face once more, and his sight returned. He took her in his arms, pulling her to him as he saw the tears in her eyes.

"Why did you return my gift?" he asked.

"Because I love you also. And because you looked so lost and afraid. No one has ever done for me what you offered to do, Cormac. I will never forget it."

"Then why are you crying?"

She did not reply. How could she tell him that until now she had never understood the loneliness of darkness?

"His anger toward you is very great," said Anduine as she and Culain sat in the sunshine. Two months had passed, and now the cooler breezes of autumn whispered in the golden leaves. Every day Cormac and Culain would work together for many hours—boxing, wrestling, dueling with sword or quarterstaff. But when the sessions were over, the youth would turn away, his feelings masked, his gray eyes showing no emotion.

"I know," answered the warrior, shielding his eyes and watching the boy gamely running on toward the stand of pine high up on the mountain's flank. "He has reason to. But he likes you, trusts you."

"I think so, my lord. But I cannot heal the anger. As I touch it, it recoils like mist before me. Will he not speak of it?"

"I have not tried to speak to him, Anduine. There would be little to gain for either of us. I first met his father on this mountain, and it was here that Uther learnt to love Laitha, my Gian Avur. Now the son follows. And still the world is at war, evil flourishes, and good men die. I am sorry about your father. Had I come sooner . . ."

"He was an old warrior," she said, smiling. "He died as he would have wished, with his sword in his hand, his enemies falling to him."

"He was brave to refuse Wotan."

"It was not bravery, my lord. He wanted a higher price for me. Wotan merely mistook greed for nobility."

"You miss very little, Anduine, for one who cannot see."

"You are leaving today?"

"Yes. You will be safe, I think, until I return. I am sorry that the cabin is so bare of luxury. It will be hard for you."

"I may just survive," she said, smiling. "Do not concern yourself."

"You are a fine woman."

Her smile faded. "And you are a good man, my lord. So why do you plan to die?"

"You see too much."

"You did not answer me."

"To ask the question means you know the answer, for the two are one."

"I want to hear you say it."

"Why, lady?"

"I want you to hear yourself. I want you to understand the futility."

"Another time, Anduine." He took her hand and kissed it softly.

"No, there will be no other time. You will not come back, and I will never meet you again."

For a while Culain was silent, and she felt the tension in him ease.

"All my life," he said at last, "all my long, long life I have been able to look at Culain and be proud. For Culain never acted basely. Culain was the true prince. My arrogance could have swamped mountains. I was immortal: the Mist Warrior, the Lance Lord from the Feragh. I was Apollo for the Greeks, Donner to the Norse, Agripash to the Hittites. But in all the interminable centuries I never betrayed a friend or broke a trust. Now I am no longer that Culain, and I wonder if ever I was."

"You speak of the queen?"

"Uther's bride. I raised her—here where we sit. She ran in these mountains, hunted and laughed, sang and knew joy. I was a father to her. I did not know then that she loved me, for she was a child of the earth and my love was a goddess of eternal beauty. But then you know the tale of the Witch Queen and her deeds." Culain shrugged. "When the battle was over, I should never have gone back. Uther and Laitha thought me dead; they were married then and, I believed, happy. But I found the last to be untrue. He ignored her, treating her with shameful disdain. He took other women and flaunted them at his palaces, leaving my Gian desolate and a laughingstock. I would have killed him, but she forbade it. I tried to comfort her. I pitied her. I loved her. I brought her happiness for a little while. Then they became reconciled, and our love was put away. She conceived a child by him—and all the past torments seemed forgotten.

"But it did not last, for his bitterness was too strong. He sent her to Dubris, telling her the sea air would help her in her pregnancy. Then he moved a young Iceni woman into his palace. I went to Gian." He chuckled, then sighed. "Foolish Culain; it was a trap. He had men watching the house. I was seen, and they tried to take me. I killed three of them—and one was an old friend.

"I took Gian to Anderida and then farther along the coast, having got a message to friends in Sicambria. A ship was due to meet us, and we sheltered in an old cave, safe from all—even the magic of Maedhlyn, Uther's Lord Enchanter."

"How did they find you?" she asked.

"Gian had a pet hound called Cabal. Uther's horse master, a crippled Brigante called Prasamaccus, released the beast outside Dubris, and it trailed us all the way to the cave. Gian was so pleased when it arrived, and I did not think—so great was her pleasure that it masked my intellect. The hound gave birth to a litter of five pups some time before Gian bore Cormac. A black and bitter day that was! The babe was dead, of that there is no doubt. But Gian left it with her Sipstrassi necklace, and somehow the magic brought him back.

"But by then the hunters had found me. I killed them all and carried Gian to the cliff top. Uther was already there, sitting on his warhorse. He was alone, and I thought of killing him. Gian stopped me once more, and I looked to the sea. There in the bay was the Sicambrian ship. I had no choice; I took Gian in my arms and leapt. I almost lost her in the waves, but at last we were safe. But she never recovered her spirit. The betrayal of Uther and the death of her son became linked in her mind as a punishment from God, and she sent me away."

"What became of her?" whispered Anduine.

"Nothing became of her. She was dead and yet living. She joined a community of God seekers in Belgica and stayed there for thirteen years, scrubbing floors, growing vegetables, cooking meals, studying ancient writings, and seeking forgiveness."

"Did she find it?"

"How could she? There is no god in the universe who would hate her. But she despised herself. She would never see me. Every year I journeyed to Belgica, and every year the gatekeeper would go to her, return, and send me away. Two years ago he told me she had died."

"And you, my lord? Where did you go?"

"I went to Africa. I became Revelation."

"And do you seek forgiveness?"

"No. I seek oblivion."

Culain sat opposite the young warrior in the watery sunshine, pleased with the progress Cormac had made in the last eight weeks. The youth was stronger now, his long legs capable of running for mile upon mile over any terrain, his arms and shoulders showing corded muscle, taut and powerful. He had outgrown the faded red tunic and now wore a buckskin shirt and woolen trews Culain had purchased from a traveling merchant passing through the Caledones toward Pinnata Castra in the east.

"We must talk, Cormac," said the Lance Lord.

"Why? We have not yet practiced with the sword."

"There will be no swordplay today. After we have spoken, I shall be leaving."

"I do not wish to talk," said Cormac, rising.

"Know your enemy," said Culain softly.

"What does that mean?"

"It means that from today you are on your own—and Anduine's life is in your care. It means that when Wotan finds you—as he will—only you and your skill will be between Anduine and the blade of sacrifice."

"You are leaving us?"

"Yes."

"Why?" asked the youth, returning to his seat on the fallen log.

"I do not answer to you for my life. But before we part, Cormac, I want you to understand the nature of the enemy, for in that you may find his weakness."

"How can I fight a god?"

"By understanding what a god is. We are not talking about the Source of All Things, we are talking about an immortal: a man who has discovered a means to live forever. But he is a man nonetheless. Look at me, Cormac. I also was an immortal. I was born when the sun shone over Atlantis, when the world was ours, when Pendarric the king opened the gates of the universe. But the oceans drank Atlantis, and the world was changed forever. Here, on this Island of Mist, you see the last remnants of Pendarric's power, for this was the northern outpost of the empire. The Standing Stones were gateways to journeys within and beyond the realm. We gave birth to all the gods and demons of the world. Werebeasts, dragons, blood drinkers—all were set free by Pendarric."

Culain sighed and rubbed at his eyes. "I know there is

too much to burden you with here. But you need to understand at least a part of a history that men no longer recall, save as legend. Pendarric discovered other worlds, and in opening the gates to those worlds he loosed beings very different from men. Atlantis was destroyed, but many of the people survived. Pendarric led thousands of us to a new realm—the Feragh. And we had Sipstrassi, the stone from heaven. You have seen its magic, felt its power. It saved us from aging but could not give us wisdom or prevent the onset of a terrible boredom. Man is a hunting, competitive animal. Unless there is ambition, there is apathy and chaos. We found ambitions. Many of us returned to the world, and with our powers we became gods. We built civilizations, and we warred one upon another. We made our dreams reality. And some of us saw the dangers . . . others did not. The seeds of madness are nurtured by unlimited power. The wars became more intense, more terrifying. The numbers of the slain could not be counted.

"One among us became Molech, the god of the Canaanites and the Amorites. He demanded the blood sacrifices from every family. Each firstborn son or daughter was consigned to the flames. Torture, mutilation, and death were his hallmarks. The agonized screams of his victims were as sweet to him as the music of the lyre. Pendarric called a council of the Feragh, and we joined together to oppose Molech. The war was long and bloody, but at last we destroyed his empire."

"But he survived," said Cormac.

"No. I found him on the battlements of Babel with his guard of demons. I cut my way through to him, and we faced each other high above the field of the fallen. Only once have I met a man of such skill, but I was at the magical peak of my strength and I slew Molech, cut his head from his shoulders, and hurled the body to the rocks below."

"Then how has he returned?"

"I do not know. But I will discover the truth, and I shall face him again."

"Alone?"

Culain smiled. "Yes, alone."

"You are no longer at the peak of your strength."

"Very true. I was almost slain twenty-five—no, twenty-six years ago. The Sipstrassi restored me, but since then I have not used its power for myself. I want to be a man again, to live out a life and die like a mortal."

"Then you will not beat him."

"Victory is not important, Cormac. True strength is born of striving. When you first ran to the pine, you could not return before the shadow passed the stick. Did you say, 'Ah, well, there is no point in running again'? No. You ran and grew stronger, fitter, faster. It is the same when facing evil. You do not grow stronger by running away. It is balance. Harmony."

"And how do you win if he kills you?" said Cormac.

"By sowing the seed of doubt in his mind. I may not win, Cormac, but I will come close. I will show him his weakness, and then a better man can destroy him."

"It sounds as if you were merely going away to die."

"Perhaps that is true. How will you fare here alone?"

"I do not know, but I will protect Anduine with my life."

"This I know." Culain dipped his hand into the leather pouch at his side and produced the Sipstrassi necklace Cormac had dropped in the circle of stones. The youth tensed, his eyes glinting with anger.

"I do not want it," he said.

"It gave you life," said Culain softly, "and whatever you think of me, you should know that your mother never recovered from losing you. It haunted her to her dying day. Add this to the burden of your hate for me. But it was not *my* gift to you—it was hers. With it you can protect Anduine far more powerfully than with the sword."

"I would not know how to use it."

Culain leaned forward. "Take it and I will show you."

"Give it to Anduine, and I will think about it after you have gone," said Cormac, rising once more.

"You are a stubborn man, Cormac. But I wish we could part as friends."

"I do not hate you, Culain," said the youth, "for you saved me from Agwaine and fought off the demons for Anduine. But had it not been for you, I would not have known a life of pain and sorrow. I am the son of a king, and I have been raised like a leper. You think I should thank you?"

"No, you are my shame brought to life. But I loved your mother and would have died for her."

"But you did not. Grysstha once told me that men will always excuse their shortcomings, but to your credit you never have. Try to understand, Culain, what I am saying. I admire you. I am sorry for you. But you are the father of my loneliness, and we could never be friends."

Culain nodded. "At least you do not hate me, and that is something to carry with me." He held out his hand, and Cormac took it. "Be on your guard, young warrior. Train every day. And remember the three mysteries: life, harmony, and spirit."

"I shall. Farewell, Revelation."

"Farewell, Prince Cormac."

◊ 6 ◊

IN THE MONTHS following the Trinovante uprising Britannia enjoyed an uneasy peace. Uther paced the halls of Camulodunum like a caged warhound, eagerly watching the roads from his private apartment in the north tower. Every time a messenger arrived, the king would hurry to the main hall, ripping the seals from dispatches and devouring the contents, ever seeking news of insurrection or invasion. But throughout the summer and into the autumn peace reigned, crops were gathered, and militiamen were sent home to their families.

Men walked warily around Uther, sensing his disquiet. Across the Gallic Sea a terrible army had ripped into the Sicambrian kingdoms of Belgica and Gaul, destroying their forces and burning their cities. The enemy king, Wotan, was named Anti-Christ by the Bishop of Rome, but that was not unusual. A score of barbarian kings had been dubbed the same name, and subsequently many had been admitted to the church.

Rome herself sent five legions to assist the Sicambrians. They were destroyed utterly, their standards taken.

But in Britain the people enjoyed the hot summer and the absence of war. Storehouses groaned under the weight of produce; the price of bread and wine plummeted. Only the merchants complained, for the rich export trade with Gaul had been disrupted by the war, and few were the trade ships docking at Dubris or Noviomagus.

Each morning Uther would climb to the north tower, lock the door of oak, and set the Sword of Power in its niche in the gray boulder. Then he would kneel before it and wait, focusing his thoughts. Dreams and visions would swirl in his mind, and his spirit would soar across the land from Pinnata Castra in the north to Dubris in the south, from Gariannonum in the east to Meriodunum in the west, seeking gatherings of armed men. Finding nothing, he would follow the coastline, spirit eyes scanning the gray waves for signs of long ships and Viking raiders.

But the seas were clear.

One bright morning he tried to cross the Gallic Sea but found himself halted by a force he could neither see nor pass, like a wall of crystal.

Confused and uncertain, he returned to his tower, opening the eyes of his body and removing the sword from the stone. Stepping to the ramparts, he felt the cool autumn breeze on his skin, and for a while his fears slumbered.

His manservant Baldric came to him at noon, bringing wine, cold meat, and a dish of the dark plums the king favored. Uther, in no mood for conversation, waved the lad away and sat at the window staring out at the distant sea.

He knew that Victorinus and Gwalchmai were concerned about his state of mind, and he could not explain the fear growing in his soul. He felt like a man walking a dark alleyway, knowing—without evidence and yet with certainty—that a monster awaited him at the next turn: faceless, formless, yet infinitely deadly.

Not for the first time in the last ten years Uther wished that Maedhlyn were close. The Lord Enchanter would have laid his fears to rest or at worst identified the danger.

"If wishes were horses, the beggars would ride," muttered Uther, shutting his mind from the memory of Maedhlyn's departure. Harsh words, hotter than acid, had poured from Uther that day. They were regretted within the hour but could not be drawn back. Once spoken, they hung in the air, carved on invisible stone, branded into the hearts of the hearers. And Maedhlyn had gone . . .

As Laitha had gone. And Culain . . .

Uther poured more wine, seeking to dull the memories and yet enhancing them. Gian Avur, Fawn of the Forest, was the name Culain had given to Laitha—a name Uther had never been allowed to use. But he had loved her and had been lost without her.

"Why, then, did you drive her into his arms?" he whispered.

There was no answer to be found in logic or intellect. But Uther knew where it lay, deep in the labyrinthine tunnels of dark emotion. The seeds of insanity were sown on that night in another world when the youth had first made love to the maid, only to have her whisper the name of Culain at the moment of Uther's greatest joy. The opposite of the alchemist's dream—gold become lead, light plunged into darkness. Even then he could have forgiven her, for Culain was dead. He could not . . . would not be jealous of a corpse. But the Lance Lord had returned, and Uther had seen the light of love reborn in Laitha's eyes.

Yet he could not send him away, for that would be

defeat. And he could not kill him, for he owed everything to Culain. He could only hope that her love for the Lance Lord would be overcome by her marriage vow to the king. And it was—but not enough. He tested her resolve time and again, treating her with appalling indifference, forcing her in her despair to the very act he feared above all others.

King of fools!

Uther, the Blood King, the Lord of No Defeat! What did it matter that armies could not withstand him when he dwelled in loneliness in a chilly tower? No sons to follow him, no wife to love him. He turned to the bronze mirror set on the wall; gray roots were showing under the henna-dyed hair, and the eyes were tired.

He wandered to the ramparts and stared down at the courtyard. The Sicambrian Ursus was strolling arm in arm with a young woman. Uther could not recognize her, but she seemed familiar. He smiled. The horse armor had been a miserable failure, becoming sodden and useless in the rain, but Ursus had proved a fine cavalry commander. The men liked his easy manner and quick wit, added to which he was not reckless and understood the importance in strategy of patience and forethought.

The king watched the easy way Ursus draped his arm over the woman's shoulder, drawing her to him in the shadows of a doorway, tilting her chin to kiss her lips. Uther shook his head and turned away. He rarely had women sent to his apartments these days; the act of loving left him with a deep sadness, a hollow empty loneliness.

His eyes scanned the green landscape, the rolling hills and the farms, the cattle herds and the sheep. All was at peace. Uther cursed softly. For years he had fostered the myth that he was the land, the soul, and the heart of

Britannia. Only his trusted friends knew that the sword gave him the power. Yet now, even without the aid of the mystic blade, Uther could feel a sinister threat growing in the shadows. The tranquillity around him was but an illusion, and the days of blood and fire were waiting to dawn.

Or are you getting old? he asked himself. Have you lied for so long about the myth that you have come to believe it?

A cold breeze touched him, and he shivered.

What was the threat? From where would it come?

"My lord?" said a voice, and Uther spun to find Victorinus standing in the doorway. "I knocked on the outer door, but there was no response," said the Roman. "I am sorry if I startled you."

"I was thinking," said the king. "What news?"

"The Bishop of Rome has agreed to a treaty with Wotan and has validated his claims to Gaul and Belgica."

Uther chuckled. "A short-lived Anti-Christ, was he not?"

Victorinus nodded, then removed his bronze helm. His white hair made him seem much older than his fifty years. Uther moved past him into the apartments, beckoning the general to sit.

"Still clean-shaven, my friend," said the king. "What will you do now that the pumice stones are no longer arriving?"

"I'll use a razor," said Victorinus, grinning. "It does not become a Roman to look like an unwashed barbarian."

"That is no way to speak to your king," said Uther, scratching at his own beard.

"But then your misfortune, sire, was to be born

without Roman blood. I can only offer my deepest sympathies."

"The arrogance of Rome survives even her downfall," said Uther, smiling. "Tell me of Wotan."

"The reports are contradictory, sire. He fought four major battles in Sicambria, crushing the Merovingians. Nothing is known of their king; some say he escaped to Italia, others that he sought refuge in Hispania."

"The strategies, man. Does he use cavalry? Or the Roman phalanx? Or just a horde, overwhelming by numbers?"

"His army is split into units. There are some mounted warriors, but in the main he relies on axmen and archers. He also fights where the battle is thickest, and it is said no sword can pierce his armor."

"Not a good trait in a general," muttered the king. "He should stay back, directing the battle."

"As you do, my lord?" asked Victorinus, raising an eyebrow.

Uther grinned. "I will one day," he said. "I'll sit on a canvas stool and watch you and Gwalchmai sunder the enemy."

"I wish you would, sire. My heart will not take the strain you put upon it with your recklessness."

"Has Wotan sent emissaries to other kings?" asked Uther.

"Not as far as we know—only the Bishop of Rome and the boy emperor. He has pledged not to lead his armies into Italia."

"Then where will he lead them?"

"You think he will invade Britain?"

"I need to know more about him. Where is he from? How did he weld the German tribes, the Norse, and the

Goths into such a disciplined army? And in so short a time?"

"I could go as an ambassador, sire. His court is now in Martius."

Uther nodded. "Take Ursus with you; he knows the land, the people, and the language. And a gift; I will arrange a suitable offering for a new king."

"Too fine a gift may be misread as weakness, sire, and you did have a treaty with Meroveus."

"Meroveus was a fool, his army the laughingstock of Europe. Our treaty was for trade, no more. You will explain to Wotan that the treaty was between the kings of Sicambria and Britain and that I acknowledge the agreement to remain active even as I acknowledge his right to the throne."

"Is that not dangerous, sire? You will be supporting the right of the conqueror against the right of blood."

"It is a dangerous world in which we live, Victorinus."

Ursus awoke in a cold sweat, his heart hammering. The girl beside him slept on under the warm blankets, her breathing even. The prince slid out from the bed and walked to the window, pulling back the velvet hangings and allowing the breeze to cool his flesh. The dream had been so real; he had seen his brother pursued through the streets of Martius and dragged into a wide hall. There Ursus had watched a tall blond-bearded warrior cut his brother's heart from his living body.

He moved to the table and found that there was still a little wine in the jar. He poured it into a clay goblet and drained it.

Just a dream, he told himself, born of his concern over the invasion of Gaul.

A bright light flashed behind his eyes, filling his head with fiery pain. He cried out and stumbled, blind and afraid, tipping the table to the floor.

"What is it?" screamed the girl. "Sweet Christos, are you ill?" But her voice faded back into the distance, and a roaring filled his ears. His vision cleared, and he saw once more the blond-bearded warrior, this time standing in a deep circular pit. Around him were other warriors, all wearing horned helms and carrying huge axes. A door above them opened, and two men dragged a naked prisoner to a set of wooden steps, forcing him to climb down into the pit. With horror Ursus saw that it was Meroveus, the king of Sicambria. His beard was matted, his hair encrusted with mud and filth; his slender body showed signs of cruel use, whip marks crisscrossing the skin.

"Well met, brother king," said the tall warrior, gripping the prisoner by his beard and hauling him upright. "Are you well?"

"I curse you, Wotan. May you burn in the fires of hell!"

"Fool! I am hell, and I lit the fires."

Meroveus was dragged to a greased and pointed stake and hoisted high in the air.

Ursus tore his eyes from the scene but could not block the awful sounds as the monarch was brutally impaled. Once more the bright light flashed, and now he was viewing a scene in a great wooden hall. Warriors surrounded a crowd, their lances aimed at men, women, and children who stood in silent terror. Ursus recognized many faces: cousins, uncles, aunts, nephews. Most of the Merovingian nobles were gathered there. Warriors in mail shirts began to throw buckets of water over the prisoners, jeering and laughing as the liquid splashed down.

It was a ridiculous scene yet tainted with a terrible menace. Once more the blond-bearded Wotan stepped forward, this time carrying a torch. Terrified screams sprang up from the prisoners as Wotan laughed and hurled the torch into the mass. Fire swept the group . . . and Ursus suddenly understood. It was not water they were drenched with . . . but oil. The lancers retired quickly as burning men ran like human torches, spreading the blaze.

The walls ran with flames, and dark smoke settled over the scene . . .

Ursus screamed and fell back, weeping piteously, into the arms of the girl.

"Dear God," she said, stroking his brow. "What is it?"

But he could not answer. There were no words in all the world.

There was only pain . . .

Two officers from the adjoining rooms entered, lifting Ursus to the wide bed. Other men gathered in the stone corridor. The surgeon was summoned, and the girl quietly gathered her clothing, dressed, and slipped away.

"What is the matter with him?" asked Plutarchus, a young cavalry officer who had befriended Ursus during the summer. "There is no wound."

His companion, Decimus Agrippa, a lean warrior with ten years of experience, merely shrugged and looked into Ursus' unblinking, unfocused eyes.

Gently he pressed the lids closed.

"Is he dead?" whispered Plutarchus.

"No, I think he is having a fit. I knew a man once who would suddenly go stiff and tremble with such a seizure. The great Julius was said to be so afflicted."

"Then he will recover?"

Agrippa nodded, then turned to the men in the corridor. "Off to your beds," he ordered. "The drama is over."

The two men covered Ursus with the linen sheet and the soft woolen blankets. "He does like luxury," said Agrippa, grinning. It was not often that the man smiled, and it made him almost handsome, thought Plutarchus. Agrippa was made for command—a cool, distant warrior whose skill and lack of recklessness led men to clamor to join his troop. In major engagements he lost fewer men than did the more reckless of his brother officers yet invariably achieved his objectives. He was known among the *Cohors Equitana* as the Dagger in the Night or, more simply, the Dagger.

Plutarchus was his second decurion, a young man fresh from the city of Eboracum and yet to prove his worth on the battlefield.

The surgeon arrived, checked Ursus' pulse and breathing, and tried to rouse him, breaking the wax seal on a phial of foul-smelling unguent and holding it below the unconscious man's nose. There was no reaction from Ursus, though Plutarchus gagged and moved away.

"He is in a deep state of shock," said the surgeon. "What happened here?"

Agrippa shrugged. "I was sleeping in the next room when I heard a man scream, then a woman. I came in with young Pluta to find the Sicambrian on the floor and the woman hysterical. I thought it was a fit."

"I doubt it," said the surgeon. "The muscles are not in spasm, and the heart is slow but regular. You!" he said to Plutarchus. "Bring a lantern to the bed." The young officer obeyed, and the surgeon opened the prince's right eye. The pupil had contracted to no more than a dot of darkness within the blue.

"How well do you know this man?"

"Hardly at all," answered Agrippa, "but Pluta has spent many days in his company."

"Is he a mystic?"

"No, I do not believe so, sir," said Plutarchus. "He has never spoken of it. He did tell me once that the House of Merovee was renowned for its knowledge of magic, but he said it with a smile, and I took him to be jesting."

"So," said the surgeon, "no speaking in strange tongues, no divining, no reading of the portents?"

"No, sir."

"Curious. And where is the woman?"

"Gone," said Agrippa. "I do not think she was desirous of more public scrutiny."

"Whores should get used to it," snapped the surgeon. "Very well; we'll leave him resting for tonight. I will send my daughter here tomorrow morning with a potion for him; he will sleep most of the day."

"Thank you, surgeon," said Agrippa solemnly, aware of the spreading grin on Plutarchus' face.

After the surgeon had departed, the younger man began to chuckle.

"You will share the cause of your humor?" Agrippa asked.

"He called his own daughter a whore. Do you not think that amusing? Half the officers have tried to entice her to bed, and the other half would like to. And here she was, alone and naked with the Sicambrian!"

"I am not laughing, Pluta. The Sicambrian has the morals of a gutter rat, and the lady deserves better. Do not mention her name to anyone."

"But she was seen by the other men in the corridor."

"They will say nothing, either. You understand me?"

"Of course."

"Good. Now let us leave our rutting ram to his rest."

Throughout the exchange between the two men Ursus had been conscious, though paralyzed. After they had gone, he lay unable to feel the soft sheet on his body, his memory hurling the visions of death to his mind's eye over and over again.

He saw Balan's heart torn from his chest and heard the agonized scream, watching helplessly as the light of life died in his brother's eyes. Poor Balan! Sweet little brother! Once he had cried when he found a fawn with a broken leg. Ursus had ended its misery, but Balan had been inconsolable for days. He should have entered the priesthood, but Ursus, using the power of an older brother's love, had talked him into the quest for riches.

Both men had grown used to the luxury of their father's palace in Tingis, but when the old man died and the size of his debts became clear, Ursus was unprepared for a life of near poverty. The brothers had used the last of the family wealth to secure passage to Sicambria, there to introduce themselves to their influential relatives. The king, Meroveus, had granted them a small farm near Martius where the court resided, but the revenues were meager.

Balan had been blissfully happy wandering the mountains, bathing in silver streams, composing poems, and sketching trees and landscapes. But the life did not suit Ursus, for there were few women to be had and a positive dearth of wide silk-covered beds.

But Balan would have been happy at the Monastery of Revelation in Tingis, sleeping on a cot bed and studying the mysteries. Now he was dead, victim of a demonic king and a greedy brother.

Toward dawn Ursus' skin began to tingle, and at last he could open his eyes. He stared for a long time at the rough-hewn ceiling, tears flowing, memories burning his soul—reshaping it until the heat of anguish fled, to be replaced by the ice of hatred.

"The Sicambrian has the morals of a gutter rat. The lady deserves better."

Balan had also deserved better from his brother.

Feeling returned to his arms and shoulders, and pushing back the bed linen, he forced himself to a sitting position and massaged his legs until he felt the blood begin to flow.

He felt weak and unsteady and filled with a sadness bordering on despair. The door opened, and Portia entered, carrying a wooden tray on which there was a bowl of fresh water, a small loaf of flat baked bread, some cheese, and a tiny copper phial stoppered with wax.

"Are you recovered?" she asked, placing the tray on the chest by the wall and pushing shut the door.

"Yes and no," he said. She sat beside him, her small body pressed to his and her arms around him. He could smell the sweet perfume in her auburn hair and feel her soft breasts against his chest. He lifted her chin and kissed her gently.

"Are you sure you are recovered? Father has sent a sleeping draft; he says rest is needed."

"I am sorry for your embarrassment last night. It must have been hard for you. Forgive me."

"There is nothing to forgive. We love each other."

Ursus winced at the words, then forced a smile. "Love can mean different things to different people. Agrippa said I have the morals of a gutter rat, and he was quite correct. He said you deserved better; he was right in that also. I am sorry, Portia."

"Do not be sorry. You did me no harm. Far from it," she said, stiffening as the realization of his rejection struck her. But she was Roman and of proud stock and would not let him see her pain. "There is food there. You should eat."

"I must see the king."

"I should dress first—and wash." Pulling away from him, she walked to the door. "You really are a fool, Ursus," she said, and the door closed behind her.

The prince washed swiftly, then dressed in shirt, tunic, and leggings of black under a pearl-gray cape. His riding boots were also stained gray and adorned with silver rings. The outfit would have cost a British cavalry commander a year's salarium, yet for the first time it gave Ursus no pleasure as he stood before the full-length bronze mirror.

Despite his messages of urgency, the king refused to see him during the morning, and the prince was left to wander the town of Camulodunum until the appointed hour. He breakfasted in the garden of an inn, then journeyed to the Street of Armorers, purchasing a new sword shaped after the Berber fashion with a slightly curved blade. Those swords were becoming increasingly fashionable with Uther's cavalry for their use from horseback. The curved blade sliced clear with greater ease than did the traditional gladius, and being longer, it increased the killing range.

The church bell tolled the fourth hour after noon, and Ursus swiftly made his way to the north tower, where Uther's manservant and squire, Baldric, bade him wait in the long room below Uther's apartments. There Ursus sat for a further frustrating hour before he was ushered in to the king.

Uther, his hair freshly dyed and his beard combed, was sitting in the fading sunshine, overlooking the fields and meadows beyond the fortress town. Ursus bowed.

"You mentioned urgency," said the king, waving him to a seat on the ramparts.

"Yes, my lord."

"I heard of your seizure. Are you well?"

"I am well in body, but my heart is sickened."

Swiftly and succinctly Ursus outlined the visions that had come to him and the nauseating slayings he had witnessed.

Uther said nothing, but his gray eyes grew bleak and distant. When the young man had concluded his tale, the king leaned back and switched his gaze to the countryside.

"It was not a dream, sire," said Ursus softly, mistaking the silence.

"I know that, boy. I know that." Uther stood and paced the ramparts. Finally he turned to the prince. "How do you feel about Wotan?"

"I hate him, sire, as I have hated no man in all my life."

"And how do you feel about yourself?"

"Myself? I do not understand."

"I think you do."

Ursus looked away, then returned his gaze to the king. "I get no pleasure from the mirror now," he said, "and my past is no longer a cause for pride."

Uther nodded. "And why do you come to me?"

"I want permission to return home and kill the usurper."

"No, that you shall not have."

Ursus rose to his feet, his face darkening. "Blood cries out for vengeance, sire. I cannot refuse it."

"You must," said the king, his voice gentle and almost sorrowful. "I will send you to Martius, but you will travel with Victorinus and a party of warriors as an embassy to the new king."

"Sweet Mithras! To face him and not to kill him? To bow and scrape before this vile animal?"

"Listen to me! I am not some farmer, responsible only for his family and his meager crop of barley. I am a king. I have a land to protect, a people. You think this Wotan will be content with Gaul and Belgica? No. I can feel the presence of his evil; I feel his cold eyes roaming my lands. Fate will decree that we face each other on some bloody battlefield, and if I am to win, I need knowledge: his men, his methods, his weaknesses. You understand?"

"Then send someone else, sire, for pity's sake."

"No. Harness your hatred and keep it on a tight rein. It will survive."

"But surely it will end his threat if I just kill him?"

"If it were that simple, I'd wish you God's luck. But it is not. The man uses sorcery, and he will be protected by man and demon. Believe me! And if you failed, they would know whence you came and have legitimate cause to wage war on Britain. And I am not ready for them."

"Very well, sire. It shall be as you say."

"Then swear it upon your brother's soul."

"There is no need . . ."

"Do it!"

Their eyes locked, and Ursus knew he was beaten. "I so swear."

"Good. Now we must have a new name for you—and a new face. Wotan has butchered the House of Merovee, and if you are recognized, your death is assured. You will meet Victorinus at Dubris. You will be Galead, a knight of Uther. Follow me." The king led Ursus into the inner apartments and drew the Sword of Power from its scabbard. As he touched the blade to the prince's shoulder, Uther's eyes narrowed in concentration.

Ursus felt a tingling sensation on his scalp and face, and his teeth began to ache. The king removed the sword and led the warrior to the oval mirror on the wall.

"Behold the latest of Uther's knights," he said with a wide grin.

Ursus stared into the mirror at the blond stranger with his close-cropped hair and eyes of summer blue.

"Galead," whispered the new knight. "So be it!"

◊ 7 ◊

THE WINTER WAS fierce in the Caledones, snowdrifts blocking trails, ice forcing its way into the cracks in the wooden walls of the cabin. The surrounding trees, stripped of their leaves, stood bare and skeletal, while the wind howled outside the sealed windows.

Cormac lay in the narrow bed with Anduine snuggled beside him and knew contentment. The door rattled in its frame, and the fire blazed brightly, dancing shadows flickering on the far wall. Cormac rolled over, his hand sliding gently over Anduine's rounded hip, and she lifted her head and kissed his chest.

Suddenly she froze.

"What is it?" he asked.

"There is someone on the mountain," she whispered. "Someone in danger."

"Did you hear something?"

"I can feel their fear."

"Their?"

"Two people, a man and a woman. The way is blocked. You must go to them, Cormac, or they will die."

He sat up and shivered. Even here in this bright, warm room, cold drafts hinted at the horror outside. "Where are they?"

"Beyond the stand of pine, across the pass. They are on the ridge leading to the sea."

"They are not our concern," he said, knowing his argument would be useless. "And I might die out there myself."

"You are strong, and you know the land. Please help them!"

He rose from the bed and dressed in a heavy woolen shirt, leather leggings, a sheepskin jerkin, and boots. The jerkin had a hood lined with wool that he drew over his red hair, tying it tightly under his chin.

"This is a heavy price to pay for your love, lady," he said.

"Is it?" she asked, sitting up, her long dark hair falling across her shoulders.

"No," he admitted. "Keep the fire going. I will try to be back by dawn."

He looked at his sword lying beside the hearth and considered carrying it with him, but it would only have encumbered him. Instead he slipped a long-bladed hunting knife behind his belt and stepped out into the blizzard, dragging the door shut with difficulty.

Since Culain's departure three months before Cormac had stuck to his training, increasing the length of his runs, working with ax and saw to build his muscles, and preparing the winter store of wood, which now stood six feet high and ran the length of the cabin, aiding the insulation on the north wall. His body was lean and powerful, his shoulders wide, his hips narrow. He set off toward the mountain peaks at an easy walk, using a six-foot quarterstaff to test the snow beneath his feet. To hurry would mean to sweat; in these temperatures the sweat would form as ice on the skin beneath his clothes and would kill him as swiftly as if he were naked. The straighter paths on the north side were blocked with drifts, and Cormac was forced to find a more circuitous route to the pine, edging his way south through the woods, across frozen streams and ponds. Huge gray wolves prowled the mountains but kept clear of the man as he made his slow, steady progress.

For two hours he pushed on, stopping to rest often, saving his strength, until at last he cleared the pine and began the long dangerous traverse of the ridge above the pass. There the trail was only five feet wide, snow covering ice on the slanted path. One wrong or careless step and he would plummet over the edge, smashing himself on the rocks below. He halted in a shallow depression sheltered from the wind and rubbed at the skin of his face, forcing the blood to flow. His cheeks and chin were covered by a fine red-brown down that would soon be a beard, but his nose and eyes felt pinched and tight in the icy wind.

The blizzard raged about him, and vision was restricted to no more than a few feet. His chances of finding the strangers were shrinking by the second. Cursing loudly, he stepped out into the wind and continued his progress along the ridge.

Anduine's voice came to him, whispering deep in his mind: "A little farther, to the left, there is a shallow cave. They are there."

He had long grown used to her powers. Ever since he had given her—albeit briefly—the gift of sight, her mystic talents had increased. She had begun to dream in vivid pictures of glorious color, and often he would allow her the use of his eyes to see some strange new wonder: swans in flight, a racing stag, a hunting wolf, a sky torn by storms.

Moving on, he found the cave and saw a man huddled

by the far wall, a young woman kneeling by him. The man saw him first and pointed; the woman swung, raising a knife.

"Put it away," said Cormac, walking in and looking down at the man. He was sitting with his back to the wall and his right leg thrust out in front of him, the boot bent at an impossible angle. Cormac glanced around. The shelter was inadequate; there was no wood for a fire, and even if he could light one, the wind would lash it to cinders.

"We must move," he said.

"I cannot walk," replied the man, his words slurred. There was ice in his dark beard, and his skin was patchy and blue in places. Cormac nodded.

Reaching down, he took the man's hand and pulled him upright; then he ducked his head to let the body fall across his shoulders and heaved him up.

Cormac grunted at the weight and slowly turned. "Follow me," he told the girl.

"He will die out there," she protested.

"He will die in here," answered Cormac.

He struggled to the ridge and began the long trek home, his burden almost more than he could bear, the muscles of his neck straining under the weight of the injured man. But the blizzard began to ease, and the temperature lifted slightly. After an hour Cormac began to sweat heavily, and his fear rose. He could feel the ice forming and the dreadful lethargy beginning. Sucking in a deep breath, he called to the young woman.

"Move alongside me." She did so. "Now, talk."

"I'm too tired . . . too cold."

"Talk, curse your eyes! Where are you from?" He staggered on.

"We were in Pinnata Castra, but we had to leave. My father broke his leg in a fall. We . . . we . . ." She stumbled.

"Get up, damn you! You want me to die?"

"You bastard!"

"Keep talking. What is your name?"

"Rhiannon."

"Look at your father. Is he alive?" Cormac hoped he
was not. He longed to let the burden fall; his legs were
burning, his back a growing agony.

"I'm alive," the man whispered.

Cursing him savagely, Cormac pushed on. They reached
the pine after two torturous hours and then began the long
climb downhill to the woods. The blizzard found fresh
strength, and the snow swirled about them, but once they
were in the trees the wind dropped.

Cormac reached the cabin just as dawn was lightening
the sky. He dropped his burden to the cot bed, which
creaked under his weight.

"The girl," said Anduine. "She is not with you."

Cormac was too weary to curse as he stumbled from
the cabin and back into the storm. He found Rhiannon
crawling across a snowdrift and heading away from the
cabin. She struggled weakly as he lifted her, then her
head sagged on his shoulder.

In the cabin he laid her before the fire, rubbing warmth
into her arms and face.

"Strip her clothes away," ordered Anduine, but Cormac's cold fingers fumbled with the leather ties, and she
came to his aid. He removed his own clothes and sat
by the fire, wrapped in a warm blanket, staring into the
flames.

"Move away," Anduine said. "Let the heat reach her."
Cormac turned and saw the naked girl. She was blond

and slim, with an oval face and a jaw that was too strong to be feminine. "Help me," asked Anduine, and together they moved her nearer to the fire. Anduine pulled the warm blanket from Cormac's shoulders and laid it over Rhiannon. "Now let us see to the father."

"You don't mind if I dress first?"

Anduine smiled. "You were very brave, my love. I am so proud of you."

"Tell me in the morning."

Stepping to the bed, Anduine pulled the blanket clear of the injured leg, which was swollen and purple below the knee. When Cormac was clothed once more, she bade him twist the limb back into place. The injured man groaned but did not wake. While Cormac held it, Anduine placed her hands on either side of the break, her face set in deep concentration. After some minutes, she began to tremble and her head sagged forward. Cormac released his hold on the man's leg and moved around to her, helping her to her feet.

"The break was jagged and splintered," she said. "It was very hard forcing it to knit. I think it is healing now, but you will need to cut some splints to support it."

"You look exhausted. Go back to bed; I'll tend to them."

She grinned. "And you, I take it, are back to the peak of your strength?"

"Assassins!" screamed the girl on the floor by the fire, sitting bolt upright. Slowly her eyes focused, and she burst into tears. Anduine knelt beside her, holding her close and stroking her hair.

"You are safe here, I promise you."

"No one is safe," she said. "No one!"

The wind howled outside the door, causing it to rattle against the leather hinges.

"They will find us," whispered Rhiannon, her voice rising.

Anduine's hand floated over the girl's face, settling softly on her brow. "Sleep," she murmured, and Rhiannon sank back to the floor.

"Who is hunting them?" asked Cormac.

"Her thoughts were jumbled. I saw men in dark tunics with long knives; her father killed two of them, and they escaped into the wilderness. We will talk to her when she wakes."

"We should not have brought them here."

"We had to. They needed help."

"Maybe they did. But *you* are my concern, not them."

"If you felt like that, why did you not drop your burden on the high mountain when you thought you were going to die?"

Cormac shrugged. "I cannot answer that. But believe me, if I thought they were a danger to you, I would have slit both their throats without hesitation."

"I know," she said sadly. "It is a side of you I try not to think about." She returned to her bed and said nothing more about the strangers.

Cormac sat by the fire, suddenly saddened and heavy of heart. The arrival of the father and daughter had cast a shadow over the mountain. The ugliness of a world of violence had returned, and with it the fear that Anduine would be taken from him.

Taking up his sword, he began to hone the edge with long sweeping strokes of his whetstone.

* * *

Anduine slept later than usual, and Cormac did not wake her as he eased from the bed. The fire had sunk to glowing ashes, and he added tinder until the flames leapt. Larger sticks were fed to the blaze, and the warmth crept across the room. Cormac knelt beside the blond-haired girl; her color was good, her breathing even. Her father was snoring softly, and Cormac moved to the bedside and stared down at the man's face. It was strong and made almost square by the dark beard, which glistened as if oiled. The nose was flat and had been twisted by some savage break in the past, and there were scars around the eyes and on the brow. Glancing down at the man's right arm, which lay outside the blankets, he saw that it, too, was crisscrossed with scars.

The snoring ceased, and the man's eyes opened. There was no sign of drowsiness in the gaze that fastened on the young man.

"How are you feeling?" Cormac asked.

"Alive," answered the man, pushing his powerful arms against the bed and sitting up. He threw back the covers and looked down at his leg, around which Cormac had fashioned a rough splint.

"You must be a skilled surgeon. I feel no pain. It is as if it were not broken at all."

"Do not trust it overmuch," said Cormac. "I will cut you a staff."

The man swung his head, staring down at his daughter by the fireside. Satisfied that she was sleeping, he seemed to relax and smiled, showing broken front teeth.

"We are grateful to you, she and I." He pulled the blankets over his naked body. "Now I will sleep again."

"Who was hunting you?"

"That is none of your concern," was the soft reply, the words eased by an awkward smile.

Cormac shrugged and moved away. He dressed swiftly in woolen tunic, leggings, and sheepskin boots, then stepped out into the open. Icicles dripped from the overhanging roof, and the slate-gray sky was breaking up, showing banners of blue. For an hour he worked with the ax, splitting wood for the store. Then he returned as the smell of frying bacon filled the air.

The man was dressed and sitting at the table, the girl beside him wrapped in a blanket. Anduine was delicately slicing the meat, her blindness obvious. Her head was tilted, her eyes seeming to stare at the far wall.

She smiled as Cormac entered. "Is it a beautiful day?"

"It will be," he said, sensing the change in the atmosphere. The man was deep in thought, his face set and his eyes fixed on Anduine.

Cormac joined them at the table, and they broke their fast in silence.

"What are your plans now, Oleg Hammerhand?" Anduine asked as the meal was finished.

"How is it, lady, that you know my name?"

"How is it that you know mine?" she countered.

Oleg leaned back in the chair. "All across the world men seek news of the Lady Anduine, the Life Giver. Some say Wotan took her, others that she died. I met a man who was close by when her father was slain. He said that a man dressed as a monk yet wielding two swords cut his way through the assassins and rescued the princess. Was that man you?" he asked, switching his gaze to Cormac.

"No. Would that it were!"

Oleg swung back to face Anduine. "Wotan has offered

a thousand gold pieces for news of your whereabouts. Can you imagine? A thousand pieces! And there has been not a word. Not a sign."

"Until now," said Anduine.

"Yes," he agreed. "But we will not betray you, lady— not for ten times ten times that amount."

"I know. It is not in your nature, Oleg." Anduine leaned toward the girl and reached out, but the girl shrank back. "Take my hand, Rhiannon."

"No," whispered the girl.

"Do it, girl," ordered Oleg.

"She is a demon!"

"Nonsense!" Oleg roared.

Anduine leaned back, withdrawing her hand. "It is all right; we all have our fears. How close behind were the hunters?"

"We lost them in the mountains," said Oleg, "but they will not give up the search."

"They want Rhiannon," said Anduine. "For she, too, has a talent."

"How did you know?" Oleg asked, his eyes fearful.

"She called me from the mountains; that is why Cormac came."

"I am sorry we have caused you trouble. We will leave as soon as my leg is mended."

"You think to escape Wotan?"

"I do not know, lady. All my life I have been a warrior, a wolf of the sea. I fear no man. And yet . . . this Wotan is not a man. His followers are crazed. They adore him, and those who are less than adoring are rooted out and slain. A kind of madness has infected the people of the Northlands. The god is returned. The grim, gray god walks among men. Can I escape him? I fear that I cannot."

"Have you seen this Wotan?" asked Cormac.

"Indeed I have. I served him for three years. He is strong, which is all we ever asked in a leader. But he is more than this. He has power in his voice and in his eyes. I have seen men cut their own throats on his order . . . and do it gladly for the honor of pleasing him. He is like strong wine; to listen to him is to be filled with a sense of glory."

"You sound like a worshiper still," whispered Anduine.

"I am, lady. But I am a man also, and a father. The brides of Wotan die. My Rhiannon is not for him."

"How did you escape?" Cormac asked.

"I was told to deliver Rhiannon to his castle in Raetia. I said that I would, but instead we boarded a merchant trireme bound for Hispania. Strong winds and fear of the following storm made the captain seek shelter near Pinnata Castra, but the storm winds were Wotan's and his assassins attacked us outside the castle. I killed two, and we fled into the blizzard."

"How many hunters are there?" Cormac wanted to know.

"Only five attacked us, but there will be more. And he has other forces to do his bidding, though I will not speak of them before the Lady Anduine."

"Do not fear for me, Oleg. I am aware of the demons; they have attacked me also."

"How, then, did you survive?"

"Through the courage of others. Cormac saved my life, as did the monk you heard of."

"Then the demons are not invincible?"

"Nothing is invincible. There is no evil that cannot be conquered, not even Wotan."

"I would like—dearly like—to believe that. But he is now the king across the water, and all the nations pay him homage. Even Rome sends gifts with ambassadors who bow and scrape."

"Uther does not bow and scrape," said Cormac. "Wotan has yet to face the Blood King."

"That I know. It is the whisper of the world, Cormac. In every tavern men wonder at the outcome. It is said that Uther has a magic sword, a gift from a god, that once it parted the sky like a tearing curtain and men saw two suns blazing in the heavens. I would like to see the day he and Wotan face each other."

"And I," agreed Cormac. "Blood King and Blood God."

Rhiannon tensed, her head jerking upright and her hands covering her face.

"What is it?" asked Oleg, his huge arm circling her shoulder.

"The hunters have found us," she whispered.

In the silence that followed Cormac could feel his heart beating hard inside his chest. His fear rose as bile in his throat, and he felt his hands trembling. All his life he had been subject to the whims of others, lashed and beaten, allowed no opportunity to stand tall and learn the virtues of pride; he had had no time to absorb the strength-giving qualities of defiance. With Culain his anger had carried him on, but now, as the enemy approached, he felt a terrible sense of despair crawling on his skin, bearing him down.

Anduine came around to stand beside him, her soft hand touching the skin of his neck, her fingers easing the knot of tension in his shoulders. Her voice whispered inside his mind.

"I love you, Cormac." The depth of her emotion warmed him like a winter fire, the ice of his panic fleeing from it.

"How many are there?" he asked aloud.

"Three," whispered Rhiannon.

"How close?"

"They are on the hillside to the south, approaching the cabin," the girl answered.

"And I have no sword!" thundered Oleg, crashing his fist to the table.

"I have," Cormac said softly. Standing, he took Anduine's hand and kissed the palm, then walked to the hearth, where the sword of Culain stood by the far wall.

"I'll come with you," Oleg said, gathering a carving knife from the table and pushing himself to his feet.

"No," said Cormac. "Wait—and deal with any left alive."

"You cannot defeat three men."

Cormac ignored him and walked into the cold sunlight. He moved swiftly to the chopping ring, laid his sword beside it, and took up the ax. The six-pound blade hammered into a chunk of wood, splitting it neatly; he lifted another piece and carried on working. After several minutes he heard the hunters moving across the yard and turned. As Rhiannon had said, there were three men, tall and bearded, their hair braided beneath bronze helms. Each wore a sheepskin cloak, and the man in the lead carried a round wooden shield edged with bronze and a longsword.

"Are you seeking shelter?" asked Cormac, sinking the ax blade into the ring.

"Are you alone?" responded the leader, his voice guttural, his eyes as cold as the snow around him.

"You are waylanders," said Cormac. "Are you lost?"

Two of the men moved toward the cabin, and Cormac lifted his sword from the ground, brushing snow from the blade. "Shelter will cost you coin," he called, and they stopped and looked to the warrior with the shield.

"Good sword," he said. "Very good." He turned to the others and spoke in a language Cormac had never heard. The men chuckled. "I like the sword," he said, turning back to Cormac.

"You have a good eye. Now, are you going to pay for shelter or move on?"

"You think I would pay to enter that cattle shed?"

"You don't enter if you don't pay."

"Do not make me angry, boy. I am cold and have walked far. You have a woman in there?"

"She'll cost extra."

The warrior grinned. "Is everything for sale in this cursed country?"

"Yes," said Cormac.

"Well, I don't want a woman. I want hot food and information."

"The nearest settlement is Deicester. You should head back down the hill and then east along the deer trails. You could be there by dawn tomorrow. Other than that, there is Pinnata Castra."

"We are looking for a man and a girl, and for that we *will* pay coin."

"Why are you looking here? There is no one else on the mountain but me and my wife."

"In that case you are of no use to me." As he turned to his comrades and spoke softly, Anduine's voice whispered inside Cormac's mind.

"He is telling his men to kill you."

Cormac took a deep breath and walked forward, smiling. "There is one place you might care to search," he said, and the three men relaxed as he approached.

"Where?" asked the leader.

"In hell," he answered, still smiling.

Suddenly Cormac's sword swept up to slash through the neck of the nearest man, and blood fountained into the air. The second tried desperately to drag his sword clear, but Cormac reversed the blade, sending it double-handed through the man's collarbone and deep into his chest. The leader leapt back, hurling his shield aside and taking a double-handed grip on his longsword.

Cormac launched a swift attack, but the Viking blocked it with ease and a vicious riposte nicked the skin of the youth's throat.

"The sword is only as good as the man who wields it," said the warrior as the two men circled.

Cormac attacked once more, slashing wildly, but the Viking blocked and countered, this time ripping through the buckskin tunic and slicing the skin of Cormac's chest. Cormac stepped back, swallowing his anger, forcing it down, and clearing his mind. The Viking was skilled, battle-hardened, and confident. He watched Cormac back away, smiled grimly, and then with dazzling speed attacked, the sword whistling for the youth's skull. Cormac blocked the cut, swiveled on his heel, and rammed his elbow into the man's head, spinning him to the ground. Then he ran in for the killer blow but slipped on the ice.

The Viking rolled to his feet. "A good trick. I shall remember it." Blood was seeping from a gash on his cheek.

The two warriors circled. Three times the Viking attacked, but each time Cormac countered swiftly. Then Cormac lunged, but the Viking's sword flashed down to block and then twisted as he rolled his wrists. Cormac's blade spun from his grasp.

"Another good trick," said the Viking, advancing on the defenseless youth. "But you will not live to remember it!"

Diving to his left, Cormac rolled and came to his feet against the chopping ring. Tearing the ax loose, he faced the Viking once more. The man grinned and backed away to where Cormac's sword lay in the snow. Stooping, he lifted it, feeling the balance. Sheathing his own sword, the warrior faced Cormac.

"To be killed by your own blade . . . not a good way to die. The gods will mock you for eternity."

Cormac's eyes narrowed, his rage returning, but he quelled it savagely. Hefting the ax, he launched a murderous swing, and the Viking leapt back. But halfway into the swing Cormac released the haft, and the ax flew from his hands, the six-pound head smashing into the Viking's face. The man stumbled back, dropping the sword, whereupon Cormac jumped forward, swept up the blade, and hammered it into the Viking's chest. The man died without a sound. Dragging the sword clear, Cormac wiped it clean of blood and returned to the cabin.

"That was well done," said Oleg. "But you need to work on your grip; you held the sword too tightly."

Cormac smiled. "Next time I'll remember."

"Next time it will not be so difficult, lad."

"How so?"

"Next time the Hammerhand will be beside you. And then you will learn something."

◊ **8** ◊

AFTER MANY WEEKS of travel Culain lach Feragh arrived at the ruined stone circle of Sorviodunum. At dawn, under a bright glowing sky, he approached the central altar and laid his silver staff on it. The sun rose to bathe the monoliths in golden light, the staff shining like captured fire.

Culain closed his eyes and whispered three words of power. The air crackled around him, blue fire rippling over his cloak and tunic. Then the sky darkened, and an emptiness smote him, a great engulfing blackness that swallowed his soul.

He awoke feeling sick and dazed.

"You are a fool, Culain," said a voice, and he turned his head. His vision swam, and his stomach heaved. "No one should seek to pass the gateway without a stone."

"Still preaching, Pendarric?" he growled, forcing himself to a sitting position. He was lying in a soft bed, covered with sheets of silk. The sun blazed brightly in the violet sky beyond the arched window. His eyes cleared, and he gazed at the broad-shouldered figure seated beside the bed.

"I rarely preach these days," said the Atlantean king, a broad grin parting the square-cut golden beard. "The more adventurous of my subjects have found various pursuits beyond the Mist, and those who remain are more interested in scholarly pursuits."

"I have come for your help."

"I did not doubt it," said the king. "When will you cease these games in the old world?"

"It is not a game—not to me."

"That, at least, is welcome news. How is the boy?"

"Boy? Which boy?"

"Uther, the boy with the sword."

Culain smiled. "The boy now has gray in his beard. They call him the Blood King, but he reigns wisely."

"I thought that he would. And the child, Laitha?"

"Are you mocking me, Pendarric?"

The king's face became stern, the blue eyes cold. "I mock no one, Culain, not even reckless adventurers like you and Maedhlyn who have ruined a world. What right have I to mock? I am the king who drowned Atlantis. I do not forget my past, and I condemn no one. Why do you ask?"

"You have not kept a watch on the old world?"

"Why should I? Goroien was the last danger, and you disposed of her and her undead son. I don't doubt Maedhlyn is still meddling with kings and princes, but he is unlikely to destroy the world. And you? For all your recklessness, you are a man of honor."

"Molech has returned," said Culain.

"Nonsense! You beheaded him at Babel; the body was consumed by fire."

"He is back."

"Maedhlyn agrees with you on this?"

"I have not seen Maedhlyn in sixteen years. But believe me, the Devil has returned."

"Let us walk in the garden—if you are strong enough. Some tales need to be told in bright sunlight."

Culain eased himself from the bed and stood, but dizziness swamped him. He took a deep breath and steadied himself.

"You will be weak for a day or so. Your body suffered terrible punishment during the journey, and you were all but dead when you appeared."

"I thought there would be sufficient power in the lance."

"There might have been—for a younger man. Why is it, Culain, that you insist on growing old? What virtue is there in dying?"

"I want to be a man, Pendarric: to experience the passing of the seasons, to feel myself a part of the life of the world. I have had enough of immortality. As you said, I have helped to ruin a world. Gods, goddesses, demons, legends—each one contributing to a future of violence and discord. I want to grow old; I want to die."

"The last, at least, is the truth," said the king. He led Culain to a side door and then down a short corridor to a terraced garden. A young man brought them a tray of wine and fruit, and the king sat on a curved seat by a bed of roses. Culain joined him.

"So, tell me of Molech."

Culain told him of the vision in the monastery and of the lightning bolt that had seared his hand. He detailed the astonishing rise to power of the king, Wotan, and his conquests in Belgica, Raetia, Pannonia, and Gaul. At last Culain sat back and sipped his wine, staring out over the gardens at the green hills beyond the city.

"You said nothing of Uther or his lady," said Pendarric.

Culain took a deep breath. "I betrayed him. I became his wife's lover."

"Did he kill her?"

"No. He would have, but we escaped to Gaul and she died there."

"Oh, Culain . . . of all the men I have known, you are the last I would expect to betray a friend."

"I offer no excuses."

"I would hope not. So, then, Molech has returned. What is it you require of me?"

"As before, an army to destroy him."

"I have no army, Culain. And if I did, I would not sanction a war."

"You know of course that he desires to kill you? That he will attack Britain and use the great gate at Sorviodunum to invade the Feragh?"

"Of course I know," snapped the king. "But there is no more to be said about war. What will you do?"

"I shall find him—and . . . fight him."

"For what purpose? The old Culain could have defeated him . . . did defeat him. But you are not the old Culain. What are you in human terms, forty, fifty?"

"Somewhat more," was the wry reply.

"Then leave him be, Culain, and return to your monastery. Study the mysteries. Live out your days and your seasons."

"I cannot," Culain said simply.

For a while the two men sat in silence, then Pendarric laid his hand on Culain's shoulder. "We will not talk again, my friend, so let me say this: I respect you; I always have. You are a man of worth. I have never heard you blame another for your own mistakes or seek to curse fate or the Source for your misfortunes. That is rare and a precious quality. I hope you find peace, Culain."

"Peace . . . death . . . Perhaps they are the same," whispered Culain.

Uther awoke in the night, his hand clawing at the air, the nightmare clinging to him in the sweat-dampened sheets. He threw them back and rolled from the bed. In his dreams dark holes had appeared in the walls of the castle, disgorging monsters with curved talons and dripping fangs that stank of death and despair. He sucked in a deep breath and moved to the window; the battlements were deserted.

"Old men and children fear the dark," whispered the Blood King, forcing a chuckle.

The breeze whispered along the castle walls, and for a moment he thought he heard his name hissing softly in the night wind. He shivered. Calm yourself, Uther!

Then the sound came again, so low that he shut his eyes and craned his head toward the window. There it was . . .

"Uther . . . Uther . . . Uther . . ."

He pushed it from his mind as a trick of the night and returned to his bed. Glancing back at the window, he saw a flickering shape floating there.

In the moment that he identified it as a man, Uther reacted. His hand swept back to the sword sheathed at the bedside, and the blade flashed into the air. He leapt toward the window and froze. Though the figure remained, it was wholly transparent and hung like trapped smoke against the moonlight.

"They are coming," whispered the figure . . .

And vanished.

Confused and uncertain, Uther threw the sword to the bed and wandered to the table by the far wall, where stood a jug of wine and several goblets. As he reached for the jug, he stumbled, his mind reeling. He fell to his knees and only then saw the mist covering the floor of his room. His senses swam, but with one desperate heave he regained his feet and half staggered, half fell toward the bed. His hand scrabbled for the sword hilt, closing around it just as the darkness seemed set to envelop him. The Sword of Power glowed like a lantern, and the mist fled, snaking back to the wall and under the door. Naked, the king dragged open the door and stepped into the corridor beyond, where Gwalchmai slept on a narrow cot.

"Wake up, my friend," said the king, nudging the sleeping man's shoulder. There was no response. He shook him harder. Nothing.

Fear touched the king, and he moved slowly down the circular stair to the courtyard. Four sentries lay on the cobbles with their weapons beside them.

"Sweet Christos!" whispered Uther. "The dream!"

There was a movement to his left, and he whirled, the sword slicing the air. The ghostly figure floated beside him once more, the face hooded, the figure blurred and indistinct.

"The sword," it whispered. "He wants the sword."

"Who are you?"

Suddenly a hand of fire swept around the figure, and the heat hurled the king from his feet. He landed on his shoulder and rolled. Dark shadows spread on the walls around him, black as caves, opening . .

Uther ran to one of the sentries, dragging the man's sword from his scabbard. Then, touching his own blade to the weapon, he closed his eyes in concentration. Fire blazed on the blades as the king staggered and stared down: in his hands were two Swords of Power, twins of shining silver steel.

The dark caves opened still farther, and the first of the beasts issued forth. Uther swung back the true blade and hurled it high into the air. Lightning blazed across the sky . . . and the Sword of Cunobelin disappeared.

The beast roared and stepped into the courtyard, its terrible jaws parted in a bestial snarl. Others crowded behind it, moving into the courtyard and forming a circle around the naked king. Men in dark cloaks came after them, gray blades in their hands.

"The sword," called one of them. "Give us the sword."

"Come and take it," said Uther.

The man gestured, and a beast raced forward. Fully seven feet tall, it was armed with a black ax. Its eyes were blood-red, its fangs yellow and long. Most men would have frozen in terror, but Uther was not like most men.

He was the Blood King.

He leapt to meet the attack, ducking under the swinging ax, his sword ripping through the creature's scaled belly. A terrible scream tore aside the silence of the night, and the other creatures howled in rage and pushed forward, but the dark-cloaked man ordered them back.

"Do not kill him!" he screamed, and Uther stepped back, wondering at this change of heart. Then he glanced down at his sword to see that the beast's blood had stained the blade . . . and ended the illusion. Once more it was a simple gladius of iron with a wooden hilt wrapped in oiled leather.

"Where is the sword?" demanded the leader, his eyes betraying his fear.

"Where your master can lay no hand upon it," Uther answered, smiling grimly.

"Damn your eyes!" screamed the man, and threw back his cloak and raised his sword of shimmering gray. The others followed his example. There were more than a dozen, and Uther was determined to take a goodly number of them as company on the journey into hell. They spread out around him and then rushed forward. Uther charged the circle, sweeping aside a frenzied thrust and burying his gladius in a man's heart. A cold blade pierced his back, and he dragged the gladius clear and spun, his sword tearing through a warrior's neck. Two more blades hammered into him, filling his chest with icy pain, but even as he fell, his sword lashed out and gashed open a man's face. Then numbness flowed through him, and death laid a skeletal finger on his soul. He felt himself floating upward, and his eyes opened.

"Now you are ours," hissed the leader, his cold gray eyes gleaming in triumph.

Uther looked down at the body that lay at the man's feet; it was his own, and there was not a mark on it. He watched as the attackers lifted their blades and saw the swords swirl and disperse like mist in the morning breeze.

"Now you will learn the true meaning of agony," said the leader. As he spoke, the huge hand of fire appeared, engulfing the king's soul and vanishing into darkness. Leaving the body where it lay, the beasts and men returned to the shadows, which closed behind them, becoming once more the gray stone of a silent fortress.

Galead, the blond knight who had been Ursus, prince of the House of Merovee, awoke in the chill of the dawn.

The room was cool, the bed empty. He sat up and shivered, wondering if it was the cool breeze that prickled his skin or the memory of those ice-blue eyes . . .

For three weeks the embassy had been kept waiting in the city of Lugdunum, assured that the new king would see them at his earliest opportunity. Victorinus had accepted the delays with Roman patience, never giving a public display of his increasing anger. The messages from Wotan had been delivered by a young Saxon called Agwaine, a tall warrior with yellow hair and a sneering manner.

The choice of Agwaine was a calculated insult, for the warrior was from the South Saxon, Uther's realm, and that made him a traitor in Victorinus' eyes.

But the Roman made good use of his enforced idleness, touring the city with Galead, listening to the talk in the taverns, watching the various regiments of Gothic warriors at maneuvers, gathering information that would aid Uther in the now-inevitable war.

On their trip from the coast they had seen the massive triremes under construction and the barges that could land an army on the south coast, there to be swelled by dissenting Saxons and Jutes longing for a victory against the Blood King.

On the twenty-second day of their wait Agwaine arrived in the hour just after dawn with a summons from Wotan. Victorinus thanked him courteously and dressed in a simple toga of white. Galead wore the leather breastplate, leggings, and greaves of a *Cohors Equitana* commander, a gladius at his side, but over this was the short white surplice of the herald, a simple red cross embroidered over the heart.

The two men were taken to the central palace and into

a long hall lined with lances on which severed heads were impaled.

Galead glanced at the rotting skulls, quelling his anger as he recognized one as Meroveus, the former king of the Merovingians. Swallowing hard, he marched slowly behind Victorinus toward the high throne on which sat the new god-king. Flanked by guards in silver armor, Wotan watched as the men approached, his eyes fixed on the white-clad Victorinus.

Reaching the foot of the dais, Victorinus bowed low.

"Greetings, my Lord King, from your brother across the water."

"I have no brothers," said Wotan, the voice rich and resonant.

Galead gazed at him, awed by the power emanating from the man. The face was handsome and framed by a golden beard, the shoulders broad, the arms thick and powerful. He was dressed in the same silver armor as his guards and was cloaked in black.

"My king," said Victorinus smoothly, "sends you a gift to celebrate your coronation." He turned, and two soldiers carried forward a square box of polished ebony. They knelt before the king and opened it. He leaned forward and lifted the silver helm from within. A gold circlet decorated the rim; the silver raven's wings were fixed to the sides as ear guards.

"A pretty piece," said Wotan, tossing it to a guard, who set it down on the floor beside the throne. "And now to the realities. I have given you three weeks to see the power of Wotan. You have used this time well, Victorinus, as befits a soldier of your rank and experience. Now go back to Britain and tell those in power that I will come to them with gifts of my own."

"My lord Uther . . ." began Victorinus.

"Uther is dead," said Wotan, "and you are in need of a king. Since there is no heir and since my brother Saxons have appealed to me for aid against your Roman tyranny, I have decided to accept their invitation to journey to Britannia and investigate their claims of injustice."

"And will you journey with your army, my lord?" Victorinus asked.

"Do you think I will have need of it, Victorinus?"

"That, my lord, will depend on the king."

"You doubt my word?" asked Wotan, and Galead saw the guards tense, their hands edging toward their swords.

"No, sire. I merely point out—with respect—that Britain has a king. When one dies, another rises."

"I have petitioned the Vicar of Christ in Rome," said Wotan, "and I have here a sealed parchment from him bestowing the kingdom of Britannia upon me, should I decide to accept it."

"It could be argued that Rome no longer exercises sovereignty over the affairs of the west," said Victorinus, "but that is for others to debate. I am merely a soldier."

"Your modesty is commendable, but you are far more than that. I would like you to serve me, Victorinus. Talented men are hard to find."

Victorinus bowed. "I thank you for the compliment. And now, with your leave, we must prepare for the journey home."

"Of course," said Wotan, rising. "But first introduce your young companion; he intrigues me."

"My lord, this is Galead, a knight of Uther."

Galead bowed, and the king stepped down from the dais to stand before him. Galead looked up into the ice-blue eyes.

"And what is your view, knight of Uther?"

"I have no view, sire, only a sword. And when my king tells me to use it, I do so."

"And if I were your king?"

"Ask me again, sire, when that day dawns."

"It will dawn, Galead. Come the spring, it will dawn. Tell me," he said, smiling and raising his arms to point at the severed heads, "what do you think of my ornaments?"

"I think they will attract flies, sire, when the spring comes."

"You recognized one of them, I think."

Galead blinked. "Indeed I did, sire, and your powers of observation are acute." He pointed to the rotting head of Meroveus. "I saw him once—when my father was visiting Gaul. It is the . . . former . . . king."

"He could have served me. I find it strange that a man will prefer to depart this life in agony rather than enjoy it in riches and pleasure. And for what? All men serve others . . . even kings. Tell me, Galead, what point is there in defying the inevitable?"

"I was always told, sire, that the only inevitability is death, and we do our best to defy that daily."

"Even death is not inevitable for those who serve me well—nor is it a release for those who oppose me. Is that not true, Meroveus?"

The rotting head seemed to sag on the lance, the mouth opening in a silent scream. "You see," Wotan said softly, "the former king agrees. Tell me, Galead, do you desire me for an enemy?"

"Life, my lord, for a soldier is rarely concerned with what he desires. As you so rightly say, all men are subject to the will of someone. For myself, I would prefer no enemies, but life is not that simple."

"Well said, soldier," replied the king, turning and striding back to the throne.

The two men backed down the hall, then turned and walked in silence to their lodgings. Once there, Victorinus slumped in a broad chair, head in hands.

"It may not be true," said Galead.

"He did not lie; there would be no point. Uther is dead. Britain is dead."

"You think Wotan will be king?"

"How do we stop him? Better that he is elected and the bloodletting be minimized."

"And you will suggest that course?"

"Do you have a better one?"

As the younger man was about to answer, he saw Victorinus' hand flicker, the fingers spreading and then closing swiftly into a fist. It was the scout's signal for silence in the presence of the enemy.

"No, sir, I think you are right," he said.

Now, in the bright morning, Galead rose and walked naked to the stream behind the lodgings. There he bathed in the cool waters that ran from the snow-covered mountains down into the valleys. Refreshed, he returned to his room and dressed for the journey ahead. There were twelve men in the party, and they met to break their fast in the dining room of the inn. Victorinus, clothed once more as a warrior commander in bronze breastplate and bronze-studded leather kilt, sat in silence. The news of Uther's death had filtered down to all the warriors, darkening their mood.

A young stable boy entered and informed Victorinus that the horses were ready, and the group made its way to the mounts, riding from the city as the sun finally cleared the mountains. Victorinus waved Galead forward, and the blond young warrior cantered his mount alongside the veteran.

The two men rode ahead of the following group, out of earshot, then Victorinus reined in and turned toward the young Merovingian.

"I want you to head for Belgica and take ship from there."

"Why, sir?"

Victorinus sighed. "Use your wits, young prince. Wotan might have been fooled by my words and the air of defeat I summoned. But he might not. Were I him, I would see that Victorinus did not reach the coast alive."

"All the more reason to stick together," said Galead.

"You think one sword can make a difference?" snapped the old general.

"No," Galead admitted.

"I am sorry, my boy. I get irritated when people try to kill me. When you get back to Britain, find Prasamaccus—he's a wily old bird—and Gwalchmai. Both of them will offer sage counsel. I do not know who will have taken charge—perhaps Petronius, though he is ten years older than I. Or maybe Geminus Cato. I hope it is the latter; he at least understands war and its nature. From the looks of the barges they will be ready to sail by the spring, and that gives little time for adequate preparation. My guess is they will land near Anderida, but they may strike farther north. Wotan will have allies at either end of the kingdom. Damn Uther to hell! How could he die at a time like this?"

"And what will you do, sir?"

"I'll continue as expected, but I will leave the road come nightfall. Sweet Mithras, what I would not give for ten of the old legions! Did you see those Roman soldiers at Wotan's court?"

"Yes. Not impressive, were they?"

"No helmets or breastplates. I spoke to one of the young men, and it seems the army voted to do away with them because they were so heavy! How did Rome ever rule the world?"

"A country is only as strong as its leaders allow it to be," said Galead. "The Goths could never have conquered without Wotan to bind them, and when he dies, they will be sundered once more."

"Then let us hope he dies soon," said Victorinus. "Once we are out of sight of the city, strike north—and may Hermes lend wings to your horse."

"And may your gods bring you home, sir."

Victorinus said nothing, but he removed his cloak and folded it across his saddle, a ritual all cavalry officers followed when riding into hostile territory.

"If I am not home by the spring, Galead, light a lantern for me at the Altar of Mithras."

Culain stood at the center of the stone circle, his silver lance in his hand.

"Are you sure this is wise, my friend?" asked Pendarric.

Culain smiled. "I was never wise, Lord King. A wise man understands the limits of his wisdom. But I believe it is my destiny to stand against the evil of Wotan. My swords may not be enough to sway the battle, but then again, they may. Unless I try, I will never know."

"I, too, will go against the dark one," said Pendarric, "but in my own way. Take this; I think you will have need of it." Culain reached out and accepted a golden stone the size of a sparrow's egg.

"I thank you, Pendarric. I do not think we will meet again."

"In that you are correct, Lance Lord. May the Source of All Things be with you always."

Pendarric raised his arms and spoke the word of power . . .

◊ 9 ◊

THE CITY OF Eboracum was in mourning when Revelation arrived at the south gate. The sentry, seeing that the white-bearded stranger was a monk carrying no weapons, merely a long wooden quarterstaff, stepped aside and waved him through.

"Is the king in residence?" asked Revelation.

"You have not heard?" said the sentry, a young militiaman bearing only a lance.

"I have been on the road for three days. I have seen no one."

"The king is dead," said the sentry. "Slain by sorcery."

Other travelers waited behind Revelation, and the guard waved him on. He moved under the gate tower and on into the narrow streets, his mind whirling with memories: the young Uther, tall and strong in the Caledones; the Blood King leading the charge against the enemy; the boy and the man so full of life. Revelation felt a terrible sadness swelling within him. He had come here to make his peace with the man he had betrayed, to seek forgiveness.

He moved through the town like a dreamer, not seeing the shops and stores and market stalls, heading for the royal keep, where two sentries stood guard, both in ceremonial black coats and dark-plumed helms.

Their lances crossed before him, barring the way.

"None may enter today," said a guard softly. "Come back tomorrow."

"I need to speak to Victorinus," said Revelation.

"He is not here. Come back tomorrow."

"Then Gwalchmai or Prasamaccus."

"Are you hard of hearing, old man? Tomorrow, I said."

Revelation's staff swept up, brushing the lances aside. The men jumped forward to overpower him, but the staff cracked against the first man's skull, bowling him from his feet, then hammered into the second man's groin, doubling him over, after which a second blow took him at the base of the neck.

Revelation walked on into the courtyard. Groups of men were sitting idly, their faces set and their misery apparent.

"You!" said Revelation, pointing at a warrior sitting on a well wall. "Where is Gwalchmai?" The man looked up and gestured to the north tower. Revelation mounted the steps and made his way up the circular stairwell to the king's apartments. There, on a bed covered with white linen, lay the body of Uther dressed in full armor and plumed helm. Beside the bed, holding the king's hand, was Gwalchmai, the Hound of the King. Tears stained his cheeks, and his eyes were red-rimmed.

He did not hear Revelation approach or react when the man's hand touched his shoulder, but at the sound of the voice he jerked as if stung and leapt to his feet.

"How did it happen, Gwal?"

"You!" Gwalchmai's hand flew to his side, but there was no sword. The eyes blazed. "How dare you come here?"

Revelation ignored him and moved to the bed. "I asked how it happened," he whispered.

"What difference does it make? It happened. A sorcerous mist filled the castle, and all fell into a deep sleep. When we awoke, the king was lying dead in the courtyard beside the body of a scaled beast. And the sword was gone."

"How long ago?"

"Three days."

Revelation lifted the king's hand. "Then why no sign of stiffening?" He slid his fingers to the king's wrist and waited. There was no pulse, yet the flesh was warm to the touch.

From the pocket of his robe he produced Pendarric's stone, which he touched to the king's brow. There was no discernible movement, but the pulse point under his fingers trembled.

"He is alive," said Revelation.

"No!"

"See for yourself, man."

Gwalchmai moved to the other side of the bed and pressed his fingers to the king's throat, just under the jawline. His eyes brightened, but the gleam died.

"Is this more sorcery, Culain?"

"No, I promise you."

"Of what worth are the promises of an oath breaker?"

"Then you must judge, Gwalchmai. There is no stiffness in the body, the blood has not fallen back from the face, and the eyes are not sunken. How do you read his condition?"

"But there is no breath, there is no heartbeat," said the Cantii tribesman.

"He is at the point of death, but he has not yet passed the dark river."

Revelation put both hands to the king's face.

"What are you doing?" asked Gwalchmai.

"Be silent," ordered Revelation, closing his eyes. His mind drifted, linking with Uther, drawing on the power of the stone he carried.

Darkness, despair, and a tunnel of black stone . . . A beast . . . Many beasts . . . a figure, tall and strong . . .

Revelation screamed and was hurled back across the room, the front of his habit ripped, blood welling from the talon tears on his chest. Gwalchmai stood transfixed as Revelation slowly rose to his feet.

"Sweet Mithras," whispered Gwalchmai.

Revelation took the stone and held it to his chest, and the wounds sealed instantly. "They have Uther's soul," he said.

"Who?"

"The enemy, Gwalchmai: Wotan."

"We must rescue him."

Revelation shook his head. "That would take a power beyond mine. All we can do is protect the body. While it lives there is hope."

"A body without a soul—what good is it?"

"The flesh and the spirit are linked, Gwalchmai, each drawing on the strength of the other. Wotan will know now that the body lives and will seek to destroy it; that is a certainty. What is puzzling, however, is why the soul was taken. I can understand Wotan's desire to kill Uther but not this."

"I care nothing for his motives," hissed Gwalchmai, "but he will die for this. I swear it."

"I fear he is too powerful for you," said Revelation. He

walked to the far wall and traced a line along it with the golden stone, past the door, onto the north wall, and on around the room until he reached his starting point. "Now we shall see," he said.

"Why have you come back?"

"I thought I had come to ask Uther to forgive me. But now I think the Source guided me here to protect the king."

"Had he been . . . alive . . . he would have killed you."

"Perhaps. Perhaps not. Fetch your weapons, Gwal, and your armor. You will need them soon."

Without a word Gwalchmai left the room, and Revelation pulled up a chair and sat beside the bed. Why had the king been taken? Molech would not idly waste such power merely to torment an enemy. And the power drain on his Sipstrassi Stones would be enormous for such a venture. He had to believe there was something to gain, something worth the loss of magic. And the body— why leave it alive?

Revelation gazed down at the king. The armor was embossed with gold, the helm bearing the crown of Britain and the eagle of Rome, the breastplate fashioned after the Greek style and embossed with the symbol of the bear. The brass-studded kilt was worn over leather leggings and thigh-high boots reinforced with copper to protect the knees of a horseman in the crashing together of mounts during a charge. The scabbard was jewel-encrusted, a gift from a rich merchant in Noviomagus, made to house the Great Sword of Cunobelin.

It was a sickening thought that the Sword of Power was now in Wotan's hands. For once it had been Culain's, and he had watched it being fashioned from pure silver Sipstrassi, the rarest form of the magical stone, a hundred times more powerful than the gold pebble Culain now carried. Without the sword Wotan was powerful enough, but with it, could any power on earth stand against him?

The door opened, and Gwalchmai entered in full armor and wearing two short swords scabbarded at the hips. Behind him came Prasamaccus, bearing his curved cavalry bow and a quiver of arrows.

"It is good to see you again," said Revelation.

Prasamaccus nodded and limped into the room, laying the bow and quiver by the wall. "Somehow," said the old Brigante, "I did not think the fall from the cliff would kill you. But when you failed to reappear . . ."

"I traveled to Mauretania on the African coast."

"And the queen?"

"She stayed in Belgica. She died there some years ago."

"It was all a terrible folly," said Prasamaccus. He held out his hand to Revelation, who took it gratefully.

"You do not hate me, then?"

"I never hated anyone in all my life. And if I were to begin, it would not be with you, Culain. I was there the first night when Uther made love to Laitha; it was in the land of the Pinrae. Later I saw the prince, as he then was, and he told me that during the lovemaking—when his emotions were at their highest point—Laitha whispered your name. He never forgot it . . . it ate at him like a cancer. He was not a bad man, you understand, and he tried to forgive her. The trouble is that if you can't forget, you can't forgive. I am sorry the queen is dead."

"I have missed you both during the years," said Revelation. "And Victorinus. Where is he?"

"Uther sent him to Gallia to discuss treaties with Wotan," said Gwalchmai. "There has been no word in a month."

Revelation said nothing, and Prasamaccus pulled up a chair and sat down beside the bed. "When will they come?" he asked.

"Tonight, I think. Perhaps tomorrow."

"How will they know the body lives?"

"I tried to reach Uther's soul. Wotan was there, and one of the beasts attacked me. Wotan will know I traced the thread of Uther's life, and they will follow it back."

"Can we stop them?" asked the Brigante softly.

"We can try. Tell me everything about how the king was found."

"He was lying in the courtyard," said Gwalchmai. "There was a nightmare beast beside him, gutted and dead and rotting at a rate you would not believe. By nightfall only the bones and the stench remained."

"That is all that was there? Just a dead beast and the king?"

"Yes . . . no . . . There was a gladius by the body; it belonged to one of the guards."

"A gladius? Did the guard drop it there?"

"I do not know. I'll find out."

"Do it now, Gwal."

"How important can it be?"

"If the king was using it, then believe me, it is important."

Once Gwalchmai had gone, Prasamaccus and Revelation walked together on the circular battlement around the north tower, staring out over the hills surrounding Eboracum.

"The land is so green and beautiful," said Revelation. "I wonder if it will ever know a time without war."

"Not so long as men dwell here," replied Prasamaccus, pausing to rest his lame leg by sitting on the battlement wall. The wind was chilly, and he drew his green cloak around his slender frame. "I thought you immortals never aged," he said.

Revelation shrugged. "All things have their seasons. How is Helga?"

"She died. I miss her."

"Do you have children?"

"We had a boy and a girl. The boy died of the red plague when he was three, but my daughter survived. She is a handsome lass; she is pregnant now and hoping for a boy-child."

"Are you happy, Prasamaccus?"

"I am alive . . . and the sun shines. I have no complaints, Culain. You?"

"I think that I am content. Tell me, has there been any word of Maedhlyn?"

"No. He and Uther parted company some years ago. I do not know the rights and wrongs of it, but it began when Maedhlyn said his magic could not discover where you were hiding with Laitha. Uther believed it was his loyalty to you that prevented him from giving aid."

"It was not," said Revelation. "I used my stone to shield us."

Prasamaccus smiled. "I am sorry about the hound. I wished we had never discovered you. But Uther was my king and my friend. I could not betray him."

"I bear no ill will, my friend. I just wish you had searched a little harder after we leapt from the cliff."

"Why so?"

"Uther's son was waiting in the cave. Laitha bore the child there, and it survived."

The color drained from the old Brigante's face. "A son? Are you sure it was Uther's?"

"Without the slightest doubt. He was raised among the Saxons; they found him by the hound and her pups, and they called him Daemonsson. Once you see him, there will be no doubt in your mind. He is the image of Uther."

"We should fetch him here. He should be the new king."

"No," said Revelation sharply. "He is not ready. Say nothing of this to Gwal or any other man. When the time is right, Uther himself will acknowledge him."

"If the king lives," whispered Prasamaccus.

"We are here to see that he does."

"Two elderly warriors and an immortal seeking to die? Not the most awe-inspiring force to be mustered in this Land of Mist!"

Gwalchmai returned just as the sun was setting, and Revelation and Prasamaccus joined him in the king's apartments.

"Well?" asked Revelation.

The white-haired Cantii shrugged. "The guard said that when the mist struck, his sword was in its scabbard, but when he awoke, it was beside the king. What of it?"

Revelation smiled. "It means that Uther killed the beast with the guard's gladius. What does that suggest to you?"

Gwalchmai's eyes brightened. "He did not have his sword."

"Exactly. He knew what they had come for and hid the blade where they could not find it. Therefore, they took him alive . . . for torture."

"Can you torture a soul?" asked Prasamaccus.

"Better than you can a body," Revelation answered.

"Think of the inner pain you have suffered over the death of a loved one. Is it not greater than any physical wound?"

"What can we do, Culain?" whispered Gwalchmai, his gaze resting on the still body of the king he had served for a quarter of a century.

"First we must protect the body, second find the Sword of Power."

"It could be anywhere," said Prasamaccus.

"Worse," admitted Revelation, "it could be *anything*."

"I do not understand you," the Cantii said. "It is a sword."

"It was fashioned from silver Sipstrassi, the most potent source of power known to the ancient world. We built the gateways with its power, fashioned the Standing Stones, created the old straight tracks your people still use. With it we left the ancient paths, stretching across many kingdoms, joining many sites of earth magic. If Uther wished, the sword could become a pebble, or a tree, or a lance, or a flower."

"Then for what do we search?" asked Prasamaccus. "Can we send Uther's knights across the land in search of a flower?"

"Wherever it is, the magic of the sword will become apparent. Let us say it is a flower: in that region plants will grow as never before, crops will flower early, and sickness will disappear. The knights must search for such signs."

"If it is in Britannia," said Gwalchmai.

"If it was easy to find, then Wotan would take it," snapped Revelation. "But think on this: When Uther was in peril, he had at best only moments to hide the sword. Knowing the king as you both do, where do you think he would send it?"

Prasamaccus shrugged. "The Caledones, perhaps, where he first met you and Laitha. Or the Pinrae, where he defeated the army of Goroien. Or Camulodunum."

"All places Wotan will search, for the king's story is well known. Uther would not make it so easy," said Revelation. "Sweet Christos!"

"What?" asked Gwalchmai.

"There are two people in the Caledones Wotan must not find. And I cannot reach them; I cannot leave here." He rose from his seat, his face gray, his eyes haunted. Prasamaccus laid a gentle hand on his shoulder.

"The boy you spoke of?"

Revelation nodded.

"And now you must choose between . . ." Prasamaccus left the sentence unfinished. He knew the torment raging inside him. Save the father or the son. Or as Culain would see it, betray one to save the other.

Behind him Gwalchmai lit the lanterns and drew the first of his swords, which he honed with an old whetstone. Revelation took up his staff and closed his eyes. The brown woolen habit disappeared, to be replaced by the black and silver armor of Culain lach Feragh. The gray beard vanished, and the hair on his head darkened. The staff became silver, and Culain twisted the haft, producing two short swords of glistening silver.

"You have made your decision, then?" whispered Prasamaccus.

"I have, may God forgive me," said the Lance Lord.

The spring was beautiful in the Caledones, the mountains ablaze with color, the swollen streams glittering in the sunlight, the woods and forests filled with birdsong. Cormac had never been happier. Oleg and Rhiannon had found and renovated the old cabin higher in the mountains, leaving Anduine and Cormac to the solitude needed by young lovers. On most mornings Oleg would join Cormac on his training runs and teach him the more subtle skills of swordplay. But once the sun passed noon, Oleg would journey back to his cabin. Of Rhiannon, Cormac saw little but enough to know she was unhappy. She had not believed her father concerning Wotan and was convinced he had prevented her from becoming a queen over the Goths. Now she stayed in the high country, wandering the hills, seeking inner peace.

But thoughts of Rhiannon rarely entered Cormac's head. He was alive, surrounded by beauty, and in love.

"Are you happy?" Anduine asked him as they sat naked by the lake in the afternoon sunshine.

"How could I not be?" he countered, stroking her cheek and leaning in to kiss her softly on the mouth. Her arm looped around his neck, pulling him down until he could feel her soft breasts pressing against the skin of his chest. His hand slid down her hips, and he marveled anew at the silky softness of her skin. Then he drew back from her.

"What is wrong?" she asked.

"Nothing," he replied, chuckling. "I just wanted to look at you."

"Tell me what you see."

"What can I tell you, my lady?"

"You could flatter me mercilessly. Tell me I am beautiful—the most beautiful woman who ever lived."

"You are the most beautiful I have ever seen. Will that suffice?"

"And do you love me only for my beauty, young sir? Or is it because I am a princess?"

"I am the son of a king," said Cormac. "Is that why you love me?"

"No," she whispered. "I love you for what you are as a man."

They made love once more, this time slowly yet with passion. At last they moved apart, and Cormac kissed her softly on the brow. He saw the tears in her eyes and pulled her to him.

"What is the matter?"

She shook her head, turning away from him.

"Tell me . . . please."

"Each time we are together like this, I fear it is the last. And one day it will be."

"No!" he said. "We will always be together. Nothing will separate us."

"Always?"

"Until the stars fall from the sky," he promised her.

"Only until then?"

"Only until then, lady. After that I might need someone younger!"

She smiled and sat up, reaching for her dress. He passed it to her, then gathered his own clothes and the sword he had worn since the attack.

"Give me your eyes, Cormac," she asked.

He leaned toward her, allowing her hand to touch his closed eyelids. Darkness descended, but this time there was no panic.

"I'll race you home," she shouted, and he heard her running steps. He grinned and walked forward six paces to the round rock, his hand feeling for the niche that pointed south. Lining himself up with the niche, he began to run, counting the steps. At thirty he slowed and carefully inched forward to the lightning-struck pine whose upper branch pointed down toward the cabin and the straight run into the clearing.

As he reached it, he heard Anduine scream, a sound that lanced his heart and filled him with a terrible fear.

"Anduine!" he yelled, his torment echoing in the mountains. He blundered on, sword in hand, not noticing that he had left the path until he tripped over a jutting root. As he fell awkwardly, the sword slipped from his grasp, and his fingers scrabbled across the grass, seeking the hilt.

He fought for calm and concentrated on the sounds around him, his fingers still questing. At last he found the blade and stood. The incline of the hill was to his left, so he slowly turned right and followed the hill downward, his left hand stretched out before him. The ground leveled, and he could smell the woodsmoke from the cabin chimney.

"Anduine!"

There was a movement to his right, heavy and slow. "Who's there?"

There was no answer, but the sound increased as hurried steps moved toward him. Cormac waited until the last second, then swung the sword in a whistling arc; the blade hammered into the attacker and then slid clear. More sounds came to Cormac then: angry voices, shuffling feet. Gripping his sword double-handed, he held it before him.

There was a sudden movement to his left—and a hideous pain in his side. He twisted and slashed out with his sword, missing his attacker.

By the wall of the cabin Anduine regained consciousness

to find herself being held tightly by a bearded man. Her eyes opened, and she saw Cormac, blind and alone in a circle of armed men.

"No!" she screamed, closing her eyes and returning his gift.

Cormac's vision returned just as a second attacker moved silently forward. The man was grinning. Cormac blocked a blow, then sent his blade slicing through the Viking's throat. The remaining seven charged in, and Cormac had no chance, but as he fell, he hacked and cut at the enemy. A sword blade pierced his back, and another tore a gaping wound in his chest.

Anduine screamed and touched her hand to her captor's chest. The man's tunic burst into flames that slid up to cover his face. Bellowing in pain, he released her, his hands beating his beard as the fire caught in his hair.

She fell, then stood and ran at the group surrounding Cormac, her hands blazing with white fire. A Viking warrior moved toward her with sword raised, but flames lanced from her hands, engulfing him. A second warrior hurled a knife that slammed into her chest. She faltered, staggered, but still came on, desperate to reach Cormac. From behind her another warrior moved in, his blade piercing her back and exiting at her chest. Blood bubbled from her mouth, and she sank to the ground.

Cormac tried to crawl to her, but a sword plunged into his back and darkness swept over him.

From the hill above Oleg Hammerhand roared in anger. The Vikings turned as he raced into the clearing with two swords in his hands.

"I see you, Maggrin," shouted Oleg.

"I see you, traitor," hissed a dark-bearded warrior.

"Don't kill him!" Rhiannon yelled from the cabin doorway.

Oleg and Maggrin rushed at each other, their blades crashing, sparks flying from the contact. Oleg spun on his heel and rammed his second sword like a dagger into the man's belly. As Maggrin fell, the four survivors attacked in a group. Oleg ran to meet them, blocking and cutting with a savage frenzy they could not match. One by one they fell before the cold-eyed warrior and his terrible blades. The last survivor broke into a run to escape his doom, but Oleg hurled a sword after him that hit him hilt-first on the back of the head, and he fell. Before he could rise, the Hammerhand had reached him and his head rolled from his shoulders.

Oleg stood in the clearing, his lungs heaving, the berserk rage dispelling. Finally he turned to Rhiannon.

"Traitress!" he said. "Of all the acts you could have committed to bring me shame, this was the worst. Two people risked their lives to save you . . . and paid for it with their own. Get out of my sight! Go!"

"You don't understand!" she shouted. "I didn't want this to happen; I just wanted to get away."

"You called them here. This is your work. Now go! If I see you after this day, I will kill you with my bare hands. *Go!*"

She ran to him. "Father, please!"

His huge hand lashed across her face, spinning her from her feet. "I do not know you! You are dead," he said.

She struggled to stand, then backed away from the ice in his eyes and ran away down the hillside.

Oleg moved first to Anduine, pulling the sword clear from her back.

"You will never know, lady, the depth of my sorrow.

May God grant you peace." He closed her eyes and walked to where Cormac lay in a spreading pool of blood.

"You fought well, boy," he said, kneeling.

Cormac groaned. Oleg lifted him and carried him into the cabin, where, after stripping the youth's blood-drenched clothes, he checked his wounds: two in the back, one in the side, one in the chest. All were deep, and each one could see a man dead, Oleg knew. But all of them? Cormac had no chance.

Knowing it was useless, Oleg gathered needle and thread and stitched the wounds. When they were sealed, he covered Cormac with a blanket and built up the fire. Then, with candles lit and the cabin warm, Oleg returned to the bed. Cormac's pulse fluttered weakly, and his color was bad—gray streaks on his face, purple rings below his eyes.

"You lost too much blood, Cormac," whispered Oleg. "Your heart is straining . . . and I can do nothing! Fight it, man. Every day will see you stronger." Cormac's head sagged sideways, his breath rattling in his throat. Oleg had heard that sound before. "Don't you die, you whoreson!"

All breathing ceased, but Oleg pushed his hand hard down on Cormac's chest. "Breathe, damn you!" Something hot burned into Oleg's palm, and he lifted his hand. The stone on the chain around Cormac's neck was glowing like burning gold, and a shuddering breath filled the wounded man's lungs.

"Praise be to all the gods there ever were," said Oleg. Placing his hand once more on the stone, he stared down at the wound in Cormac's chest. "Can you heal that?" he asked. Nothing happened. "Well, keep him alive, anyway," he whispered.

Then he rose and took a shovel from the back of the cabin. The ground would still be hard, but Oleg owed at least that to Anduine, the Life Giver, the princess from Raetia.

◊ 10 ◊

A S THE NIGHT wore on, Gwalchmai slept lightly on
his chair at the bedside, his head resting on the
wall. Prasamaccus and Culain sat silently. The Brigante
was recalling his first meeting with the Lance Lord, high
in the Caledones, when the dark-cloaked Vampyres
sought their blood and the young prince escaped through
the gateway to the land of the Pinrae. The boy, Thuro—
as he then was—became the man Uther in a savage war
against the Witch Queen. He and Laitha had wed there,
and she had brought him the gift of the sword; two young
people ablaze with the power of youth, the confidence
that death was an eternity away. Now, after a mere
twenty-six summers, the Blood King lay still, Gian
Avur—the beautiful Laitha—was gone, and the kingdom
Uther had saved faced destruction by a terrible foe. The
words of the Druids echoed through Prasamaccus' mind.

*"For such are the works of man that they are written
upon the air in mist and vanish in the winds of history."*

Culain was lost in thoughts of the present. Why had
they not slain the king once his soul was in their posses-
sion? For all his evil, Molech was a man of great intellect. News of Uther's death would demoralize the

kingdom, making his invasion plans more certain of success. He worried at the problem from every angle.

Wotan's sorcerer priests had come to kill the king and take the sword. But the sword was gone. Therefore, they took Uther's soul. Perhaps they thought—not without justification—that the body would die.

Culain pushed the problem from his mind. Whatever the reason, it was a mistake, and the Lance Lord prayed it would be a costly one. Though he did not know it, it had proved more than costly to the priest who had made it, for his body now hung on a Raetian battlement, his skin flayed, crows feasting on his eyes.

A glowing ball of white fire appeared in the center of the room, and Prasamaccus nocked an arrow to his bow. Culain stretched his sword across the bed and touched Gwalchmai's shoulder. The sleeper awakened instantly. Taking the golden stone, Culain touched it to both of Gwalchmai's blades, then moved to Prasamaccus and emptied his quiver, running the stone over each of the twenty arrowheads. The glowing ball collapsed upon itself, and a gray mist rolled out across the room. Culain waited, then lifted the stone and spoke a single word of power. A golden light pulsed from him, surrounding the two warriors and the body of the king. The mist filled the room . . . and vanished. A dark shadow appeared on the far wall, deepening and spreading until it became the mouth of a cave. A cold breeze blew from the opening, causing the lanterns to gutter. Moonlight streamed through the open windows, and in that silver light Gwalchmai saw a beast from the pit emerge from the cave. Scaled and horned, with long curved fangs, it pushed out into the room. But as it touched the lines of magic Culain had laid, lightning seared its gray body and flames engulfed it. It fell back into the cave, hissing in pain.

Three men leapt into the room. The first fell with an arrow in his throat. Culain and Gwalchmai darted forward, and within moments the other assassins both lay dead upon the floor.

The two warriors waited with swords raised, but the cave mouth shrank to become a shadow and faded from sight.

Gwalchmai pushed the toe of his boot at a fallen assassin, turning the body to its back. The flesh of the face had decomposed, and only a rotting corpse lay there. The old Cantii warrior recoiled from the sight. "We fought dead men!" he whispered.

"It is Wotan's way of gaining loyalty. The bravest of his warriors are untouched by death . . . or so they believe."

"Well, we beat them," said Gwalchmai.

"They will return, and we will not be able to hold them. We must take the king to a place of safety."

"And what place is safe from the sorcery of Wotan?" asked Prasamaccus.

"The Isle of Crystal," Culain answered.

"We cannot carry the king's body halfway across the realm," argued Gwalchmai. "And even if we could, the holy place would not accept him. He is a warrior; they will have no dealings with those who spill blood."

"They will take him," said Culain softly. "It is, in part, their mission."

"You have been there?"

Culain smiled. "I planted the staff that became a tree. But that is another story from another time. Nowhere on land is the earth magic more powerful or the symbols more obscure. Wotan cannot bring his demons to the Isle of Crystal. And if he journeys there himself, it will be as a man, stripped of all majesty of magic. He would not dare."

Gwalchmai stood and looked down at the seemingly lifeless body of Uther. "The question is irrelevant. We cannot carry him across the land."

"I can, for I will travel the ancient paths, the *lung mei*, the way of the spirits."

"And what of Prasamaccus and me?"

"You have already been of service to your king, and you can do no more for him directly. But Wotan's army will soon be upon you. It is not my place to suggest your actions, but my advice would be to rally as many men to Uther's banner as you can. Tell them the king lives and will return to lead them on the day of Ragnorak."

"And what day is that?" Prasamaccus asked.

"The day of greatest despair," whispered Culain. He stood and walked to the western wall. There he knelt, stone in hand, and in the near silence that followed both men heard the whispering of a deep river, the lapping of waves on unseen shores. The wall shimmered and opened.

"Swiftly now!" said Culain, and Gwalchmai and Prasamaccus lifted the heavy body of the Blood King and carried it to the new entrance. Steps had appeared, leading down into a cavern and a deep, dark river. A boat was moored by a stone jetty; gently the two Britons lowered the king into it. Culain untied the mooring rope and stepped to the stern.

As the craft slid away, Culain turned. "Get back to the turret as swiftly as you can. If the gateway closes, you'll be dead within the hour."

As swiftly as the limping Prasamaccus could move,

the two men mounted the stairs. Behind them they could hear weird murmurings and the scrabbling sounds of talons on stone. As they neared the gateway, Gwalchmai saw it shimmer. Seizing Prasamaccus, he hurled him forward and then dived after him, rolling to his knees on the rugs of Uther's room.

Behind them now was merely a wall bathed in the golden light of the sun rising above the eastern hills and shining through the open window.

Victorinus and the twelve men of his party rode warily but without incident during the first three days of their journey. But on the fourth, as they approached a thick wood with a narrow path, Victorinus reined in his mount.

His second aide, Marcus Bassicus, a young man of good Romano-British stock, rode alongside him.

"Is anything wrong, sir?"

The sun above them was bright, the pathway into the woods shrouded by the overhanging trees. Victorinus took a deep breath, aware of the presence of fear. Suddenly he smiled.

"Have you enjoyed life, Marcus?"

"Yes, sir."

"Have you lived it to the full?"

"I think so, sir. Why do you ask?"

"It is my belief that death awaits, hidden in those trees. There is no glory there, no prospect of victory. Just pain and darkness and an end to joy."

The young man's face became set, and his gray eyes narrowed. "And what should we do, sir?"

"You and the others must make your choice, but I must enter those woods. Speak to the men, explain to them that we are betrayed. Tell them that any who wish to flee may do so without shame; it is no act of cowardice."

"Then why must you ride on, sir?"

"Because Wotan will be watching, and I want him to know that I do not fear his treachery, that I welcome it. I want him to understand the nature of the foe. He has conquered Belgica, Raetia, and Gaul and has the Romans on bended knee before him. Britannia will not be as these others."

Marcus rode back to the waiting men, leaving the general staring at the entrance to his own grave. Victorinus lifted the round cavalry shield from the back of his saddle and settled it on his left arm. Then, looping the reins of his warhorse around the saddle pommel, he drew his saber and without a backward glance touched his heels to his mount and moved on. Behind him the twelve soldiers took up their shields and sabers and rode after him.

Within a clearing just inside the line of trees two hundred Goths drew their weapons and waited.

"You say the king is alive," said Geminus Cato, pushing the maps across the table and rising to pour a goblet of mixed wine and water. "But you will forgive my cynicism, I hope."

Gwalchmai shrugged and turned from the window. "I can offer you only my word, General. But it has been considered worth respecting."

Cato smiled and smoothed the close-cropped black beard that shone like an oiled pelt. "Allow me to review the facts that are known. A tall man, dressed in the robes of a Christian, assaulted two guards and made his way unobstructed to the king's tower. This man, you say, is the legendary Lancelot. He declared the body to be alive and used sorcery to remove it from the tower."

"In essence that is true," Gwalchmai admitted.

"But is he not also the king's sworn enemy? The Great Betrayer?"

"He is."

"Then why did you believe him?"

Gwalchmai looked to Prasamaccus, who was sitting quietly at the table. The crippled Brigante cleared his throat.

"With the utmost respect, General, you never knew the Lance Lord. Put from your mind the interminable stories regarding his treachery. What did he do? He slept with a woman. Which of us has not? He alone saved the king when the traitors slew Uther's father. He alone journeyed to the Witch Queen's castle and killed the Lord of the Undead. He is more than a warrior of legend. And his word, on this matter, I believe utterly."

Cato shook his head. "But you also believe the man is thousands of years old, a demigod whose kingdom is under the great western sea."

Prasamaccus swallowed the angry retort that welled within him. Geminus Cato was more than a capable general; he was a skilled and canny soldier, respected by his men though not loved, and, with the exception of Victorinus, the only man capable of fielding a force against the Goths. But he was also of pure Roman stock and had little understanding of the ways of the Celts or the lore of magic that formed their culture. Prasamaccus considered his next words with care.

"General, let us put aside for a moment the history of Culain lach Feragh. Wotan has tried, perhaps success-fully, to assassinate the king. His next move will be to invade, and when he does so, he will not find himself short of allies once it is known that Uther will not stand against them. Culain has given us time to plan. If we spread the word that the king lives—and will return—it will give the Saxons, Jutes, and Angles a problem to consider. They have heard of the might of Wotan, but they *know* the perils of facing the Blood King."

Cato's dark eyes fixed on Prasamaccus, and for several minutes the silence endured; then the general returned to his seat.

"Very well, horse master. Tactically I accept that it is better for Uther to be alive than dead. I shall see that the story is disseminated. But I can spare no knights to seek the sword. Every officer of worth is out scouring the countryside for volunteers, and all militiamen are being recalled." He pulled the maps toward him and pointed to the largest, the land survey commissioned by Ptolemy hundreds of years before. "You have both traveled the land extensively. It is not difficult to imagine where Wotan will land in the south, but he has several armies. Were I in his place, I would be looking for a double assault, perhaps even a triple. We do not have the numbers to cover the country. So where will he strike?"

Gwalchmai gazed down on the map of the land then called Albion. "The Sea Wolves have always favored the coastline here," he said, stabbing his finger to the Humber, "at Petvaria. If Wotan follows this course, he will be below Eboracum, cutting us off from our forces in the south."

Cato nodded. "And if the Brigantes and Trinovantes rise to support him, the whole of Britain will be sliced into three war zones: from the Wall of Hadrian to Eboracum, from Eboracum to Petvaria—or even Durobrivae, if they sail in by the wash—and from there to Anderida or Dubris.

"At best we can raise another ten thousand warriors, bringing our total mobile force to twenty-five thousand. Rumors tell us that Wotan can muster five times as many men, and that is not counting the Saxon rebels or the Brigantes in the north. What I would not give for Victorinus to return with reliable intelligence!" He looked up from the map. "Gwalchmai, I want you to journey to Gaius Geminus in Dubris."

"I cannot, General," said Gwalchmai.

"Why?"

"I must seek the sword."

"This is no time for chasing shadows, seeking dreams."

"Perhaps," admitted the old Cantii warrior, "yet still I must."

Cato leaned back and folded his brawny arms across his leather breastplate. "And where will you seek it?"

"In Camulodunum. When the king was a boy, he loved the hills and woods around the city. There were special places he would run to and hide from his father. I know those places."

"And you?" said Cato, turning.

Prasamaccus smiled. "I shall journey to the Caledones mountains. It was there he met his one love."

Cato chuckled and shook his head. "You Celts have always been a mystery to me, but I have learned never to argue with a British dreamer. I wish you luck on your quest. What will you do if you find the blade?"

Gwalchmai shrugged and looked to Prasamaccus. The Brigante's pale eyes met the Roman's gaze. "We will carry it to the Isle of Crystal, where the king lies."

"And then?"

"I do not know, General."

Cato was silent for a while, lost in thought. "When I was a young man," he said at last. "I was stationed at Aquae Sulis, and often I would ride the country near the isle. We were not allowed there, on orders from the king, but once—because it was forbidden—three officers and I took a boat across the lakes and landed by the highest hill. It was an adventure, you see, and we were young. We built a fire and sat laughing and talking. Then we slept. I had a dream there in which my father came to me and we spoke of many things. Mostly he talked of regret, for we had never been close after my mother died. It was a fine dream, and we embraced; he wished me well and spoke of his pride. The following morning I awoke refreshed. A mist was all about us, and we sailed back to where our horses were hobbled and rode to Aquae Sulis. We were immediately in trouble, for we had returned without our swords. None of us could remember removing them, and none had noticed that we rode without them."

"The isle is an enchanted place," whispered Prasamaccus. "And when did your father die?"

"I think you know the answer to that, Prasamaccus. I have a son, and we are not close." He smiled. "Perhaps one day he will sail to the isle."

Prasamaccus bowed, and the two Britons left the room.

"We cannot undertake this task alone," said Gwalchmai as they emerged into the sunlight. "There is too much ground to cover."

"I know, my friend. But Cato is right. Against the power of Wotan he needs all his young men, and only ancients like us can be spared."

Prasamaccus stopped. "I think that is the answer, Gwal. Ancients. You recall the day when Uther split the sky and marched out of the mist leading the Ninth?"

"Of course. Who could forget it?"

"The legate of the lost legion was Severinus Albinus. Now he has a villa at Calcaria, less than half a day's ride from here."

"The man is over sixty!" objected the Cantii.

"And how old are you?" snapped Prasamaccus.

"There is no need to ram the dagger home," said Gwalchmai. "But he is a rich Roman and probably fat and content."

"I doubt it. But he will know the whereabouts of other survivors of the Ninth. They were Uther's legion, sworn to him by bonds stronger than blood. He brought them from the Vales of the Dead."

"More than a quarter of a century ago. Most of them will have died by now."

"But there will be some who have not. Maybe ten, maybe a hundred. We must seek them out."

Severinus Albinus still looked every inch the Roman general he had been until a mere five years previously. His back was spear-straight, his dark eyes eagle-sharp. For him the past twenty-five years had been like living a dream, for he and all his men of the Ninth Legion had been trapped in the hell of the Void for centuries before the young prince, Uther Pendragon, rescued them and brought them home to a world gone mad. The might of Rome—preeminent when Severinus had marched his men into the Mist—was now but a shadow, and barbarians ruled where once the laws of Rome had been enforced by legions whose iron discipline made defeat unthinkable. Severinus had been honor-bound to serve Uther and had done it well, training native British troops along imperial lines, fighting in wars for a land about which he cared nothing. Now he was at peace in his villa, reading works of ancient times that, for him at least, were reminders of a yesterday that had swallowed his wife and children and all that he knew and loved. A man out of his time, Severinus Albinus was close to contentment as he sat in his garden reading the words of Plutarch.

His personal slave, Nica, a Jew from the Greek islands, approached him.

"My lord, there are two men at the gate who wish to speak with you."

"Tell them to come tomorrow. I am in no mood for business."

"They are not city merchants, lord, but men who claim friendship."

Severinus rolled the parchment and placed it on the marble seat beside him. "They have names, these friends?"

"Prasamaccus and Gwalchmai."

Severinus sighed. "Bring them to me and fetch wine and fruit. They will stay the night, so prepare suitable rooms."

"Shall I heat the water, lord, for the guest baths?"

"That will not be necessary. Our guests are Britons, and they rarely wash. But have two village girls hired to warm their beds."

"Yes, lord," answered Nica, bowing and moving away as Severinus stood and smoothed his long toga, his contentment evaporating. He turned to see the limping Prasamaccus shuffling along the paved walkway, followed by the tall, straight-backed Cantii tribesman known as the King's Hound. Both men he had always treated with respect, as the king's companions deserved, but he had hoped never to see them again. He was uncomfortable with Britons.

"Welcome to my home," he said, bowing stiffly. "I have ordered wine for you." He gestured to the marble seat, and Prasamaocus sank gratefully to it while Gwalchmai stood by, his powerful arms crossed at his chest. "I take it you are here to invite me to the funeral."

"The king is not dead," said Prasamaccus.

Severinus covered his shock well as the scene was interrupted by a servant bearing a silver tray on which were two goblets of wine and a pitcher of water. He laid it on the wide armrest of the seat and silently departed.

"Not dead? He lay in state for three days."

"He is in the Isle of Crystal, recovering," said Gwalchmai.

"I am pleased to hear it. I understand the Goths will be moving against us, and the king is needed."

"We need your help," said Gwalchmai bluntly. "And the men of the Ninth."

Severinus smiled thinly. "The Ninth no longer exists. The men took up their parcels of land and are now citizens, none less than fifty years old. As you well know, the king disbanded the Ninth, allowing them a well-earned retirement. War is a challenge for young men, Gwalchmai."

"We do not need them for war, Severinus," said Prasamaccus. "The Sword of Power is gone—it must be found." The Brigante told the general about the attack on the king and Culain's theory of the sword. Through it all Severinus remained motionless, his dark eyes fixed on Prasamaccus' face.

"Few men," said Severinus, "understood the power of the sword. But I saw it slice the air like a curtain to free us from the Mist, and Uther once explained the riddle of how he always knew where the enemy would strike. The sword is as valuable as the king. It is all very well to seek the Ninth, but there is no time to scour the land. You talk of a site where magic is suddenly powerful. In peacetime perhaps the quest would have some meaning, but in war? There will be columns of refugees, enemy troops, hardship, pain, and death. No, a random search is not the answer."

"Then what is?" asked Gwalchmai.

"Only one man knows where the sword was sent. We must ask him!"

"The king lies in a state close to death," said Prasamaccus. "He cannot speak."

"He could not when last you saw him, Prasamaccus. But if Culain took him to the magic isle, perhaps he is now awake."

"What do you suggest, General?"

"I will get word to the men of the Ninth. But do not expect a large gathering; many are now dead, and others have returned to Italia, hoping to find some link with their pasts. And we will start our journey tomorrow to the southwest."

"I cannot travel with you, General," said Prasamaccus. "I must go to the Caledones."

Severinus nodded. "And you, Gwalchmai?"

"I will ride with you. There is nothing for me here."

"There is nothing for any of us here," said Severinus. "The world is changing. New empires grow, old ones die. The affairs of a nation are like the life of a man; no man and no empire can for long resist decline."

"You think the Goths will win?" stormed Gwalchmai.

"If not the Goths, then the Saxons or the Jutes. I urged Uther to recruit Saxon warriors for his legions, to allow them a degree of self-government. But he would not listen. In the South Saxon alone there are thirty thousand men of sword-bearing age. Proud men, strong men. This realm will not long survive Uther."

"We have not suffered a defeat in twenty-five years," said Gwalchmai.

"And what is that to history? When I was young, in the days of Claudius, Rome ruled the world. Where are the Romans now?"

"I think age has weakened your courage."

"No, Gwalchmai; four hundred years in the Mist has strengthened my wisdom. There is a guest room for each of you. Go now—we will talk later."

The Britons retired to the villa, leaving the old general in the garden, where Nica found him. "Is there anything you need, lord?"

"What news from the merchants?"

"They say that a great army is gathering across the water and that Wotan will be here within weeks."

"What do the merchants plan?"

"Most have hidden their wealth. Some have reinvested in Hispania and Africa. Still more are preparing to welcome the Goths. It is the way of the world."

"And you, Nicodemus?"

"Me, lord? Why, I will stay with you."

"Nonsense! You have not spent ten years building yourself a fortune merely to die as my slave."

"I do not know what you mean, lord."

"This is no time for denials. You risked my capital with Abrigus, and he brought home a cargo of silks that netted me a handsome sum. You took a commission of one hundred silver pieces, which you reinvested skillfully."

Nica shrugged. "How long have you known?"

"About six years. I am leaving tomorrow, and I do not think I will return. If I do not come home within the year, then the villa is yours—and all my capital; there is a sealed parchment to that effect lodged with Cassius. My slaves are to be freed, and an amount has been set aside for the woman Trista; she has been good to me. You will see all this is done?"

"Of course, lord, but naturally I hope you will have a long life and return speedily."

Severinus chuckled. "And still you lie, you rogue! Get ready my sword and the armor of combat—not the ornamental breastplate but the old leather cuirass. As to the mount, I will take Canis."

"He is getting old, lord."

"We are all getting old, Nica. But he's wily and fears nothing."

The boat slid through the dark waters, Culain sitting silently at the tiller, until at last the tunnel widened into a cavern hung with gleaming stalactites. The waters bubbled and hissed, and the walls glimmered with an eldritch light. Culain steered the craft through a maze of natural pillars and out onto a wide mist-smeared lake. The stars were bright, the moon shining over the distant tor, on which stood a round tower. The air was fresh and cool, and the Lance Lord stretched and drew in a deep breath as the peace of the isle swept over him. His eyes roamed the landscape, seeking the once-familiar forms of the Sleeping Giants, the Questing Beast, the Centaur, the

Dove, and the Lion, hidden for two thousand years but potent still.

The craft moved on into the tree-shadowed bay, toward the campfire that twinkled in the distance like a resting star. As the boat neared the land, seven hooded figures rose from around the fire and advanced in a line toward the shore.

"Why have you called us?" asked a woman's voice.

"I have a friend here in need of your help."

"Is your friend a man of peace?"

"He is the king."

"Is that an answer?"

"He is the man who declared the Isle of Crystal to be sacred, and he has protected its sanctity and its freedom."

"The isle needs no *man* to declare it sacred or swords to protect its freedom."

"Then look upon him simply as he is, a man whose soul has been stolen and whose body is in peril."

"And where would you have us take him?" asked the woman.

"To the round hall in the circle of the great moon, where no evil may dwell, where the two worlds join in the sign of the sacred fish."

"You know many of our mysteries."

"I know *all* of your mysteries and more besides."

Without another word the women moved forward and effortlessly lifted the king from the craft. In two lines, the body almost floating between them, the hooded women set off into the shadows with Culain following. A figure in white emerged from the trees, a hood drawn over her face.

"You cannot travel farther, warrior."

"I must remain with him."

"You cannot."

"You think to stop me?"

"You will stop yourself," she told him, "for your presence weakens the power that will keep him alive."

"I am not evil," he argued.

"No, Culain lach Feragh, you are not evil."

"You know me, then? That is good, for you must also know that I planted the thorn and began the work you now continue."

"You began it, yes, but not in faith; it was but one more of your games. You told the sisters that you know all their mysteries and more besides. Once that was the truth, but it is no longer. You think you chose this place, Culain? No. It chose you."

"Forgive my arrogance, lady. But let me stay. I have much to atone for. And I am lost and have nowhere to go."

Moonlight bathed the bay, making the white-robed priestess almost ethereal, and the warrior waited as she considered his words. Finally she spoke.

"You may stay on the isle, Culain, but not at the round hall." She pointed up at the great tor and the tower that stood there. "There you may rest, and I will see that food is brought to you."

"Thank you, lady. It is a weight lifted from my heart."

She turned and was gone. Culain climbed the ancient path that circled the tor, rising higher and higher above the land and lakes below. The tower was old and had been old when he had been a child in Atlantis. The wooden floors had rotted, and only the huge stones remained, carefully fashioned with a precision now lost to the world and interlocked without the aid of mortar. Culain lit a fire with some of the rotten wood and settled down to sleep beneath the stars.

◊ **11** ◊

CORMAC AWOKE TO a barren landscape of skeletal trees and dusty craters. Beside him lay his sword, and behind him was a tunnel that rose up through a mountain. Sitting up, he looked into the tunnel. At the far end, high in the heart of the mountain, he saw a flickering glow and yearned to walk toward it and bathe in the light.

But just then he became aware of another figure and swung, sword in hand, to see an old man sitting on a flat rock; his beard was white, and he was dressed in a long gray robe.

"Who are you?" asked Cormac.

"No one," the man answered with a rueful smile. "Once, though, I was someone and had a name."

"What is this place?"

The man shrugged. "Unlike me, it has many names and many secrets. And yet, like me, it is nowhere. How did you come here?"

"I . . . there was a fight . . . I . . . cannot remember clearly."

"Sometimes that is a gift to receive with gratitude. There is much I would like to unremember."

"I was stabbed," said Cormac, "many times." Lifting

his shirt, he examined the pale flesh of his chest and back. "But there are no scars."

"The scars are elsewhere," said the man. "Did you fight well?"

"No. I was blind . . . Anduine! I must find her." He stood and moved toward the tunnel.

"You will not find her there," the man said softly, "for that way lies blood and fire and life."

"What are you saying, old man?"

"I am stating the obvious, Cormac, son of Uther. Your lady has gone before you on this long gray road. Do you have the courage to follow?"

"Courage? You are making my head spin. Where is she?"

The old man rose and pointed to the distant mountains beyond the black river that wound across the foot of the valley below. "She is there, Cormac, where all new souls gather. The Mountains of the Damned."

"I ask you again, old man. What is this place?"

"This, young prince, is the place of nightmares. Here only the dead may walk. This is the Void, and here dwells chaos."

"Then . . . I . . ."

"You are dead, Prince Cormac."

"No!"

"Look around you," said the old man. "Where is life? Is there grass or any living tree? Is there a sign of any animal or bird? Where are the stars that should grace the sky?"

"And yet I still think and feel, and I can wield my sword. This is a dream, old man; it does not frighten me."

The man rose and smoothed his gray robe. "I am

journeying to those mountains. Do you wish me to give a message to your lady?"

Cormac looked back at the tunnel and the beckoning light. Every emotion in him screamed to run toward it, to escape the pitiless gray of the land around him. But Anduine was not here. He looked to the mountains.

"You say she is there, yet why should I believe you?"

"Only because you do. I would not lie to you, young prince. I served your father and his father and grandfather. I was the Lord Enchanter."

"Maedhlyn?"

"Yes, that was one of my names in the light. Now I am no one."

"So you also are dead?"

"As dead as you, Prince Cormac. Will you travel with me on the gray road?"

"Will I truly find Anduine?"

"I do not know. But you will walk her path."

"Then I will join you."

Maedhlyn smiled and walked down the hillside to the dark river. He raised his arms and called out, and a black barge came into sight, steered by a monstrous figure with the head of a wolf and eyes that gleamed red in the pale half-light of eternal dusk. Cormac raised his sword.

"You will not need that," whispered Maedhlyn. "He is only the ferryman and will offer no harm to you."

"How can he harm a dead man?" asked Cormac.

"Only your body has died. Your spirit can still know pain and, worse, extinction. And there are many beasts here and once-men who will seek to harm you. Keep your sword ready, Cormac. You will have need of it."

Together they climbed into the barge, which moved

out onto the river under the skilled silent poling of the ferryman.

The boat came to rest against a stone jetty, and Maedhlyn climbed clear, beckoning Cormac to follow him. The ferryman sat still, his red eyes fixed on the youth and his hand extended.

"What does he want?"

"The black coin," said Maedhlyn. "All travelers here must pay the ferryman."

"I have no coin."

The old man was troubled. "Search your pockets, young prince," he ordered. "It must be there."

"I tell you I have nothing."

"Search anyway!"

Cormac did as he was bidden, then spread his arms. "As I said, I have nothing but my sword."

Maedhlyn's shoulders sagged. "I fear I have done you a terrible injustice, Cormac." He turned to the ferryman and spoke in a language the youth had never heard. The beast seemed to smile; then he stood and turned the barge, poling it back onto the river.

"What injustice?"

"You are not, it seems, dead, though how you have come here is a mystery. All souls carry the black coin."

"There is no harm done. He carried us over."

"Yes, but he will not take you back, and that is the tragedy."

"It is not wide, Maedhlyn. If necessary I can swim across."

"No! You must never touch the water; it is the essence of hell itself. It will burn what it touches, and the pain will last an eternity."

Cormac approached the old man, placing his arm over Maedhlyn's shoulder.

"It is no tragedy. I have no wish to live without Anduine, and she has already passed the river. Come, let us walk. I wish to reach the mountains before dark."

"Dark? There is no dark here. This is how the Void is and always will be. There is no sun and no moon, and the stars are a distant memory."

"Let us walk, anyway," snapped Cormac.

Maedhlyn nodded, and the two set off.

For many hours they continued on their way until at last weariness overcame the prince. "Do you never tire?" he asked the Enchanter.

"Not here, Cormac. It is another sign of your bond to life. Come, we will sit up there on the hillside; I will light a fire, and we will talk."

They camped within a circle of boulders. Maedhlyn gathered dead wood, and the small fire blazed brightly. The Enchanter seemed lost in thought, and Cormac did not disturb him. After a while Maedhlyn stretched and smiled grimly.

"It would have been better, young prince, to have met under the sun, in the woods around Eboracum or in the palace at Camulodunum. But men must make of events what they can. I taught your father when he was your age, and he was swift in learning. He became a man who could bend almost any situation to his will. Perhaps you also are such a man."

Cormac shook his head. "I was raised as a demon's son, shunned by all. The man who was a father to me was slain, and I fled. I met Culain, and he saved me. He left me to protect Anduine, and I failed. That is the story of Cormac. I do not think I am as Uther was."

"Do not judge yourself too harshly, young prince. Tell me all of the story, and I will be your judge."

As the fire flickered to glowing ash, Cormac told him of his early life with Grysstha, of the kiss from Alftruda that had led to Grysstha's murder, of the meeting with Culain, and of the battle with the demons to protect Anduine. Lastly he outlined the rescue of Oleg and his daughter and the fight with the Vikings that had ultimately caused the attack on the cabin.

Maedhlyn listened quietly until the story was complete, then added fresh fuel to the fire.

"Uther would have been proud of you, but you are too humble, Prince Cormac; I would guess that has much to do with the tribulations of your childhood. Firstly, when Alftruda's brothers attacked you, you defeated them all—the act of a warrior and a man of courage. Secondly, when the demons came, you fought like a man. And when you carried Oleg from the mountain, you once more showed the power of your spirit. And yes, you failed; the forces against you were too powerful. But know this, child of Uther, to fail is not so terrible. The real act of cowardice is never to try."

"I think, Maedhlyn, I would sooner have been less heroic and more successful. But there is no point now in worrying about it. I will have no opportunity to redeem myself."

"Do not be too sure of that," said the Enchanter softly. "This world, damnable as it is, has many similarities to the one you have left."

"Name them."

"The lord of this world is Molech, once a man but now a demon. You know him better as Wotan. This was his realm for nigh two thousand years."

"Wotan? How is that possible?"

"Through one man's stupidity. My own. But let me tell the story in my own time. You know, of course, of the Feragh, the last living fragment of Atlantis?"

"Yes, Culain told me."

"Well, in those glorious days there were many young men who yearned for adventure. And we had the power of the stones, and we became gods to the mortals. One such young man was Molech. He reveled in dark emotions, and his pleasures would turn most men's stomachs; torture, pain, and death were as wine to him. He turned his world into a charnel house. It was too much for any of us to bear, and the Feragh turned against him. Our king, Pendarric, led a war that saw Molech humbled. Culain fought him on the towers of Babel and killed him there, beheading him and hurling the body to the rocks to be burned."

"Then how did he return?"

"Be patient!" snapped Maedhlyn. "Molech, like all of us, could use the stones to become immortal. But he went one step further than we had; he took a ring of silver Sipstrassi and embedded it in his own skull, under the skin, like an invisible crown. He became Sipstrassi, needing no stone. When Culain killed him, I took the head. No one knew what I had done. I burned the flesh from it and kept it as a talisman, an object of great power. It aided me through the centuries that followed. I knew Molech's spirit still lived, and I communed with it and with the dead of his realm, learning much and using the knowledge well. But in my arrogance I did not realize that Molech was also using me and that his power was growing.

"Some years ago, just after you were born, Uther and I

suffered a parting of the ways. I journeyed to the lands of the Norse and there met a young woman who wished to be my student. I allowed her into my house and into my heart. But she was a servant of Molech, and she drugged me one night and placed the skull on my head. Molech took my body, and my spirit was sent here. Now he torments me with my own stupidity, and the murderous excesses we fought so hard to destroy have returned to plague the world. And this time he will not be defeated."

"Culain still lives. He will destroy him," said Cormac.

"No, Culain is a shadow of the man who once was. I thought that Uther and the Sword of Power might be strong enough, but Wotan outthought me there also. He has taken the Blood King."

"Killed him?"

"No. Would that he had!"

"I do not understand you," said Cormac.

"Uther is here, Prince Cormac, in the Void. Held in chains of soulfire."

"I care only for Anduine," said Cormac. "While I can admire the strength and skills of the man who sired me, all I know is that he hounded my mother to her eventual death. I do not care about his suffering." He rose smoothly to his feet. "I have rested enough, Maedhlyn."

"Very well," whispered the Enchanter. His hand floated over the fire, and the blaze died instantly. "It is a long walk and a road fraught with peril. Keep to the path. No matter what happens, Cormac, keep to the path."

Together they set off on the wide road. On either side the pitiless landscape stretched to a gray horizon, the land broken only by ruined trees and jutting black boulders, jagged and stark. Dust rose about their feet, drying Cormac's throat and stinging his eyes.

"This is a soulless place," he said, bringing a wry chuckle from Maedhlyn.

"That is exactly the opposite of the truth, young man. All that lives here *are* the souls of the departed. The problem we face is that the majority of those condemned here are evil. And here a man's true nature is what is seen. Take the ferryman. He was a man once, but now he has the shape of the beast he hid in life."

"Anduine has no place here," said Cormac. "She is gentle and kind; she has harmed no one."

"Then she will pass on along the road. Do not fear for her, Cormac. There is a cosmic balance to this place, and not even Molech could disturb it for long."

As they rounded a bend in the road, they saw a young girl whose foot was caught in a snare. "Help me!" she called, and Cormac stepped from the road to where she lay. As he reached her, a towering figure loomed from behind a rock.

"Look out!" yelled Maedhlyn, and Cormac spun, his sword slashing in a murderous arc that cleaved the side of the scaled beast.

With a hissing scream that sprayed black blood over Cormac's shirt the monster vanished. Behind him the girl rose silently, fingers extended like claws. Maedhlyn hurled a slender dagger that took her between the shoulder blades, and Cormac whirled as she fell to her knees. Her eyes were as red as blood, her mouth was lined with pointed fangs, and a serpent's tongue slid between her blue lips. Then she, too, vanished.

"Get back to the road," ordered Maedhlyn, "and bring my dagger." The blade lay in the dust. Cormac scooped it up and rejoined the Enchanter.

"What were they?"

"A father and daughter. They spent their lives robbing and killing travelers on the road between Verulamium and Londinium. They were burned at the stake twenty years before you were born."

"Does nothing good live here?"

"A man finds good in the most unlikely places, Prince Cormac. But we shall see."

They journeyed on for what seemed like an eternity. Without the stars or moon to judge the hours, Cormac lost all sense of passing time, yet eventually they reached the mountains and followed the path to a wide cave where torches blazed.

"Be on your guard here, for there is no protection," warned Maedhlyn.

Inside the cave scores of people were sitting, sleeping, or talking. The newcomers were ignored, and Maedhlyn led the prince down a series of torchlit tunnels packed with souls, halting at last in a central cavern where a huge fire burned.

An elderly man in a faded brown habit bowed to the Enchanter. "God's peace to you, Brother," he said.

"And to you, Albain. I have here a young friend in need of goodness."

Albain smiled and offered his hand. He was a frail, short man with wispy white hair framing his bald head like a crown above his ears. "Welcome, my boy. What you seek is in short supply. How may I help you?"

"I am searching for my wife; her name is Anduine." He described her to the old monk, who listened attentively.

"She was here, but I fear she was taken away. I am sorry."

"Taken? By whom?"

"The Loyals came for her. We had no time to hide her."

"Molech's guards," Maedhlyn explained. "They serve him here as they served him in life, for the promise of a return to the flesh."

"Where did they take her?"

Albain did not answer but looked at Maedhlyn.

"She will be at the keep—Molech's fortress. You cannot go there, Cormac."

"What is there to stop me?" he asked, gray eyes blazing.

"You truly are Uther's son," said Maedhlyn, caught between sorrow and pride.

Several figures moved from the shadows.

"Uther's son?" said Victorinus. "And is that you, Maedhlyn?"

"So the war has begun," Maedhlyn whispered.

"Not yet, wizard, but soon. Tell me, is he truly Uther's son?"

"Yes. Prince Cormac, meet Victorinus, Uther's ablest general."

"I wish I could say well met, Prince Cormac." He turned once more to Maedhlyn. "Albain told us that the king's soul is held at the keep . . . that they are torturing him. Can it be true?"

"I am sorry, Victorinus. I know you were his friend."

"Were? Death does not change my friendship, Maedhlyn. There are thirteen of us here, and we will find the king."

"The open ground before the keep," said Maedhlyn, "is patrolled by hounds of great size. They have teeth like daggers and skin like steel; no sword will slay them. Then, within the first wall, live the Loyals, two hundred at least—all formidable warriors during their lives.

Beyond the second wall I have never seen, but even the Loyals fear to go there."

"The king is there," said Victorinus, his face set, his eyes stubborn.

"And Anduine," added Cormac.

"It is madness! How will you approach the keep? Or do you think your thirteen swords will cut a path for you?"

"I have no idea, Maedhlyn; I am only a soldier. But once you were the greatest thinker in all the world, or so you told me."

"Hell is no place for flattery," said the Enchanter. "But I will think on it."

"Does Molech have no enemies?" Cormac asked.

"Of course he has, but most of them are like he is: evil."

"That does not concern me. Are they powerful?"

"Believe me, Cormac, this is not a course to pursue."

"Answer me, damn you!"

"Yes, they are powerful," snapped Maedhlyn. "They are also deadly, and even to approach them could cost you your soul. Worse, you could end up like your father—wrapped in chains of fire and tortured until you are naught but a broken shell, a mewling ruined thing."

"Why should they do this to me?"

"Because you are your father's son. And Molech's greatest enemy here is Goroien, the Witch Queen defeated by Uther, and her lover-son Gilgamesh, slain by Culain. Now do you understand?"

"I understand only that I want to meet her. Can you arrange it?"

"She will destroy you, Cormac."

"Only if she hates me more than she desires to defeat Molech."

"But what can you offer her? She has her own army and slave beasts to do her bidding."

"I will offer her the keep—and the soul of Wotan."

"Talk to them, Albain," said Maedhlyn as the small group sat in a corner of the stalactite-hung cavern. "Explain what they are risking." The old man looked at Victorinus, his face showing his concern.

"There are many here who will pass no farther on the road. They exist as beasts in this terrible twilight. Others are drawn on toward what some believe is a beautiful land with a golden sun and a blue sky. I myself believe in that land and encourage people to travel there. But to do so you must hold to the path."

"Our king is held here," said Victorinus. "We have a duty toward him."

"Your duty was to give your lives for him, and you did that. But not your souls."

"I will not speak for the others, Albain, only for myself. I cannot journey farther while the king needs me, not even for the promise of paradise. You see, of what worth would paradise be to me if I spent it in shame?"

Albain reached across and took Victorinus by the hand. "I cannot answer that for you. All I know is that here—in this land of death and despair—there is still the promise of hope for those who travel on. Some cannot, for their evil has found a home here. Others will not, for their fears are very great and it is easier perhaps to hide in the eternal shadows. But this ghastly world is not all there is, and you should not deny yourself the journey."

"Why have you not journeyed on?" asked Cormac.

Albain shrugged. "One day perhaps I will. For now there is work for me among the haunted and the lost."

"As indeed there is work for us," said Cormac. "I am not a philosopher, Albain, but my love is here, and you say she is held by Molech. I will not allow that. Like Victorinus, I could not live in any paradise with that on my conscience."

"Love is a fine emotion, Prince Cormac, and there is precious little of it here. Let me argue from another standpoint. To defeat Molech you seek the aid of Goroien, who was as evil as the man you desire to destroy. Can a man wed himself to the power of evil and remain untouched by it? What will happen when the fire of your purity touches the ice of her malice?"

"I do not know. But Molech's enemies should be my friends."

"Friends? How much do you know of Goroien?"

"Nothing beyond Maedhlyn telling me she was an enemy to Uther."

"She was an immortal who held her eternal beauty by sacrificing thousands of young women, watching as their blood ran over her magic stone. She brought her dead son back to life—and made him her lover. His name was— and is—Gilgamesh, the Lord of the Undead. That is what you are seeking to ally yourself with."

Cormac shook his head and smiled. "You do not understand, Albain. You speak of my purity? I would sacrifice a world to free Anduine; I would see a million souls writhe in agony to see her safe."

"And would she desire this, young prince?"

Cormac looked away for a moment. "No, she would not," he admitted, "and perhaps that is why I love her so deeply. But I will seek Goroien."

"She will destroy you, and that is only if you *can* reach her. To do so you must leave the road and journey across the Shadowlands. There the most vile of creatures dwell, and they will haunt your every step."

Victorinus raised his hand, and all eyes turned to him. "I appreciate your advice, Albain, and your warnings. But the prince and I will leave the road to seek the Witch Queen." He turned to his aide, Marcus. "Will you travel with me?"

"We died with you, sir," said the young man. "We'll not leave you now."

"Then it is settled. What of you, Maedhlyn?"

"The witch hates me more than any of you, but yes—I will go. What else is there for me?"

Albain rose and gazed sadly at the fifteen men. "I wish you God's luck. There is no more to say."

Cormac watched the little man weave his way through the crowded cavern. "How did he come to be here, Maedhlyn?"

"He followed the right god at a time when Rome was ruled by the wrong one. Let us go."

◊ **12** ◊

THREE INVASION FLEETS landed on the coasts of Britannia in the fourth week of the spring. Eleven thousand men came ashore at Segundunum near the easternmost fortress of the nearly derelict Wall of Hadrian. The town was sacked, with hundreds of citizens put to the sword.

The second fleet—led by Wotan's ablest general, Alaric—disgorged eight thousand men at Anderida on the south coast, and this army was further swelled by two thousand Saxons recruited by the renegade Agwaine. Refugees packed the roads and tracks toward Londinium as the Goths swept along the coastline toward Noviomagus.

The third fleet beached at Petvaria, having sailed unchallenged along the mouth of the Humber. Twenty-two thousand fighting men came ashore, and the British defense force of twelve hundred men fled before them.

In Eboracum, less than twenty-five miles away, the city was in panic.

Geminus Cato, left with little choice, gathered his two legions of ten thousand men and marched to engage the enemy. Fierce storms lashed the legions, and during the first night of camp many men swore they had seen a demonic head outlined against the thunderclouds and lit by spears of lightning. By morning desertions had reduced Cato's fighting force by more than a thousand.

His scouts reported the enemy closing in just after dawn, and Cato moved his men to the crown of a low hill half a mile to the west. There trenches were hastily dug and spiked, and the horses of the officers were removed to a picket line in a nearby wood, behind the battle site.

The storm clouds disappeared as swiftly as they had come, and the Goths came into sight in brilliant sunshine that blazed from their spear points and raised axes. Cato felt the fear spread along the line as the sheer size of the enemy force made an impact on the legions.

"By all the gods, they're a pretty bunch," shouted Cato. A few men sniggered, but the tension did not break.

A young soldier dropped his gladius and stepped back. "Pick it up, boy," said Cato softly. "It'll gather rust lying there."

The youth was trembling and close to tears. "I don't want to die," he said.

Cato glanced at the Goths who were gathering for the charge and then walked to the boy, stooping to gather his sword. "Nobody does," he said, pushing the hilt into the soldier's hand and guiding him back into line.

With a roar that echoed the previous storm, the Goths hurled themselves at the line.

"Archers!" bellowed Cato. "Take your positions!"

The five hundred bowmen in their light leather tunics ran forward between the shield bearers and formed a line along the hilltop. A dark cloud of shafts arched into the air and down into the charging mass. The Goths were heavily armored and the casualties were few, yet the charge faltered as men fell and tripped those who were following.

"Retire and take up spears!"

The bowmen pulled back behind the shield wall, dropped their bows and quivers, and in pairs took up the ten-foot spears lying in rows behind the heavily armored legionaries. The first man in each pair knelt hidden behind a shielded warrior, holding the spear three feet from the point. The second man gripped the shaft at the base, awaiting the order from Cato.

The charging Goths were almost at the line when Cato raised his arm.

"Now!"

As the spearmen surged forward, the hidden spears, directed by the kneeling men at the front, flashed between the shields, plunging into the front ranks of the attacking warriors, smashing shields to shards, and cleaving chain mail. The unbarbed spears were dragged back and then rammed home again and again.

The slaughter was terrifying, and the Goths fell back dismayed.

Three times more they charged, but the deadly spears kept them at bay. The ground before the line was thick with enemy dead and with wounded writhing in agony with their ribs crushed, their lifeblood oozing into the soft earth.

An officer moved across the Goths' front line and spoke to the waiting warriors. Five hundred men flung aside their shields and advanced.

"What are they doing, sir?" asked Cato's aide, Decius. Cato did not reply. It did not become an officer in the midst of a battle to admit that he had no idea.

The Goths surged up the hill, screaming the name of

Wotan. The spears plunged into them, but each stricken warrior grabbed the shaft of the weapon that was killing him, trapping the spear in his own body. The main army attacked once more, this time crashing against the British shield wall with tremendous force.

For a moment the wall split, and several warriors forced their way into the line. Cato drew his gladius and rushed at them; he was joined by a young legionary, and together they closed the breach. As the Goths fell back, Cato turned to the legionary and saw that it was the boy who earlier had dropped his sword.

"You did well, lad." Before the boy could reply, a terrifying roar went up from the Gothic ranks and the enemy surged toward the line.

The battle lasted the full day with neither side triumphant, yet at dusk Cato had no choice but to pull back from the hill. He had lost 271 men, with another 94 wounded. The enemy losses, he calculated, were around two thousand. In military terms it was a victory, but realistically Cato knew it had gained the Britons little. The Goths now knew—if they ever had been in doubt—that Uther's army was not as poorly led as the Merovingian forces across the water. And the Britons knew the Goths were not invincible. Apart from those two points nothing had been gained from the day, and Cato marched his men back along the road toward Eboracum, having already chosen the site for the next battle.

"Is it really true, sir?" asked Decius as the two men rode ahead of the legions. "Is the king alive?"

"Yes," answered Cato.

"Then where is he?"

Cato was weary and not for the first time wished he had another aide. But Decius was the son of a rich merchant and had paid for the appointment with a beautiful villa outside Eboracum.

"The king will let us know his plans when he is ready. Until then we will do what he asks of us."

"But several men saw the corpse, sir. And the funeral arrangements were being made."

Cato ignored the comment. "When the night camp is made, I want you to tour the fires. The men fought well today. Make yourself known among them—compliment them, tell them you have never seen such bravery."

"Yes, sir. For how long should I continue to do this?"

Cato bit back his anger and thought of his villa. "Never mind, Decius. You set up my tent and I'll talk to the men."

"Yes, sir. Thank you."

Galead's dreams were dark and filled with pain. Awakening in the cold dawn, he stared at the ashes of the previous night's fire. He had seen in his dreams Victorinus and his twelve warriors ride into the wood to be surrounded by the Goths—led by the traitor Agwaine—and had watched the old general die as he had lived, with cold dignity and no compromise.

Shivering, he rekindled the fire. His news was of little worth to Britain now. The invasion fleets would sail within days, the king was dead, and the power of Wotan was beyond opposition. Yet could feel no hate, only a terrible burden of sorrow dragging down his spirit.

Beside him lay his sword, and he stared at it, loath to touch it. What was it, he wondered, that led men to desire such weapons, that filled them with the need to use them against their fellows, hacking and cutting and slaying?

And for what? Where was the gain? Few soldiers grew

rich. Most returned to the poor farms and villages where they had grown up, and many lived out their lives without limbs or with terrible scars that served as grim reminders of the days of war.

A sparrow landed beside him, pecking at the crumbs of the oatcake he had eaten at dusk the day before. Another joined it. Galead sat unmoving as the birds hopped around the scabbarded sword.

"What do they tell you?" asked a voice.

Galead looked across the fire to see a man seated there, wrapped in a cloak of rich rust-red. His beard was golden and heavily curled, and his eyes were deep blue.

"They tell me nothing," he answered softly, "but they are peaceful creatures, and I am happy to see them."

"Would they have fed so contentedly beside Ursus, the prince who desired riches?"

"If they had, he would not have noticed them. Who are you?"

"I am not an enemy."

"This I already knew."

"Of course. Your powers are growing, and you are rising above the sordid deeds of this world."

"I asked who you were, stranger."

"My name is Pendarric."

Galead shivered as he heard the name, as if deep inside himself the name echoed in a distant hall of memory. "Should I know you?"

"No, though I have used other names. But we walk the same paths, you and I. Where you are now I once stood, and all my deeds seemed as solid as morning mist—and as long-lasting."

"And what did you decide?"

"Nothing. I followed the heart's desire and came to know peace."

Galead smiled. "Where in these lands can I find peace? And were I to try, would it not be selfish? My friends are about to suffer invasion, and my place is with them."

"Peace does not rest within a realm, or a city, or a town, or even a crofter's hut," said Pendarric. "But then, you know this. What will you do?"

"I will find a way to return to Britain. I will go against the power of Wotan."

"Will it give you satisfaction to destroy him?"

Galead considered the question. "No," he said at last. "Yet evil must be countered."

"With the sword?"

Galead looked down at the weapon with distaste. "*Is* there another way?"

"If there is, you will find it. I have discovered a wonderful truth in my long life: Those who seek with a pure heart usually find what they are looking for."

"It would help me greatly to *know* what I am looking for."

"You talked about countering evil, and in essence that is a question of balance. But the scales are not merely linear. A great amount of evil does not necessarily require an equivalent amount of good to equalize the balance."

"How can that be true?" Galead asked.

"An angry bear will suffer a score of arrows and still be deadly, but a touch of poison, and it falls. Sometimes an apparently meaningless incident will set in motion events that will cause either great suffering or great joy."

"Are you saying there is a way to bring down Wotan without the sword?"

"I am saying nothing that simple. But it is an interesting

question for a philosopher, is it not? Wotan feeds on hatred
and death, and you seek to combat him with swords and
shields. In war a soldier will find it all but impossible not
to hate the enemy. And so, do you not give Wotan even
more of what he desires?"

"And if we do not fight him?"

"Then he wins and brings even more death and despair
to your land and many others."

"Your riddle is too deep for me, Pendarric. If we fight
him, we lose. If we do not, we lose. Yours is a philoso-
phy of despair."

"Only if you cannot see the *real* enemy."

"There is something worse than Wotan?"

"There always is, Galead."

"You speak like a man of great wisdom, and I sense
you have power. Will you use that power against
Wotan?"

"I am doing exactly that at this moment. Why else
would I be here?"

"Are you offering me a weapon against him?"

"No."

"Then what is the purpose of your visit?"

"What indeed?" answered Pendarric.

His image faded, and Galead was alone once more.
The birds were still feeding by the sword as the knight
turned to look at them, but as he moved, they fluttered
away in panic. He stood and strapped the blade to his
side, covered the fire with earth, and saddled his horse.

The coast was a mere eight miles through the woods,
and he hoped to find a ship that might land him on the
shores of Britain. He rode the narrow trails through the
forest, lost in thought, listening to the birdsong, enjoying
the sunlight that occasionally lanced through the gaps in

the overhanging trees. His mood was more tranquil after Pendarric's appearance, though the sorrow remained.

Toward the middle of the morning he met an elderly man and two women standing alongside a handcart with a broken wheel. The cart was piled with possessions: clothes, chests, and a very old chair. The man bowed as he approached, the women standing nervously as Galead dismounted.

"May I offer assistance?" he asked.

"That is truly kind," said the man, smiling. His hair was long and white, though darker streaks could still be seen in his forked beard. One of the women was elderly, the other young and attractive with auburn hair streaked with gold; her right eye was bruised, and her lip cut and swollen. Galead knelt by the cart and saw that the wheel had come loose and had been torn away from the joining pin at the axle.

He helped them unload the cart, then lifted it so that the wheel could be pushed back in place. Using the back of a hatchet blade, he hammered the joining pin home and then reloaded the cart.

"I am very grateful," said the man. "Will you join us for our midday meal?"

Galead nodded and sat down by the roadside as the young woman prepared a fire. The older woman busied herself taking pans and plates from the back of the cart.

"We do not have much," said the old man, seating himself beside Galead. "Some oats and salt. But it is filling, and there is goodness in the food."

"It will suffice. My name is Galead."

"And I am Caterix. That is my wife, Oela, and my daughter, Pilaras."

"Your daughter seems to be in pain."

"Yes. The journey has not been kind to us, and I pray to the lord that our troubles may now be over."

"How was she hurt?"

Caterix looked away. "Three men robbed us two days ago. They . . . assaulted my daughter and killed her husband, Doren, when he tried to aid her."

"I am sorry," Galead said lamely.

The meal was eaten in silence after a short prayer of thanks from Caterix. Galead thanked the family for the hospitality and offered to ride with them to the coast, where they had friends. Caterix accepted the offer with a bow, and the small group followed slowly as Galead rode ahead.

As dusk flowed into evening Galead, rounding a bend in the trail, saw a man sitting with his back to a tree. He rode forward and dismounted. The man was bleeding heavily from a wound in his chest, and his face was pale, the eyelids and lips blue from loss of blood. Ripping open the dirty tunic, Galead stanched the wound as best he could. After several minutes Caterix came upon the scene; he knelt beside the wounded man, lifting his wrist and checking his pulse.

"Get him to the cart," he said. "I have some cloth there for bandages and a needle and thread." Together they half lifted, half dragged the man to a rounded clearing by a silver stream. The two women helped clean the wound, and Caterix expertly sewed the jagged flesh together. Then they wrapped the man in blankets warmed by the fire.

"Will he live?" asked Galead.

Caterix shrugged. "That is in the lord's hands. He has lost much blood."

In the night Galead awoke to see the girl Pilaras kneeling by the wounded man. Moonlight glinted from the knife in her hand.

She sat motionless for a long moment, then raised the knife, resting the point on the sleeping man's neck. Suddenly her head sagged forward, and Galead saw that she was weeping. She lifted the knife and replaced it in the sheath at her side, returning to her blankets by the cart.

Galead lay back and returned to his dreams. He watched as the invasion ships landed on the coast of Britain, saw the Goths begin their march toward the cities, and, over it all, saw two visions that haunted him: a demonic head filling the sky, surrounded by storm clouds and lightning, and a sword shining like a midnight lantern.

Despite his dreams, he awoke refreshed. The wounded man was still sleeping, but his color was better. Galead washed in the stream and then approached Caterix, who was sitting beside the victim.

"I must leave you," said Galead. "I need to find a ship to take me home."

"May the lord guide you and protect you on your journey."

"And you on yours, Caterix. It was a fine deed to save the man's life."

"Not fine at all. What are we if we do not aid our fellows in their times of trial?"

Galead rose and walked to his horse, then on impulse returned to Caterix.

"Last night your daughter held a knife to this man's throat."

He nodded. "She told me this morning. I am very proud of her."

"Why did she do it?"

"This is the man who raped her and killed her husband."

"And you saved him? Sweet Mithras, he deserves death!"

"More than likely," answered Caterix, smiling.

"You think he will thank you for saving him?"

"His thanks are not important."

"Yet you may have saved him only to allow him to butcher other innocent people—to rape more young girls."

"I am not responsible for his deeds, Galead, only my own. No man willingly allows those he loves to suffer hurt and pain."

"I do not disagree with that," said Galead. "Love is a fine emotion. But he is not someone you love."

"Of course he is. He is a brother."

"You know him?"

"No, I do not mean a brother of the flesh. But he—like you—is my brother. And I must help him. It is very simple."

"This is no way to deal with an enemy, Caterix."

The old man looked down at the wounded robber. "What better way is there of dealing with enemies than making them your friends?"

Galead walked back to his horse and stepped into the saddle. He tugged on the reins, and the beast began to walk along the trail. Pilaras was gathering herbs at the wayside, and she smiled as he passed.

Touching his heels to the horse's sides, he rode for the coast.

Culain sat beneath the stars on his sixteenth night at the Isle of Crystal. Every morning he would wake to find food and drink on a wooden tray outside the tower; every evening the empty dishes would be removed. Often he would catch a glimpse of a shadowy figure on the path below, but always he would walk back inside the tower, allowing his nocturnal visitors the solitude they so obviously desired.

But on this night a moon shadow fell across him as he sat, and he looked up to see the woman in white, her face shrouded by a high hood.

"Welcome, lady," he said, gesturing her to seat herself. As she did so, he saw that beneath the hood she wore a veil. "Is there need for such modesty even here?" he asked.

"Especially here, Culain." She threw back the hood and removed the veil, and his breath caught in his throat as the moonlight bathed the pale face he knew so well.

"Gian?" he whispered, half rising and moving toward her.

"Stay where you are," she told him, her voice stern and lacking all emotion.

"But they told me you were dead."

"I was tired of your visits, and I was dead to you." There were silver streaks in her hair and fine lines about the eyes and mouth, but to Culain the queen had lost none of her beauty. "And yet now you are here once more," she continued, "and once more you torment me. Why did you bring *him* to me?"

"I did not know you were here."

"I have spent sixteen years trying to forget the past and its tragedies. I thought I had succeeded. You, I decided, were a young girl's fantasy. As a child I loved you and in so doing destroyed my chance for happiness. As a lonely queen I loved you and in so doing destroyed my son. For several years I hated you, Culain, but that passed. Now there is only indifference—both to you and to the Blood King my husband became."

"You know, of course, that your son did not die?"

"I know many things, Lance Lord. But what I desire to know most is when you will leave this isle."

"You have become a hard woman, Gian."

"I am not Gian Avur, not your little Fawn of the Forest. I am Morgana of the Isle, though I have other names, I am told. You should know how that feels, Culain, you who were Apollo, and Aeneas, and Cunobelin the king, and so many valiant others."

"I have heard the leader of this community called the Fey Witch. I would never have dreamed it was you. What has happened to you, Laitha?"

"The world changed me, Lance Lord, and I care no longer for it or for any creature that lives in it."

"Then why are you here in this sacred place? It is a center for healing and peace."

"And so it remains. The sisters are spectacularly successful, but I and others spend our time with the true mysteries: the threads that link the stars, the patterns that weave through human lives, crisscrossing and joining, shaping the world's destiny. I used to call it God, but now I see it is greater than any immortal dreamed of by man. Here in this—"

"I have heard enough, woman. What of Uther?" Culain cut in.

"He is dying," she hissed, "and it will be no loss to the world when he passes."

"I never thought to see evil in you, Gian; you were always a woman of exquisite beauty." He laughed grimly. "But then, evil comes in many guises and does not have

to be ugly. I have sat here in silent penance for many
nights, for I believed that when I began this community,
it was for selfish motives. Well, lady, perhaps they were
selfish. Yet the isle was still fashioned with love and for
love, and you—with your search for mysteries I knew a
thousand years before you were born—you have per-
verted it. I'll stay on this tor no longer . . . or await your
bidding." He rose smoothly, gathered his staff, and began
the long climb down toward the circle of huts.

Her voice rang out behind him, an edge of cold triumph in her words.

"Your boat is waiting, Culain. If you are on it within
the hour, I may not allow the Blood King to die. If you
are not, I will withdraw the sisters from him and you may
take the corpse where you will."

He stopped, suffering the taste of defeat. Then he
turned.

"You were always willful and never one to admit an
error. Very well, I will go and leave Uther to your tender
mercies. But when you pause in your studies of the mysteries, think on this: I took you in as a tiny child and
raised you as a father. I offered nothing to make you feel
there should be more. But you it was who whispered my
name as you lay with Uther. You it was who bade me
stay at Camulodunum. It is there that my guilt begins,
and I will carry it. But perhaps when you look down from
your gilded tower, you will see that tiny scrap of your
own guilt and find the courage to lift it to your eyes."

"Are you done, Lance Lord?"

"I am done, Morgana."

"Then leave my isle."

◊ 13 ◊

"**W**E LEAVE THE road here," said Maedhlyn as the party crested a low dusty hill. "And there is the realm of Goroien," he continued, pointing to a distant range of forbidding mountains.

The landscape was pitted and broken, but many shadows moved furtively between the dead trees and the cracked boulders. Some slunk on all fours, others flew on black wings, still more slithered or ran.

Cormac took a deep breath, willing himself to step from the sanctuary of the road. He glanced at Victorinus, who smiled and shrugged.

"Let us go," said the prince, drawing his sword.

The fifteen men, weapons ready, moved off into the gloom, and at once the shadows converged on them. There were beasts with slavering jaws, men with hollow fangs and red-rimmed eyes, wolves whose faces shifted and changed like mist, becoming human, then bestial. Above them flew giant bats, wheeling and diving, their leather wings slicing the air over the heads of the marchers. But none came within range of the bright swords.

"How far?" asked Cormac, walking beside Maedhlyn at the head of the column.

"Who can judge time here?" replied the former Enchanter. "But it will take long enough."

Gray dust rose about their feet as they walked on, flanked by an army of shadows drawing ever closer.

"Will they attack us?" Victorinus whispered.

Maedhlyn spread his hands. The man at the rear of the column screamed as taloned claws wrenched at his cloak, pulling him from his feet.

Victorinus whirled. "Sword circle!" he called, and with their blades held high, the warriors leapt into the ranks of the beasts and surrounded their fallen comrade.

The creature holding him vanished as a gladius cleaved its heart. "Marching formation," said Victorinus, and as the small group of warriors formed in two lines, the shadows moved back.

On and farther on they marched, until the road could no longer be seen and the dust hung around them like a storm cloud, blurring their vision and masking the distant mountains.

Twice more the shadows moved in, but each time the bright swords of the Britons forced them back.

At last they came to higher ground on which stood an ancient stone circle, blackened and ruined. The shadows ringed the foot of the hill, and it was with a sense of relief that the weary group sat down among the stones.

"Why will they not come here?" asked Victorinus.

"I am not the fount of all human knowledge," snapped Maedhlyn.

"You always claimed you were."

"I would like you to know, Victorinus, that of all Uther's followers you were the one whose company I enjoyed least."

"Cutting words, Enchanter," answered Victorinus,

grinning. "Perhaps now you'll have an eternity in my company."

"Hell, indeed," commented Maedhlyn.

"This must have once been a living land," said Cormac. "There were trees, and we have crossed a score of dried-out streambeds. What changed it?"

"Nothing changed it, Cormac," Maedhlyn replied. "For it does not exist. It is an echo of what once was; it is a nightmare."

"Does our presence not prove its existence?" asked Marcus Bassicus, moving to sit alongside them.

"Did you ever dream you were somewhere where you were not?" countered Maedhlyn.

"Of course."

"And did that dream prove the existence of the dreamscape?"

"But we are all sharing this dream," Marcus argued.

"Are we? How can you know? Perhaps we are just figments of your nightmare, young Marcus. Or perhaps you are all appearing in mine."

Victorinus chuckled. "I knew it would not be long before you began your games." He turned to the other men, who were sitting by and listening intently. "I once saw this man spend two hours arguing the case that Caligula was the only sane man ever to walk the earth. At the end we all believed him, and he laughed at us."

"How could you not believe me?" asked Maedhlyn. "Caligula made his horse a senator, and I ask you, did the horse ever make a wrong decision? Did it seek to seize power? Did it argue for laws that robbed the poor and fed the rich? It was the finest senator in Roman history."

Cormac sat listening to the chatter, and a slow, burning anger began to seize him. All his life he had lived with fear—of punishment, of humiliation, of rejection. Those chains had held him in thrall since his first memories, but the fire of his anger cut through them. Only two people had ever loved Cormac Daemonsson, and both were dead. From deep inside him a new Cormac rose and showed him his life from another viewpoint. Maedhlyn had been right: Cormac Daemonsson was not a failure or a loser. He was a man—and a prince by right and by blood.

Power surged in his heart, and his eyes blazed with its heady strength.

"Enough!" stormed Cormac, rising. "This talk is like the wind in the leaves. It achieves nothing and is merely noise. We are here, and this place is real. Now let us move on."

"He would have made a good king," whispered Victorinus as he and Maedhlyn followed Cormac down the hill.

"This is a fine place to learn arrogance," agreed the Enchanter.

At the foot of the hill Cormac advanced on the shadow horde. "Back!" he ordered, and they split before him, creating a dark pathway. He marched into it, looking neither to the left nor to the right, ignoring the hissing and the gleaming talons. Then, sheathing his sword, he strode on, eyes fixed on the mountains.

A tall figure in a black breastplate stepped into his path. The man was wearing a winged helm that covered his face—all but the eyes, which gleamed with a cold light. In his hands were two short swords, about his waist was a kilt of dark leather, and on his shins were black greaves. He stood in perfect balance on the balls of his feet, poised to attack.

Cormac continued to walk until he stood directly before the warrior.

"Draw your sword," said the man, his voice a metallic echo from within the helm. Cormac smiled and considered his words with care. When he spoke, it was with grim certainty.

"If I do, it will be to kill you."

"That has been done before, but not by the likes of you."

Cormac stepped back, and the sword of Culain flashed into his hand.

The warrior stood very still, staring at the blade. "Where did you come by that weapon?"

"It is mine."

"I am not questioning its ownership."

"And I am weary of this nonsense. Step aside or fight!"

"Why are you here?"

"To find Goroien," answered Maedhlyn, pushing forward to stand between the warriors.

The man sheathed his blades. "The sword earns you that right," he told Cormac, "but we will speak again when the queen is done with you. Follow me."

The tall warrior led them across the arid valley to a wide entrance carved into a mountain. There torches blazed and guards stood by, bearing silver axes. Deep into the heart of the mountain they walked until they came to a huge doorway before which stood two massive hounds. The warrior ignored them and pushed open the doors. Inside was a round hall that was richly carpeted and hung with rugs, curtains, and screens. At the center, lounging on a divan, lay a woman of exquisite beauty. Her hair was golden, highlighted by silver; her eyes were pale blue, matching the short shift she wore; and her skin was pale and wondrously smooth. Cormac swallowed hard as the warrior advanced to the divan and knelt before her. She waved him aside and summoned Cormac.

As he approached, he saw her shimmer and change to a bloated, scaled creature, diseased and decaying, then back to the slim beauty he had first seen. His steps faltered, but still he came on.

"Kiss my hand," she told him.

He took the slender fingers in his own and blanched as they swelled and disgorged maggots into his palm. His thoughts fixed on Anduine, he steeled himself as his head bent and his lips touched the writhing mass.

"A brave man, indeed," she said. "What are you called?"

"Cormac Daemonsson."

"And are you the son of a demon?"

"I am the son of Uther, high king of Britain."

"Not a name to conjure friendship here," she said.

"Nor is he a friend to me; he hounded my mother to her death."

"Did he indeed?" Her gaze wandered to the figure of Maedhlyn at the back of the hall. "And there is my old friend Zeus. You are a long way from Olympus . . . such a very long way. I cannot tell you how pleasant it is to see you," she hissed.

Maedhlyn bowed gravely. "I wish I could echo the sentiment," he called.

She returned her gaze to Cormac. "My first thought is to watch you scream, to listen to your howls of torment, but you have aroused my curiosity. And events of interest are rare for Goroien now. So speak to me, handsome prince—tell me why you sought the queen."

"I need to assault the keep," he said simply.

"And why should that interest me?"

"Simply because Wotan—Molech—is your enemy."

"Not enough."

"It is said, my lady, that he has the power to return his followers to a life of flesh and blood. Could it not be that were you to control the keep, you would also have that power?"

As she lay on the divan, she stretched out once more. Cormac longed to tear his eyes from the shimmering figure of beauty and decay.

"You think I have not tried to defeat him? What do you bring me that could make the difference?"

"First, let me ask what prevents you from taking the keep."

"Molech's power is greater than my own."

"And if he were not here?"

"Where else would he be?"

"In the world of flesh, my lady."

"That is not possible. I was among those who destroyed him at Babel; I saw Culain cut the head from the body."

"Yet he is returned, thanks to the man Maedhlyn. The same could be done for you."

"Why are you offering me this, when your very blood should scream its hatred for me?"

"Because the woman I love was murdered on account of this Molech, and even now he has her soul at the keep."

"But there is something else, yes? Something that brings Maedhlyn to me—and those other men of Uther's."

"He also has the king's soul in chains of fire."

"Now I see. And you want Goroien to free Uther? You are mad." She raised one hand, and guards moved in from all around the hall.

"Molech is alive," said Cormac softly. "He calls himself Wotan now, and he plans to invade Britain. Only Uther has the power to destroy him. If, when that happens, you are in control of the keep, will Molech's soul not come unwittingly to you?"

She waved back the guards. "I will consider the questions you have raised. Maedhlyn! Join the prince and myself in my chambers. The rest of you may wait here."

For an hour in the queen's private chambers, as she lay on a silk-covered bed, Maedhlyn talked of the return to life of the man Molech. Cormac noted that the tale was slightly different from the story Maedhlyn had told him. In this version Maedhlyn was far less at fault and was defeated only by an act of treachery. Cormac said nothing as the Enchanter spoke but watched the shimmering queen, trying to gauge the emotions in her ever-changing face.

As Maedhlyn finished speaking, Goroien sat up. "You always were an arrogant fool," she said, "and at last you pay the price. But then, there was no Culain to save you this time. Wait in the outer rooms." Maedhlyn bowed and left the chamber. "Now you, Prince Cormac."

"Where should I begin?"

"How did the son of Uther come to be known as the son of a demon?"

And he told her. Her eyes blazed as he spoke of Culain's love for the queen, but she remained still and silent until at last he spoke of the day on the mountain when the Vikings had come and Anduine had been slain.

"So," she whispered, "you are here for love? Foolish, Cormac."

"I never claim to be wise, my lady."

"Let us test your wisdom," she said, leaning forward with her face close to his. "You have given me all that you have, is that not correct?"

"It is."

"So you are of no further use to me?"

"That is true."

"Did not Maedhlyn tell you that I was not to be trusted? That I was evil?"

"Yes."

"Then why did you come here?"

"He also said Culain lach Feragh once loved you."

"And what difference does that make?" she snapped.

"Perhaps none. But I love Anduine, and I know what that means. She is part of me, and I of her. Apart from her I am nothing. I do not know if evil people can love or, if they do, how they can remain evil. But I do not believe Culain would love anyone who did not possess a measure of goodness."

"As you say, Prince Cormac, you are not wise. Culain loved me for my beauty and my wit. And he betrayed me, just as he betrayed Uther. He wed another . . . and I killed her. He had a daughter, Alaida; he tried to save her by allowing her to marry the king of Britain, but I found her and she, too, died. Then I tried to kill her son, Uther, but there I failed. And now, you tell me, he is a prisoner and facing death . . . and *his* son sits in my fortress asking a favor. What do you offer me so that I will grant you aid? Think carefully, Cormac. A great deal rests on your answer."

"Then I am lost, my lady, for I can offer you nothing else."

"Nothing," she echoed. "Nothing for Goroien? Leave me and join your friends. I will have an answer for you in a little while."

He looked into her gleaming eyes, and his heart sank.

The fishing boat beached in the moonlight in the shelter of a rounded bay close to Anderida. Galead thanked the skipper, gave him two small golden coins, and clambered over the side, wading through the calf-deep water to the rocky beach. He climbed a narrow path to the cliff top, then turned to watch the boat bobbing out on the Gallic Sea.

The night air was cool, the sky clear. Galead pulled his long cloak about his shoulders and sought the shelter of the trees, halting in a hollow where the light from his fire could not be observed from more than a few yards in any direction. He slept uneasily and dreamed of a sword floating over water and of a light in the sky like a great glowing silver sphere speeding across the heavens. Waking at midnight, he added fuel to the fire; he was hungry and finished the last of the smoke-dried fish the boatman had supplied.

It had been twelve days since Caterix had rescued the robber, and Galead found his thoughts constantly straying to the little man. He rubbed at the bristles on his chin and pictured a hot bath with scented water and a slave girl to dry him and oil his body, soft hands easing the tension from his muscles. Groaning as desire surged in him, he quelled it savagely.

Gods, it was an age since he had last felt soft flesh beneath him and warm arms encircling his back. For several minutes Prince Ursus returned, haunting his mind.

"What are you doing in this forsaken land?" Ursus asked him.

"I am honor-bound," Galead told him.

"And where is the profit in it, fool?"

He transferred his gaze to the flames, unable to answer. He wished Pendarric would appear and sat quietly waiting until the dawn. But there was nothing.

The day was overcast, and Galead set off in the direction the fisherman had indicated, heading west along the coast. Three times he saw deer and once a large buck rabbit, but with no bow there was no opportunity for swift hunting. Once he had known how to set a snare, but his lack of patience would never allow him to sit for hours in silent hope.

Throughout the morning he walked until he saw, slightly to the north, smoke curling into the air. He turned toward it and, cresting a hill, saw a village in flames. Bodies littered the ground, and Galead sat down staring at the warriors in their horned helms as they moved from home to home, dragging out women and children, looting, and killing. There were maybe fifty raiders, and they stayed for more than an hour. When at last they moved off to the north, nothing stirred in the village but the snaking smoke from the gutted homes.

Galead rose wearily and made his way to the Saxon hamlet, halting by each of the bodies. None lived. A smashed pot still contained dried oats, and those Galead scooped into a linen cloth, knotting it and tying it to his belt. Farther on, in the center of the devastated settlement, he found a ham charred on one side; with his knife he cut several slices and ate them swiftly.

Glancing to his right, he saw two children lying dead

in the doorway of a hut, their arms entwined, their dead eyes staring at him. He looked away.

This was war. Not the golden glory of young men in bright armor carving their names in the flesh of history. Not the Homeric valor of heroes changing the face of the world. No, just an awful stillness, a total silence, and an appalling evil that left dead children in its wake.

Carving several thick sections from the ham, he threw the joint aside and walked from the settlement, once more heading west. At the top of a rise he looked back. A fox had stolen into the village and was tugging at a corpse. Above the scene the crows were circling . . .

Something in the bush to his right moved, and Galead swung, his sword snaking out. A child screamed, and the knight threw away his weapon.

"It's all right, little one," he said softly as the girl covered her face with her hands. Leaning into the bush, he lifted her out, cradling her to his chest. "You are safe." Her arms circled his neck, and she clung to him with all her strength. Stooping, he lifted his sword and sheathed it, then turned from the village and continued on his way.

The child was no more than six years old, her arms painfully thin. Her hair was yellow streaked with gold, and he stroked it as he walked. She said nothing, scarcely moving in his arms.

By midafternoon Galead had covered some twelve miles. His legs ached with walking, and his arms were weary from carrying the child. As he topped a short rise, he saw a village below: eighteen rounded huts in a wooden stockade. There were horses in a paddock, and cattle grazed on the slopes. Slowly he made his way down the hill. A young boy saw him first and ran into the village, then a score of men armed with axes strode out to meet him. The leader was a stocky warrior with an iron-gray beard.

The man spoke in the guttural language of the Saxon.

"I do not speak your language," Galead answered.

"I asked who you are," said the man, his accent thick and harsh.

"Galead. This child is Saxon; her village was attacked by the Goths, and all were slain."

"Why would the Goths attack us? We share the same enemies."

"I am a stranger here," said Galead. "I am a Merovingian from Gaul. All I know is that warriors with horned helms slaughtered the people of this child's village. Now, can I bring her in—or shall we move on?"

"You are not an Uther man?"

"I have said what I am."

"Then you may enter. My name is Asta. Bring her to my home; my wife will take care of her."

Galead carried the child to a long hall at the center of the village, where a sturdy woman tried to prize the child from his arms. She screamed and clung on, and although Galead whispered gentle words to her, she would not leave him. The woman just smiled and fetched warm milk in a pottery cup. As Galead sat at a broad table, the girl in his lap drinking the milk, Asta joined them.

"You are sure it was the Goths?"

"There were no Romans in the attack."

"But why?"

"We cannot talk now," said Galead, indicating the silent child, "but there were many women in the settlement."

Asta's blue eyes gleamed with understanding, and his face darkened. "I see. And you observed this?"

"Unfortunately, yes."

The man nodded. "I have sent one rider to scout the village and follow the raiders and three others to settlements close by. If what you say is true, then the Goths will rue this day."

Galead shook his head. "You do not have the men, and any attempt you make to fight will result in more slaughter. If I may advise you, have scouts out, and when the Goths approach, hide in the hills. Does your king not have any forces here?"

"Which king is that?" snapped Asta. "When I was a young warrior, the Blood King crushed our forces, allowing the boy—Wulfhere—the title of king of the South Saxon. But he is no king; he lives like a woman—even to having a husband." Asta spit his contempt. "And the Blood King? What would he care that Saxon women are . . . abused?"

Galead said nothing. The child in his arms had fallen asleep, so he lifted her and carried her to a cot by the far wall near the burning log fire, where three warhounds lay sleeping on the hay-strewn floor. He covered the child with a blanket and kissed her cheek.

"You are a caring man," said Asta as he returned to the table.

"Tell me of the Goths," said Galead.

Asta shrugged. "Little to tell. Around eight thousand landed here, and they destroyed a Roman legion. The main part of the army has headed west; around a thousand remain."

"Why west? What is there for them?"

"I do not know. One of our young men rode with them for a while, and he said their general wanted to know the best route to Sorviodunum. My man did not know. That is across the country."

"Was the king, Wotan, with them?"

Once more the Saxon shrugged. "What is your interest?"

"Wotan destroyed my whole family in Gaul, and my interest is to see him die."

"They say he is a god. You are mad."

"I have no choice," Galead answered.

◇ 14 ◇

"**T**HE SOUTH IS virtually ours, sire," said Tsurai, his flat brown eyes staring at the marble floor.

Wotan said nothing as he watched the man, seeing the tautness in his flat Asiatic face and the tension in the muscles of his neck. Sweat was beading the man's brow, and Wotan could almost taste his fear.

"And the north?"

"Unexpectedly, sire, the Brigantes have risen against us. A small group of our men strayed to one of their holy sites where there were some women dancing."

"Did I not say there was to be no trouble with the tribes?"

"You did, sire. The men have been found and impaled."

"Not enough, Tsurai. You will take their officers and impale them also. What regiment were they?"

"The Balders, sire."

"One in twenty of them will be beheaded."

"Lord, I know you are all-wise, but permit me to say that men at war are subject to many vices of the passions . . ."

"Do not preach to me," said Wotan softly. "I know all the deeds men are capable of. It is nothing that a few women are raped, but obedience to my will is the paramount duty of all my people. A Saxon village was also attacked yesterday."

"It was, lord?"

"It was, Tsurai. The same punishment must be exacted there—and very publicly. Our Saxon allies must see that Wotan's justice is swift and terrible. Now tell me of Cato in the Middle Lands."

"He is a skillful general. Three times now he has fought holding actions, and our advance on Eboracum is not as swift as we had hoped. But still," he continued hurriedly, "we are advancing, and the city should fall within days."

"I did not expect the assault of Eboracum to succeed as swiftly as my generals thought it would," said Wotan. "It is of no matter. What have you discovered as to the whereabouts of the Blood King's body?"

"It is on the Isle of Crystal, my lord, close to Sorviodunum."

"You are certain?"

"Yes, lord. Geminus Cato has an aide called Decius, and he in turn has a mistress in Eboracum. He told her that a man called the Lance Lord took the king's body to the isle to restore it."

"Culain," whispered Wotan. "How I long to see him again!"

"Culain? I do not understand, sire."

"An old friend. Tell Alaric to proceed on Sorviodunum but to send two hundred men to the isle. I want the head of Uther on a lance; that body should have been cut into pieces in the first attack."

"The enemy is saying, lord, that the king will come again."

"Of course they are. Without Uther and the sword they are like children in the dark."

"Might I ask, lord, why you do not slay his spirit? Would that not solve any problem of his return?"

"I desire the sword, and he alone knows where it lies. As long as his body lives, he has hope burning in his heart and defies me. When it dies, he will know and I will milk his despair. Go now."

Alone once more, Wotan locked the door of his windowless chamber and settled back on the broad bed. Closing his eyes, he forced his spirit to plummet into darkness . . .

His eyes opened in a torchlit room of cold stone, and he rose from the floor and took in his surroundings: the empty-eyed statues, the colorless rugs and hangings. How he hated this place for its pale shadow of reality. In the corner were a jug and three goblets. During the long centuries he had passed here he had often poured the red, tasteless liquid, pretending it was wine. Everything here was a mockery.

He strode to the outer hall. Everywhere men leapt to their feet in surprise, then dropped to their knees in fear. Ignoring them all, he walked swiftly to the dais on which stood the throne of Molech. For some time he listened to the entreaties of those who served him here: the pleas for a return to the flesh, the promises of eternal obedience. Some he granted, but most he refused. At last he left the throne room and walked down the curved stairwell to the dungeons. A huge beast with the head of a wolf bowed as he entered, its tongue lolling from its long jaws and dripping saliva to the stone floor.

Wotan moved past him to the last dungeon, where Uther hung by his wrists against the far wall. Tongues of flame licked at his body, searing and burning—the flesh repaired itself instantly, only to be burned again. Wotan dismissed the flames, and the king sagged against the wall.

"How are you faring, Uther? Are you ready to lie to me again?"

"I do not know where it is," whispered Uther.

"You must. You sent it."

"I had no time. I just hurled it, wishing it gone."

"The man who first saw you said he heard you call a name. What was that name?"

"I do not remember, I swear to God."

"Was it a friend? Was it Culain?"

"Perhaps."

"Ah, then it was not Culain. Good! Who, then? Who could you trust, Blood King? It was not Victorinus. Whose name was on your lips?"

"You'll never find it," said Uther. "And if I were freed from here, I could not find it, either. I sent the sword to a dream that can never be."

"Tell me the dream!"

Uther smiled and closed his eyes. Wotan raised his hand, and once more fire surged over Uther, forcing a bloodcurdling scream of agony. The flames disappeared, and the blackened skin was replaced instantly.

"You think to mock me?" hissed Wotan.

"Always," said Uther, tensing himself for the next torture.

"You will find that always is a very, very long time, Uther. I am tired of fire. You should have some company." As Wotan stepped back to the doorway, holes appeared in the dungeon walls and rats poured out, swarming over the helpless king to bite and tear at his flesh.

Wotan strode from the dungeon, screams echoing behind him in the corridor.

He moved back to the upper levels and found the captain of his Loyals waiting by the throne. The man bowed as he entered.

"What do you want, Ustread?"

"I have something for you, lord. I hope it will make amends for my failure in Raetia."

"It needs to be something rather greater than you can find here," said Wotan, still angry from his talk with the stubborn king.

"I hope you will find I do not exaggerate, lord." Ustread clapped his hands, and two soldiers entered, holding a girl between them.

"A woman? What use is that here? I can . . ." Wotan stopped as he recognized the princess. "Anduine? How?" He walked forward, waving away the guards, and she stood silently before him.

"What happened to you, Princess?"

"Your men killed me. I was in the mountains of the Caledones, and they stabbed me."

"They will pay. Oh, how they will pay!"

"I do not wish them to pay. What I wish is to be released. I am no longer of value to you; there is nothing left to sacrifice."

"You misunderstood me, Anduine. You were never for sacrifice. Come with me."

"Where?"

"To a private place where no harm will come to you." He smiled. "In fact, quite the reverse."

The child screamed in the night, and Galead awoke instantly. Rising from his blankets by the dying fire, he went to her, lifting her to his arms.

"I am here, little one. Have no fear."

"Mudder tod," she said, repeated the words over and over. Asta's wife crossed the hall, a blanket around her shoulders. Kneeling by the bedside, she spoke to the child for some minutes in a language unknown to the Merovingian. The girl's face was bathed in sweat, and the woman wiped it clear as Galead laid her down once more. Her tiny hands gripped the front of Galead's tunic, her eyes fearful. *"Vader! Vader!"*

"I won't leave you," he said. "I promise." Her eyes closed, and she slept.

"You are a gentle man, very rare for a warrior," said the woman. She stood and moved to the fire, adding wood and fanning the blaze to life. Galead joined her, and they sat together in the new warmth.

"Children like me," he said. "It is a good feeling."

"My name is Karyl."

"Galead," he replied. "Have you lived here long?"

"I came from Raetia eight years ago, when Asta paid my father. It is a good land, though I miss the mountains. What will you do with the child?"

"Do? I thought to leave her here, where she will be looked after."

Karyl gave a soft, sad smile. "You told her you would not leave her. She believed you, and she is much troubled. No child should suffer the torment she has endured."

"But I cannot look after her. I am a warrior in the midst of a war."

Karyl ran her hands through her thick, dark hair; her face in profile was not pretty, but there was a strength that made her a handsome woman.

"You have the sight, have you not, Galead?" she whispered, and a shiver touched him.

"Sometimes," he admitted.

"As do I. The men here were going to join the Goths, but I bade Asta wait, for the signs were strange. Then you came, a man who wears a face that is not his own but who cares for a Saxon child. I know you are an Uther man, but I have not told Asta. Do you know why?"

"No."

"Because Asta will also be an Uther man before this is over. He is a good man, my husband, a strong man. And these Goths are seduced by evil. Asta will summon the Fyrrd when he learns that what you said is true. And the Saxon warriors will rise."

"There are no swords," said Galead. "Uther forbade any Saxon to bear arms."

"What is a sword? A cutting tool. We Saxons are an ingenious people, and our warriors now are skilled in the use of the ax. They will rise and aid the Blood King."

"You think we can win?"

She shrugged. "I do not know. But you, Galead, have a part to play in the drama . . . and it will not be with a sword."

"Speak plainly, Karyl. I was never good at riddles."

"Take the child with you. There is a woman you must meet: a cold, hard woman. She is the gateway."

"The gateway to what?"

"As to that, I can help you no further. The child's name is Lectra, though her mother called her Lekky."

"Where can I take her? You must know a place."

"Take her to your heart, warrior. She is now your daughter, and that is how she sees you—as her father. Her mother's husband went to Raetia to serve Wotan while she was still pregnant, and Lekky has waited long years to see him. In her tortured mind you are that man, come home to look after her. Without you I do not think she will survive."

"How do you know all this?"

"I know because I touched her, and you know I do not lie."

"What was she saying when she woke?"

"*Mudder tod?* Mother dead."

"And *Vader*? Father?"

Karyl nodded. "Give me your hand."

"Then you would know all my secrets."

"Does that frighten you?"

"No," he said, stretching out his arm, "but it will lessen me in your eyes."

She took his hand, sat silently for several moments, and then released it.

"Sleep well, Galead," she said, rising.

"And you, lady."

"I will sleep better now," she told him, smiling.

He watched her walk back to the far end of the hall and vanish into the shadows of the rooms beyond. Lekky whimpered in her sleep, and Galead took his blanket and lay down alongside her. She opened her eyes and cuddled into him.

"I am here, Lekky."

"Vader?"

"Vader," he agreed.

Goroien was alone in her mirrorless room, her mind floating back to the days of love and glory. Culain had been more than a lover, more than a friend. She remembered her father forbidding her to see the young warrior and how she had trembled when he had told her he had ordered his young men to hunt him down and kill him. Thirty of her father's finest trackers had set off into the mountains in the autumn. Only eighteen had returned;

they said they had cornered him in a deep canyon, and then the snows had blocked the passes—and no man could live in that icy wilderness for long.

Believing her lover dead, Goroien had refused all food. Her father had threatened her and whipped her, but he could not defeat her. Slowly she lost her strength, and death was very close on that midwinter night.

Semidelirious and bedridden, she had not seen the drama that had followed.

During the Feast of Midwinter, the great door had opened and Culain lach Feragh had stridden down the center of the hall to stand before the thane.

"I have come for your daughter," he had said, ice clinging to his dark beard.

Several men leapt to their feet with swords ready, but the thane waved them back.

"What makes you believe you can leave here alive?" the thane asked.

Culain stared around the long tables at the fighting men; then he laughed, and his contempt stung them all.

"What makes you think I could not?" he countered. An angry roar greeted the challenge, but once more the thane quelled it.

"Follow me," he said, leading the warrior to where Goroien lay. Culain knelt by the bedside, taking her hand, and she heard his voice.

"Do not leave me, Goroien. I am here; I will always be here."

And she had recovered, and they had been wed. But that was in the days before the fall of Atlantis, before the Sipstrassi had made them gods. And in the centuries that followed each had taken many lovers, though always returning at the last to the sanctuary of each other's arms.

What had changed them? she wondered. Was it the power or the immortality? She had borne Culain a son, though he never knew it, and Gilgamesh had inherited almost all of his father's skill with weapons. Unfortunately, he had also inherited his mother's arrogance and amorality.

Now Goroien's thoughts turned to the last years. Of all obscenities, she had brought Gilgamesh back from the dead and taken him for her lover. In doing so she had doomed herself, for Gilgamesh suffered a rare disease of the blood that even Sipstrassi could not cure. And her immortality could no longer be assured by Sipstrassi alone. Blood and death kept her in the world of the flesh. In that period, as she had told Cormac, she had grown to hate Culain and had killed his second wife and his daughter.

But at the very end, when Culain lay dying after his battle with Gilgamesh, she had given her own life to save him, dooming herself to this limitless hell.

Now her choice was simple. Did she aid Cormac or destroy him? All that formed the intellect of the former Witch Queen screamed at her to destroy this boy who was the seed of Uther, who in turn was the seed of Culain through his daughter, Alaida. The seed of her destruction! But her heart went out to the young man who had walked into the Void for the woman he loved. Culain would have done that.

For Goroien . . .

What had the boy said? A chance to return to the flesh? Did he think that would attract her? How could he know it was the last gift she would consider?

Gilgamesh entered and removed his helm. His face was scaled and reptilian; gone was the beauty he had known in life.

"Let me have the boy," he said. "I yearn for his life."

"No. You will not have him, Gilgamesh. We will journey together to the keep, and then we will storm it. You will fight alongside Cormac, and regardless of the danger to yourself, you will keep him alive."

"No!"

"If you love me—if you ever loved me—you will obey me now."

"Why, Mother?"

She shrugged and turned away. "There are no answers."

"And when we have taken the keep? If indeed we can."

"Then we will free Uther also."

"In return for what?"

"In return for nothing. That is the prize, Gilgamesh: nothing. And I cannot think of anything I would rather have."

"You make no sense."

"Did you ever love me?"

He lifted his helm, his head bowing. "I loved nothing else," he said simply. "Not life, not combat."

"And will you do this for me?"

"You know I will do whatever you ask."

"Once I was a queen among the gods," she said. "I was beautiful, and men thought me wise. I stood with Culain at Babel, and we brought down Molech and believed we had defeated a great evil, and men said they would sing of me throughout the ages. I wonder if they still do."

Gilgamesh replaced his helm and backed from the room.

Goroien did not see him go. She was remembering that fine spring day when she and Culain had wed by the great oak, when the world was young and the future unlimited.

◊ **15** ◊

FOR FIVE DAYS the dwindling force of Geminus Cato's two legions had withstood the ferocious charges of the Goths, retreating under cover of darkness and taking up fresh positions farther back along the road to Eboracum. The men were weary to the point of exhaustion, and Cato called his commanders to a meeting on the fifth night.

"Now," he told them, "is the time for courage. Now we attack."

"Insanity!" said Decius, his disbelief total. "Now is the time to retreat. We have fewer than six thousand men, some of whom are too tired to lift their shields."

"And to where shall we retreat? Eboracum? It is indefensible. Farther north to Vinovia? There we will meet a second army of Goths. No. Tonight we strike!"

"I will not be a party to this!" said Decius.

"Then go back to Eboracum!" snapped Cato. "Ten villas could not make me keep you here another moment."

The young man rose and left the group, and Cato switched his attention to the remaining eight officers. "Anyone else?" No one moved. "Good. Now, for five days we have offered the Goths the same strategy: hold and withdraw. They will be camped between the two rivers, and we will come at them from both sides. Agrippa, you will lead the right column. Strike through to the tent that bears Wotan's banner. His generals will be at the center. I will move from the left with sword and fire."

Agrippa, a dark-eyed young man with ten years of warfare behind him, nodded. "Decius did have a point," he said. "It will still be six thousand against twice that number. Once we attack, there can be no retreat. Win or die, General."

"Realistically, our chances are slim. But the divine Julius once destroyed an army that outnumbered him by a hundred to one."

"So his commentaries tell us," said Agrippa.

"Come in on a wide front and re-form inside their camp. Once you have dispatched the generals, try to forge a link with my column."

"And if we cannot?"

"Then take as many of the bastards with you as you can."

Cato dismissed the group, and the officers roused their men. Silently the Roman army broke camp, leaving in two columns for the march.

Three miles away the Goths had spread their tents across a wide flat area between two stretches of water. There were scores of fires, but few men were still awake. Sentries had been posted, but most of them were dozing at their posts or asleep behind bushes. No one feared an army that moved backward day by day.

In the tent of the general Leofric the Gothic commanders sat on captured rugs of silk, swilling wine and discussing the fall of Eboracum and the treasure that lay there. Leofric sat beside a naked young British girl captured earlier that day by outriding scouts; her face was bruised from a blow one of the riders had given her before they raped her. But she was still pleasing to Leofric; he had taken her twice that day and planned to return for one more bout before passing her on to the men the next day. His hand cupped her breast, squeezing hard. She winced and cried out, and Leofric grinned. "Tell me how much you love me," he said, his grip tightening.

"I love you! I love you!" she screamed.

"Of course you do," he said, releasing her, "and I love you—at least for tonight." The men around him laughed. "Tomorrow," he said, "there will be women for all of us—not village peasants like this wench but highborn Roman cows with their pale skin and tinted lips."

"You think Cato will retreat to the city?" asked Bascii, Leofric's younger brother.

"No, he cannot hold the walls. I think he will split his force and make for Vinovia, trying to gather men from among the Trinovante, but he will not succeed. We will have a hard job chasing him down, but he will fall. He has nowhere to go."

"Is it true there are walls covered with gold in Eboracum?" Bascii asked.

"I doubt it, but there is treasure there, and we will have it!"

"What kind of treasure?"

"The kind you find here," he said, forcing the girl back and opening her legs. She closed her eyes as shouts of encouragement rose from the men around him. Leofric opened his breeches and mounted her.

Her torment continued interminably as first Leofric, then Bascii, and then the others took her by turn. Pain followed pain . . . followed humiliation. At last she was hurled aside, and the men returned to their tents.

Suddenly a trumpet blast pierced the night. Drunk and staggering, Leofric stumbled to the entrance to see Roman warriors streaming into his camp. Dumbfounded, he fell back, scrabbling for his sword.

All was chaos as in tight, disciplined formations the Romans surged into the camp. Men ran from their tents only to be ruthlessly cut down. Without preparation or organization the Goths, most of them without armor, fought desperately in isolation.

Cato's men, moving from the left flank, put the torch to the tents. The wind fanned the flames to an inferno that swept across the open ground.

On the right Agrippa's force sliced through the Gothic ranks, forming a wedge that cut like a spear toward Leofric's tent. For all his drunkenness, the general was a warrior of great experience; he saw at once the desperate gamble Cato had taken and knew he could turn the tide. His battle-trained eye swept the scene. There! Bascii's men had formed a shield wall, but what they needed to do was to strike against the Roman wedge, blocking it and the advance. The flames would stop the Romans from linking, and sheer weight of numbers would destroy them. Poor Bascii would never think of such a stratagem. Leofric stepped from the tent . . . and something struck him a wicked blow in the back. He stumbled and fell to his knees, his head spinning as he rolled to his back.

The British girl knelt over him, a knife in her hand and a wide smile of triumph on her mouth as the blade hovered over Leofric's eyes.

"I love you," said the girl.

And the knife plunged down.

* * *

Cato stood over the body of Leofric, the dagger hilt still jutting from the eye. "The last of them are fleeing toward Petvaria," said Agrippa. "Lucius and three cohorts are harrying them."

"I wonder what happened here," Cato said.

"I do not know, sir. But my congratulations on a famous victory!"

"Why congratulate me? You did your part, as did every man who served under me. By the gods, this place is beginning to stink!"

Cato's dark eyes swept the field. Everywhere lay corpses, some burned black by the inferno that roared over the tents, others lying where they had fallen, cut down by the swords of the legions. The British dead had been carried to a hastily dug ditch; the Goths, stripped of their armor and weapons, were being left for the crows and the foxes.

"Twelve thousand of the enemy were slain," said Agrippa. "The survivors will never re-form into an army."

"Do not say never. They will return one day. Now we have to consider whether to march the men south to reinforce Quintas or north to prevent the Goths from marching on Eboracum."

"You are tired, sir. Rest today and make your decision tomorrow."

"Tomorrow may be too late."

"My old commander used to say: 'Weary men make mistakes.' Trust his judgment, sir, and rest."

"Now you quote my own words to me. Is there no respect left?" Cato asked, grinning.

"I have ordered your tent to be set up beyond the hill.

The stream narrows in a hollow there, surrounded by oaks."

Prasamaccus reined in his horse. To the north was the semiruined Wall of Antoninus, and before it a great battle was being fought. Thousands of Brigante warriors had encircled an army of Goths, and the carnage was awesome. Neither side fought with any strategy; it was merely a savage and chaotic frenzy of slashing swords, axes, and knives.

He steered his mount away from the scene; his practiced eye could see that there would be no victors that day and that both sides would withdraw from the field bloodied and exhausted. As a Brigante himself, he knew what would happen then. The next day the tribesmen would renew their assault and continue to attack until the enemy had perished or was victorious.

Moving west, he passed through the turf wall at a place where it had collapsed alongside a ruined fort. He shivered, whispered a prayer to the ghosts that still walked there, and rode on toward the northwest and the mountains of the Caledones.

His journey had been largely without incident, though he had seen many refugees and heard terrifying stories of the atrocities committed by the invading army. Some had been exaggerated; most were stomach-turning. The elderly Brigante had long since ceased to be surprised at the horrors men could inflict on their neighbors, yet he thanked his gods that such stories could still inspire both horror and sorrow in him.

That night he camped by a fast-moving stream and moved out at first light on the steady climb to the cabin where he had first met Culain lach Feragh. It had not changed, and the welcoming sight of smoke from the short chimney lifted his spirits. As he dismounted, a huge man stepped from the cabin, bearing a sword.

Prasamaccus limped toward him, hoping that his advanced years and obvious infirmity would sway the stranger into a more relaxed stance.

"Who are you, old man?" asked the giant, stepping forward and pressing the point of the blade to Prasamaccus' chest.

The Brigante gazed down at the blade, then up into the pale eyes of the warrior. "I am not an enemy."

"Enemies come in many guises." The man looked weary, dark rings circling his eyes.

"I am looking for a young man and a woman. A friend said they were here."

"Who was that friend?"

"His name is Culain; he brought them here to keep them safe."

The man laid down the sword, turned, and walked inside the cabin, with Prasamaccus following. Within, he saw a wounded man lying on a narrow bed. The Brigante stood over him and saw that the wounds had sealed well, but there was a deathly pallor to his skin and he seemed to be barely breathing. On his chest lay a black stone with hairline streaks of gold.

"He has been like that for weeks. I can do nothing more."

"And the girl?"

"Buried outside. She died trying to save him."

Prasamaccus stared at the wounded man's face, seeing the image of Uther: the same high cheekbones and strong jaw, the same long straight nose and thick brows.

"The magic is almost gone," he said.

"I guessed that," said the man. "At the beginning it was gold streaked with black, but as the days passed, the black lines grew. Will he die?"

"I fear that he will."

"But why? The wounds are healing well."

"Recently I saw another warrior in a like condition," said Prasamaccus. "They said his spirit was gone from his body."

"But that is the same as being dead," argued Oleg, "and this boy is alive."

Prasamaccus shrugged and lifted Cormac's wrist. "The pulse is very weak."

"I have some broth here if you are hungry," said Oleg, moving to the table. Prasamaccus limped to a chair and sat.

After they had both eaten, Oleg told the Brigante about the fight outside the cabin and how his own daughter Rhiannon, had betrayed them. Prasamaccus listened in silence, reading the pain in Oleg's eyes.

"You love your daughter very much," he remarked.

"Not anymore."

"Nonsense. We raise them, we hold them, we understand them, we weep at their weaknesses and their sorrows. Where is she now?"

"I do not know. I sent her away."

"I see. I thank you, Oleg, for helping the prince."

"Prince?"

"He is the son of Uther, high king of Britain."

"He did not talk like a nobleman."

"No, nor did life allow him to live like one."

"Is there nothing we can do?" asked Oleg.

"If we could, I would take him to where his father lies, but it is too far; he would not survive the journey."

"Then all we can do is sit and watch him die? I will not accept that."

"Nor should you," said a voice from the doorway, and both men swung toward the sound, Oleg lurching upright and reaching for the sword.

"That will not be necessary," said the stranger, pushing shut the door and moving into the room. He was tall and broad-shouldered, with hair and beard of spun gold. "Do you remember me, Prasamaccus?"

The old Brigante sat very still. "The day Uther found his sword . . . you were there, helping Laitha. But you have not aged."

"I was there. Now I am here. Put down your sword, Oleg Hammerhand, and prepare for a journey."

"Where are we going?"

"To the Isle of Crystal," replied Pendarric.

"This man says it is the length of the realm," said Oleg. "It will take weeks."

"Not by the roads he will travel," Prasamaccus told him.

"What roads are those?" Oleg asked as Pendarric moved into the clearing before the cabin.

"The spirit paths," answered the Brigante.

Swiftly Oleg made the sign of the protective horn and followed his limping companion to the clearing. Pendarric held a measuring rod and was carefully chalking a series of interlocking triangles around a central circle. He looked up from his knees.

"Make yourselves useful," he said. "Dress the boy in warm clothes and then carry him out here. Be careful not to tread on the chalk lines or in any way disturb them."

"He is a sorcerer," whispered Oleg.

"I think he is," agreed Prasamaccus.

"What shall we do?"

"Exactly what he says."

Oleg sighed. They dressed the unconscious Cormac, and Oleg lifted him carefully from the bed, carrying him outside to where Pendarric waited in the center of what appeared to be a curious star. Oleg trod carefully across the lines and laid the body down beside the tall sorcerer. Prasamaccus followed, bringing Oleg's sword and another blade.

When all were inside the circle, Pendarric raised his arms and sunlight glinted from a golden stone in his right hand. The air cracked around them, and a shimmering light began that suddenly blazed so brightly that Prasamaccus shielded his eyes. Then it was gone . . .

And the trio stood within a stone circle on the crest of a hill crowned with trees.

"This is where I leave you," said Pendarric. "May good fortune attend you at the end of your journey."

"Where are we?" asked Oleg.

"Camulodunum," said Pendarric. "It was not possible to move straight to the isle. From here you will appear at the center of the settlement, for it has been designed to imitate the setting of the stones. An old friend awaits you, Prasamaccus. Give her my love."

Pendarric stepped from the circle and gestured. Once more the air shimmered, and the next sight to greet their eyes was that of three astonished women sitting in a round hall, watching over the body of Uther.

"Our apologies, ladies," said Prasamaccus, bowing. Oleg lifted Cormac and carried him to the large round table on which the king lay, where he gently laid him down beside his father. Prasamaccus approached and gazed at the two bodies with great tenderness.

"Such a tragedy that they have never met until now."

One of the women left the room; the others remained deep in prayer.

The door opened, and a tall figure dressed in white entered. Behind her came the woman who had left.

Prasamaccus limped forward. "Lady, once more I must apolo—" He stumbled to a halt as Laitha approached.

"Yes, Prasamaccus, it is I. And I am becoming increasingly angry about being haunted by shadows from a past I would as soon forget. How many more bodies do you intend to bring to the isle?"

He swallowed hard and could find no words as she swept past him and looked down on the face of Cormac Daemonsson.

"Your son, Gian," whispered Prasamaccus.

"I can see that," she said, reaching out and stroking the soft beard. "How like his father he is."

"Seeing you makes me very happy," he told her. "I have thought of you often."

"And I you. How is Helga?"

"She died. But we were very contented together, and I have no regrets."

"Would that I could say the same! That man," she said, pointing at Uther, "destroyed my life. He robbed me of my son and any happiness I could have had."

"In doing so he robbed himself," said the Brigante. "He never stopped loving you, lady. It is just . . . just that you were not meant for each other. Had you known Culain was alive, you would not have wed him. Had he been less proud, he could have put Culain from his mind. I wept for you both."

"My tears dried a long time ago," said Laitha, "as I lay on a ship bound for Gaul with my son dead behind me— or so I thought." She was silent for a moment. "Both you and your companion must leave the isle. You will find Culain camped on the hillside across the lake; there he waits for news of the man he betrayed."

Prasamaccus looked into her eyes. Her hair was still dark, though a silver streak showed at one temple, and her face was beautiful and curiously ageless. She did not look like a woman in her forties, but her eyes were flat and lifeless and there was a hardness to her that Prasamaccus found disturbing.

She looked down at the bodies once more, her face expressionless, then transferred her gaze to the Brigante.

"There is nothing of me in him," she said. "He is Uther's get and will die with him."

They found Culain sitting cross-legged on the top of a hill. Behind him was a narrow causeway that led back to the isle, which was clearly visible now that the tide was low. He rose and embraced Prasamaccus.

"How did you come here?"

"I brought Cormac."

"Where is he?"

"Alongside the king."

"Sweet Christos!" whispered Culain. "Not dead?"

"Close to it. Like Uther. Only a fading stone keeps his heart beating."

Prasamaccus introduced Oleg, who outlined once more the drama that had seen the death of Anduine. Culain sank back to the earth, staring to the east. The Brigante placed his hand on Culain's shoulder. "It was not your doing, Lance Lord. You are not responsible."

"I know, and yet I might have saved them."

"Some things are beyond even your great powers. At least Uther and his son are still alive."

"For how long?"

Prasamaccus said nothing.

"There are other matters to concern us," said Oleg softly, pointing to the east, where a large group of armed men could be seen riding at speed toward the hill.

"Goths!" said Prasamaccus. "What can they want here?"

"They are here to kill the king," said Culain, rising smoothly and taking up his silver staff. Twisting it at the center, he produced two short swords, then spun and ran toward the causeway. Halfway down the hill he turned and called to Prasamaccus.

"Hide, man! This is not the place for a cripple."

"He's right," said Oleg, "though he could have been less blunt. There are some bushes down there."

"What of you?"

"I owe Cormac my life. If those men seek to kill the king, I don't doubt they'll also butcher the boy."

Without another word he sped down the hill to the mud-covered causeway; it was a mere six feet wide, and the footing was treacherous. Carefully Oleg made his way some thirty feet along it to where Culain stood waiting.

"Welcome," said Culain. "I applaud your courage—if not your wisdom."

"We cannot hold this bridge," said Oleg. "Weight of numbers will force us back, and once we are on level ground, they will overwhelm us."

"Now would be an exceptionally good time to think of a second strategy," observed the Lance Lord as the Goths drew rein at the end of the causeway.

"I was just making conversation," replied Oleg. "Do you object to me taking the right side?"

Culain smiled and shook his head. Oleg moved warily to the right as the Goths dismounted and several of them moved onto the causeway.

"They do not appear to have any bowmen in their ranks," said Oleg.

An arrow sliced through the air, and Culain's sword flashed up, swatting it aside just before it reached Oleg's chest.

A second followed, then a third. Culain ducked the one, then blocked the other with his sword.

"You are very skilled," said Oleg. "Perhaps you can teach me that trick on another day."

The Goths charged before Culain could reply. They could only come two abreast. Culain moved forward, blocking a slashing cut and disemboweling the first man. Oleg ducked under a wild slash and hammered his fist to the other warrior's jaw, spinning him unconscious to the water, where he sank without a struggle, his heavy armor dragging him to the bottom.

Culain's swords were shimmering arcs of silver steel as he wove a terrible web of death among the warriors who were pushing forward. Beside him Oleg Hammerhand fought with all the skill he could muster. Yet both men were forced inexorably toward the isle.

The Goths fell back momentarily, and Culain, breathing hard, steadied himself. Blood was flowing from a shallow cut to his temple and a deeper wound in his shoulder. Oleg had suffered wounds to his thigh and side. Yet still they stood.

From the hillside Prasamaccus could only watch in sad admiration as the two men tried to do the impossible. The sun was sinking in glory behind them, and the water shone red in the dusk. Once more the Goths surged forward, only to be met by cold steel and courage.

Culain slipped, and a sword pierced his side, but his own blade swept up through the enemy's groin, and the man screamed and fell back. Scrambling to his feet, Culain blocked another blow and slashed his second sword in a vicious cut through his attacker's throat. Oleg Hammerhand was dying. One lung was pierced, and blood frothed over his beard; a sword blade jutted from his belly, the wielder dead from an instinctive riposte.

But with a bellowing roar of rage and frustration Oleg charged into the Goths' ranks, his great weight smashing men from their feet. Swords cut at him from every side, and even as he died, his fist crashed into a man's neck to snap it instantly. As he fell, Culain rushed into the fray, his blades cleaving and killing. Dismayed, the Goths fell back once more.

Prasamaccus closed his eyes, tears streaming down his cheeks. He could not bear to watch the death of the Lance Lord, nor did he have the courage to turn away. Then a sound came from his right: marching men. Prasamaccus drew his hunting knife and limped into their path, ready to die. The first man he saw was Gwalchmai, walking beside Severinus Albinus. Behind them came the survivors of Uther's Ninth Legion, gray-haired veterans long past their prime yet still with the look of eagles. Gwalchmai ran forward.

"What is happening, my friend?"

"Culain is trying to hold the causeway. The Goths seek the body of the king."

"Ninth to me!" shouted Severinus, his gladius snaking clear of its bronze scabbard. With a roar the eighty men gathered alongside him, taking up positions as if the years of retirement had been but a midsummer dream.

"Wedge formation!" called Albinus, and the soldiers at the outer edges fell back, forming the legendary spear point. "War pace! Forward!" The wedge moved out onto open ground before the causeway, where the great mass of the Goths still waited for a chance to mount the mud-covered bridge. Enemy warriors saw the approaching force and gazed in disbelief. Some even smiled at the sight of the gray-haired veterans, but their smiles vanished as the iron swords cleaved their ranks, the wedge plunging onto the causeway itself.

A giant Goth hurled himself at Albinus, only to find his wild cut neatly blocked and a gladius slicing into his neck. "Horns!" shouted Albinus. The veterans swung the line into the feared bull's horns and half encircled the dismayed Goths. They fell back in disorder, seeking to regroup on higher ground. "At them!" shouted Albinus, and the men at the center of the line charged. It was too much for the Goths, who broke and ran. On the causeway Culain, bleeding from a dozen wounds, saw the men facing him leap into the water rather than encounter the veterans of the Ninth. Despite their struggles to reach the shore, many of them were hauled below the surface by the weight of their armor. Culain fell to his knees, a terrible weariness sweeping over him.

His swords slipped from his hands.

Gwalchmai ran to him, catching him even as he toppled toward the water.

"Hold the causeway. They will return," Culain whispered.

"I will carry you to the isle; they'll heal you."

Gwalchmai's huge arms gathered him up, and the old

Cantii warrior staggered along the causeway to where several women were watching the battle.

"Help me!" he said, and they came forward hesitantly, taking his burden. Together they carried the dying man to the round hall.

Laitha watched them come, her face without expression as they laid him down on the mosaic floor with a rolled cloak under his head.

"Save him," said Gwalchmai. A woman opened Culain's tunic, looked at the terrible wounds, and closed it again. "Magic! Use your magic!"

"He is beyond magic," said another woman softly. "Let him pass peacefully."

Prasamaccus joined them, kneeling by Culain's side.

"You and Oleg killed thirty-one of them. You were magnificent," he said. "And Albinus has his men guarding the causeway and others patrolling the lake. More are coming every day; we will protect the king and his son."

Culain's eyes opened. "Gian?"

"She is not here," said Prasamaccus.

"Tell her . . ." Blood bubbled from his ruptured lungs.

"Culain? Dear God! Culain?"

"He is gone, my friend," said Gwalchmai.

Prasamaccus closed the dead eyes and pushed himself wearily to his feet. In the doorway he saw Laitha, her eyes wide.

"He asked for you," he said, his voice accusing. "And you could not grant him even that. Where is your soul, Gian? You wear the robes of a Christian. Where is your love?"

Without a word she turned and was gone.

◊ 16 ◊

LEKKY, HER HAIR washed and her thin body scrubbed by Karyl, sat on a horse, gazing down from a great height at the countryside around her. Behind her sat her father, the tallest and strongest man in the world. Nothing could harm her now. She wished her father had not forgotten how to speak the language of their people, but even so, his smile was like the dawn sun and his hands were soft and very gentle.

She glanced down at her new tunic of gray wool edged with black thread. It was warm and soft, just like the small sheepskin boots Karyl had given her. She had never worn footwear of any kind, and the sensation was more pleasant than she could ever have imagined as she wriggled her toes against the soft wool. Her father tapped her shoulder and pointed into the sky.

Swans were flying in a V formation, their long necks straight as arrows.

The horse Asta had given them was an elderly mare of sixteen hands, swaybacked and slow. But Lekky had never ridden a horse, and to her it was a charger of infinite strength that could outride any of the warhorses of the Goths.

They stopped for a meal when the sun was at its height,

and Lekky ran around the clearing in her new boots, never having to worry about sharp stones beneath her feet. And her father played a silly game, pointing at obvious objects such as the trees and sky and roots and giving them strange names. They were easy to remember, and he seemed pleased when she did so.

In the afternoon, close to dusk, she saw Goths in the distance riding toward them on the road. Father steered the mare into the trees, and they dismounted until the Goths had passed. But she was not frightened; there were fewer than twenty of them, and she knew Father could kill them all.

Later they camped in a shallow cave, and he wrapped her in blankets and sat with her, singing songs in his strange, melodious language. He was not a good singer—not like old Snorri—but she lay calmly in the firelight, staring up at the most wonderful face in the world, until at last her eyes drifted closed and she slipped into a dreamless sleep.

Galead sat and watched her for a long time. Her face was oval and pretty. One day she would be a beauty, and boys would come from miles around to pay court at her door, especially if she kept the habit of tilting her head and smiling knowingly, as she had when he had tried to teach her the basics of his language.

His smile faded. What are you thinking of, you fool? he asked himself. The country was at war, and even if by some miracle the Goths were beaten back, the Saxons would rise, or the Jutes, or the Angles, or any of the multitude of tribesmen. What chance would Lekky have of living a gentle life?

He settled down beside her, banked up the fire, and

rested his head on his arm. Sleep came swiftly, but with it came dreams . . .

He saw a giant figure outlined against the stars, clouds swirling around its knees. The head was terrible, with eyes of fire and teeth of sharp iron, and its hand was reaching slowly for a great sword that floated blade-downward in the sky. On the other side of the blade, turned away from it, was a beautiful woman. Then above the scene appeared a blazing, moving star like a great silver coin racing across the heavens. The giant warrior cowered from the star, and the sword seemed to shrink. The scene shifted, and he watched the Blood King, naked and alone in the courtyard at Eboracum. As the beasts issued from the yawning tunnel, he hurled his sword into the air and called out a single word.

Then Galead found himself sitting in a terraced garden, the sense of peace and tranquillity total. He knew who would be there.

"Welcome," said Pendarric.

"I could stay here forever," Galead said, and Pendarric smiled.

"I am glad you can feel the harmony. What have you learned, young knight?"

"Little that I did not know. What became of the old man, Caterix?"

"He found his friends and is safe."

"And the robber?"

"Returned to the forest."

"To kill again?"

"Perhaps, but it does not lessen the deed. You are journeying to the Isle of Crystal?"

"Yes."

"Uther is there."

"Alive?"

"That is yet to be established. You must find the lady Morgana and tell her to follow once more the advice of Pendarric. Do you understand your dreams?"

"No, save that the giant is Wotan and the sword is Uther's."

"The star is a comet that moves across the heavens once in every man's lifetime. It is made of Sipstrassi, and when it comes close, it draws its magic back to its heart. A long time ago a piece of that comet crashed into our world, giving birth to magic. Now, as it passes once more, it will draw some of that magic away. There will be a moment, Galead—and you will know it—when the fate of the world hangs in the balance. When that moment comes, tell the sword wielder to give you his blade. Raise it high and wish for whatever you will."

"Why is it that you never speak plainly? Is this all a game to you?"

Pendarric shook his head. "Do you not think I would gladly give you the wisdom to help the world? But that is not the way the mystery is passed on. It never was. For each man life is a journey toward knowledge and answers to the eternal questions: Who am I? Why am I here? If I tell you to go to a certain place and speak a word of power, what have you learned save that Pendarric is a sorcerer? But if I say to you to go to a certain place and say what is in your heart, and that proves to be a word of power, then you have learned something far greater. You will have stepped to the circle of mystery, and you will progress to its center. Caterix understood this when he aided the robber, though his heart urged him to let the man die. You also may come to understand."

"And if I do not?"

"Then evil will be triumphant, and the world will remain the same."

"Why must that responsibility be mine?"

"Because you are the one least able to cope with it. You have journeyed far, Prince Ursus, from the grasping, lecherous prince to the knight Galead who rescues a child. Continue on your journey."

Galead awoke soon after dawn. Lekky slept on, and he prepared a bowl of hot oats mixed with honey from the food store Karyl had supplied. After breakfast he saddled the mare, and they set off toward the northwest.

In the middle of the morning, as he rode into a small wood, he found himself facing a dozen riders, all wearing the horned helms of the Goths. He drew rein and stared at the cold-eyed men while Lekky shrank against him, shivering with fear.

The leader rode forward and spoke in Saxon.

"I am from Gaul," Ursus answered in the Sicambrian tongue.

The man looked surprised. "You are a long way from home," he said. The other riders moved closer, swords in their hands.

Galead prepared to hurl Lekky from the saddle and fight to the last.

"Indeed I am. But then, so are you."

"Who is the child?"

"An orphan. Her village was destroyed, and her mother slain."

"Such is war," said the man, shrugging. He rode still closer. Lekky's eyes were wide with terror as he leaned in toward her, and Galead tensed, his hand edging toward his sword.

"What is your name, little one?" the rider asked in Saxon.

"Lekky."

"Do not be frightened."

"I am not frightened," she said. "My father is the greatest of killers and will slay you all if you do not go away."

"Then I think we had better go away," he said, smiling. Straightening in the saddle, he returned his gaze to Galead.

"She is a brave girl," he said, switching to Sicambrian. "I like her. Why does she say you are her father?"

"Because I now have that honor."

"I am Saxon myself," said the man, "so I know what an honor it is. Be good to her."

Waving his arm, the man led the riders past the astonished Galead and continued on his way. The Goths rode on for several hundred yards, then the leader reined in once more and stared back at the single rider.

"Why did we not kill him?" asked his second in command. "He was not Saxon."

The leader shrugged. "Damned if I know! I left this cursed country seven years ago and swore I would never come back. I had a pregnant wife here. And I have been thinking of finding her—and my son. I was just thinking of her when the rider appeared, and it caught me off my guard."

"We could always ride back and kill him."

"No, let him go. I liked the child."

Wotan led Anduine through a maze of corridors to a small group of rooms deep in the heart of the fortress. At the center of the main room was a dark round table on which sat a skull with a circlet of what appeared to be silver embedded in the bone of the brow. He pulled a chair close to the table.

"Sit!" he commanded, and placed one hand on the skull and the other on Anduine's head. She felt a great drowsiness seeping over her and in a moment of panic fought against it, but the need to sleep was overpowering, and she faded into it.

Wotan closed his eyes . . .

. . . and opened them in his tent outside Vindocladia, less than a day's march from the Great Circle at Sorviodunum.

"Tsurai!" he called. At once, the tent flap opened and his aide stepped into view, his swarthy features taut with fear. Wotan smiled.

"Fetch the girl Rhiannon."

"Yes, lord."

Minutes later two men ushered the girl into the tent, where Wotan now sat on the wooden throne. He dismissed the guards and gazed down on her face as she knelt before him.

"You led my guards to the traitor Oleg," he said, "but he escaped?"

"Yes, my lord."

"And his companions were slain?"

She nodded dumbly, aware of the glint in his eye and the chilling sibilance of his words.

"But you did not mention the names of his companions."

"They were not traitors, lord, merely Britons."

"You lie!" he hissed. "One of them was the princess from Raetia."

Rhiannon scrambled to her feet, desperate to escape the burning eyes. He lifted his hand, and as she reached the tent entrance, she felt a numbing force close around her waist, dragging her back.

"You should not have lied to me, pretty one," he whispered as she was hurled to the ground at his feet. His hand descended to touch her brow, and her eyes closed.

He lifted the sleeping body and laid it on the silk covers of the bed beyond the throne. His hands covered her face, and his eyes closed in concentration. When he opened them and removed his hands, the features of Rhiannon had disappeared, to be replaced by the oval beauty that had been Anduine. He drew a deep breath, calming himself for the call, then placed his thumbs gently on the eyes of the sleeping woman. A shuddering breath filled her lungs, and her hands twitched.

He stood back. "Awake, Anduine," he said.

She sat up and blinked, then rose from the bed, moving to the tent flap and staring in silent wonder at the sky. When she turned back, there were tears in her eyes.

"How did you do this?" she asked.

"I am a god," he told her.

Deep in the abyss of the Void, Rhiannon also opened her eyes . . .

And her screams were pitiful.

Galead and Lekky arrived at the lake at sundown two days after the veterans of the Ninth had secured the causeway, which was now under water as the tide was at its height. As was the Roman way, a temporary fort had been established within the clearing: earth walls had been thrown up, patrolled by straight-backed warriors of the deadliest fighting force ever to march into battle.

Galead was stopped at the entrance by two sentries, one of whom fetched Severinus Albinus. The general had twice met Ursus but had never seen the blond warrior the Merovingian had become. Dismounting, Galead explained that he had been with Victorinus in Gaul. Then he was led to a timber structure and told to wait for Gwalchmai. Lekky was given some soup, and Galead settled down beside her at a rough-hewn table. After an hour Gwalchmai entered with Prasamaccus alongside him. Lekky was asleep in Galead's lap, her head resting on his chest.

"Who is it you say you are?" asked the tall Cantii.

"I was Ursus, but the king used his power to change my face so that I would not be recognized as a Merovingian noble. My name is now Galead. I was sent with Victorinus."

"And where is he?"

"He feared treachery and bade me make my own way. I think he is dead."

"And how do we know you are no traitor?"

"You do not," he said simply. "And I would not blame you for your fears. A man appeared to me and told me to come to the isle; he said I should seek the woman who ruled here. I think it is important that I at least meet her; you can have me guarded."

"Who was this man?" Gwalchmai asked.

"He said his name was Pendarric."

"What did he look like?" asked Prasamaccus.

"Golden hair, around thirty years old, maybe more."

"And what were you to say to the lady?" continued the Brigante.

"I was to urge her to once more follow the advice of Pendarric."

"Do you know what was meant?"

"No."

Prasamaccus sat down, and both Britons questioned Galead at length about his journey and the instructions he had received from Uther. At last satisfied, they led him to a shallow-hulled boat, and with Lekky still asleep in his arms, Galead sat at the stern and felt the peace of the isle sweep over him.

They beached the boat in a tree-shadowed bay and walked up to the settlement. Galead saw that it was constructed as a great circle of twelve huts built in a ring about a round hall. The perimeter was walled with timber, though not like a fort, more like a high fence. Several women in dark robes moved across the clearing, ignoring the newcomers, who walked to a hut on the western side of the circle. Inside there were rugs and blankets, pottery jugs, and a small iron brazier glowing with coals. Galead laid Lekky down and covered her with a blanket.

"Your sword," said Gwalchmai as Galead straightened. Pulling it clear, he handed it hilt first to the Cantii. Prasamaccus then searched Galead swiftly and expertly for any concealed weapons.

"Now you may see the king," Prasamaccus told him.

The three men made their way to the hall, and Galead stood silently, looking down on the two bodies lying side by side on the round table.

Three women sat close by, their heads bowed in prayer. Galead turned to Prasamaccus.

"Is there nothing we can do?"

The Brigante shook his head. The far door opened, and Laitha entered. Prasamaccus and Gwalchmai both bowed, and she approached Galead.

"Yet another wanderer," she said. "And what do you desire?"

"You are the Lady of the Isle?"

"I am Morgana."

He gave her Pendarric's message and saw her smile. "Well," she said, "that is a simple matter, for he once told me to raise my hand high in the air and grasp whatever I found." She lifted a slender arm, clenched her fist, and brought it down to hold it before Galead's face. Her fingers opened. "There! Nothing. Do you have any other messages?"

"No, my lady."

"Then go back to your little war," she snapped. He watched her depart and noticed that she had not even glanced at the bodies.

"I do not understand," he said.

Prasamaccus moved to his side. "A quarter of a century ago, in a world that was not this one, she stood on a hilltop and raised her arm. Her hand seemed to disappear, and when she withdrew it, she held the Sword of Power. With it she rescued Uther and the Ninth Legion from the Void and brought about the downfall of the Witch Queen. And Uther won back his father's kingdom."

"Then she is the queen?"

"She is."

"Pendarric was wrong, it seems. Who is the young warrior beside the king?"

"His son, Cormac. Are you a man given to prayer?"

"I am beginning to learn."

"This is a good place to practice," said the Brigante, lowering his head.

Lekky awoke in the hut; it was dark, and wind whistled in the thatch above her.

"Vader?" Fear sprang in her heart; the last thing she

remembered was eating the soup the soldier had given her. She threw back the blanket and ran outside, but there was no one in sight; she was alone. *"Vader?"* she called again, her voice starting to tremble. Tears flowed, and she ran into the clearing, where suddenly a tall figure in white appeared before her like a spirit of the dark.

Lekky screamed and stepped back, but the woman knelt before her. "Do not be afraid," she said, her Saxon heavily accented but her voice warm. "No harm can come to you here. Who are you?"

"My name is Lekky. Where is my father?"

"First let us go inside, away from the cold." She held out her hand, and Lekky took it, allowing herself to be led into a second hut, where a warm fire glowed in an iron brazier. "Would you like some milk?" Lekky nodded, and the woman poured the liquid into a pottery goblet.

"Now, who is your father?"

Lekky described him in glowing terms.

"He is with his friends and will come for you soon. How is it that a small girl like you rides with such a warrior? Where is your mother?"

Lekky turned away, her lips tightening, her eyes filling with tears. Morgana reached out and took her hand. "What happened?"

The child swallowed hard and shook her head. Morgana closed her eyes and stroked the girl's blond hair. Drawing on the power of the mysteries, she linked with the child and saw the raiders, the slaughter, and the terror. She saw also the man Galead.

She drew the child to her, hugging her and kissing her brow. "It is all right. Nothing can harm you here, and your father will soon return."

"We will always be together," said Lekky, brightening. "And when I am big, I shall marry him."

Morgana smiled. "Little girls do not marry their fathers."

"Why?"

"Because . . . by the time you grow up, he will be very old and you will desire a younger man."

"I won't care how old he is."

"No," whispered Morgana, "neither did I."

"Do you have a husband?"

"No . . . yes. But I was like you, Lekky. I lived in a village, and it was . . . attacked. A man rescued me, too, and raised me and taught me many things. And . . ." Her voice faltered, her vision blurring.

"Don't be sad, lady."

Morgana forced a smile. "We must see about getting you settled down; otherwise your father will come back to his hut and be worried."

"Did you marry him?"

"In a way. Just like you, I loved him as a child does. But I never grew up, and he never grew old. Now I'll take you home."

"Will you sit with me?"

"Yes, of course I will."

Hand in hand they returned to the hut. The fire had almost died, and Morgana added fuel, shaking out the ash pan to allow air to get to the flames. Lekky snuggled down in her blanket.

"Do you know any stories?"

"All my stories are true ones," said Morgana, sitting beside her, "and that means they are sad. But when I was young, I found a fawn in the forest. It had a broken leg. My . . . father was going to kill it, but he saw that I was very unhappy, so he set the leg and bound it with splints.

Then he carried it home. For weeks I fed the fawn, and one day we took off the splints and watched it walk. For a long time the fawn lived near our cabin, until it grew into a strong stag. Then it went away into the mountains, where, I am sure, it became the prince of all stags. From that time he always called me Gian Avur, Fawn of the Forest."

"Where is he now?"

"He . . . went away."

"Will he come back?"

"No, Lekky. Go to sleep now. I will stay here until your father returns."

Morgana sat quietly by the brazier, hugging her knees, her memory replaying the events of her youth. She had loved Culain in just the way Lekky loved Galead, with the simple all-consuming passion of a child whose knight had come for her. And now she knew it was not Culain who was wholly at fault. He had sacrificed many years to raise her and had always acted nobly. But she, from the moment he had arrived at Camulodunum, had used all her wiles to pierce his loneliness. She it was who had drawn him into betraying his friend. Yet Culain had never reproached her, accepting all the guilt.

What had he said that day on the tor? "The scrap of guilt" at her feet. Well, she had raised it to her face and taken it to her heart.

"I am sorry, Culain," she whispered. "I am sorry."

But he was dead now and could not hear her.

And her tears melted the years of bitterness.

Goroien stepped into the audience hall, dressed in armor of blazing silver with two short swords strapped to her slender hips. Cormac, Maedhlyn, and the Romano-Britons all stood.

"I will aid you, Cormac," she said. "In a while Gilgamesh will come to you and tell you that the army of the Witch Queen is ready to march."

Cormac bowed deeply. "I thank you, lady."

The queen said no more and left the hall without a backward glance.

"What did you say to her?" asked Maedhlyn.

Cormac waved away the question. "How can we be sure that Wotan will be absent from the keep? You said the men there are called Loyals, but they would not be loyal to something they never saw."

"Very shrewd, Prince Cormac," said the Enchanter.

"Leave the empty compliments," snapped Cormac. "Answer the question."

"We cannot be sure, but we know he lives in the world of flesh, and that will take most of his time. We have all seen both worlds. In which would you choose to live, Cormac?"

"I mean to keep faith with Goroien," said Cormac, ignoring the question, "and that means that I need to know what you plan. You have been wonderfully helpful, Maedhlyn. You were there when I arrived in this forsaken land ... as if you were expecting me. And that nonsense with the coin—you knew I was not dead."

"Yes," admitted Maedhlyn, "that is true, but my loyalty was to Uther—to bring him back."

"Not true. Not even close," said the prince. By then Victorinus and the other Britons were listening intently, and Maedhlyn was growing increasingly nervous. "What you desire, wizard, is to regain your body. You can do that only if we take Wotan's soul."

"Of course I wish to return to the flesh. Who would not? Does that make me a traitor?"

"No. But if Uther is released and returns to the world, he will attempt to kill Wotan. And that would doom you here forever, would it not?"

"You are building a house of straw."

"You think so? You did not wish us to come to Goroien; you argued against attacking the keep."

"That was to save your souls!"

"I wonder."

Maedhlyn stood, his pale eyes scanning the group. "I have aided those of your blood, Cormac, for two hundred years. What you suggest is shameful. You think I am a servant of Wotan? When Uther was in danger, I managed to escape this world briefly and warn him. That is why he still lives, for he managed to hide the Sword of Power. I am no traitor, nor have I ever been."

"If you wish to come with us, Maedhlyn, then convince me of it."

"You are right; I knew you were not dead. Sometimes I can breach the Void and glimpse the world of flesh. I saw you fall in the Caledones woods, and I also saw the huge man with you carry you into the hut and lay you on the bed. You wore a stone, and its power was unwittingly unleashed by your companion. He told it to keep you alive. It did—and it does. But I knew you were on the point of death, and I traveled to the gateway to await you. And yes, I want to return to the world, but I would not sacrifice Uther's life to achieve it. There is nothing more that I can say."

Cormac swung on Victorinus. "You know this man, so you choose," he said.

Victorinus hesitated, his gaze locked on Maedhlyn's.

"He always had his own game, but he is right when he says there is no treachery in him. I say we should take him with us."

"Very well," said Cormac, "but watch him carefully."

The door opened, and Gilgamesh entered. He was fully armored in black and silver, a dark helm once more covering his face. He approached Cormac, and as their eyes met, Cormac felt his hatred like a blow.

"The army is assembled, and we are ready to march."

Cormac smiled. "You do not like this situation, do you?"

"What I like is of no consequence. Follow me." He turned on his heel and strode from the room.

Outside the mountain entrance a vast horde of men and shadow beasts were gathered: red-eyed creatures with sharp fangs, monsters with wings of leather, scaled men with pallid faces and cruel eyes.

"Mother of Mithras!" whispered Victorinus. "These are our allies?"

Goroien stood at the center of the mass, surrounded by a score of huge hounds with eyes of fire.

"Come, Prince Cormac," she called. "March with Athena, goddess of war!"

◊ 17 ◊

THE KEEP LOOMED like a black tomb over the land-scape of the Void, a vast single-towered fortress with four crenellated battlements and a gateway shaped like the mouth of a demon, rimmed with fangs of dark iron.

Around it loped huge hounds, some as large as ponies, but of Molech's army there was nothing to be seen.

"I do not like the look of that gateway," said Victorinus, standing beside Cormac at the center of the shadow horde.

"Well you might not," said Goroien. "The teeth snap shut."

"Is there a mechanism that operates them?" Cormac asked.

"There is," said Maedhlyn. "Molech based that design on one I created for him at Babel; there are a series of wheels and levers behind the gateway."

"Then some of us must scale the walls," Cormac said.

"No," said Goroien, "it will not be necessary to climb them." Raising her hand, she called out in a language un-known to the Britons, and the beasts around her made way for a group of tall men, their skins ivory pale, dark wings growing from their shoulders. "These will bear you to the battlements."

"Do they know we are here, do you think?" whispered one of the Britons.

"They know," said Goroien.

"Then let us waste no more time," said Cormac.

Goroien threw back her head, and a high-pitched chilling howl issued from her throat. Her hounds leapt forward, hurtling across the dark plain. From the keep came an answering howl, and the beasts of Molech ran to meet them.

"If you cannot keep the gate open, we are lost," Goroien told Cormac, and the prince nodded.

Winged creatures with cold eyes moved behind the Britons, looping long arms around their chests. Dark wings spread, and Cormac felt himself sag into the creature's arms as it rose into the air. Dizziness struck him, and the beating of the wings sounded like a coming storm in his ears. High above the keep they soared, and now Cormac could see the armored warriors of Molech's Loyals manning the battlements. Arrows flew up toward him, arcing away as the winged beast rose above their range. Again and again the beast dropped within range, only to soar once more as the shafts were loosed. Around him Cormac could see the other winged carriers using the same tactic.

Then, without warning, they dropped together, and Cormac heard several screams from among the Britons as the keep rushed toward them. The bowmen on the walls let fly with their last shafts but hit nothing, and men scattered as the diving beasts spread their wings and beat them frantically to slow their fall. Cormac felt the arms around him loosen as he was still ten feet above the battlements. Bracing himself and bending his knees, he was ready when the creature released him and landed lightly, his sword sliding into his hand. Around him the other

Britons gathered themselves, and alongside him appeared the dark-armored Gilgamesh.

The winged carriers departed, and for a moment there was no movement on the battlements. Then, seeing how few the attackers were, the Loyals charged. With a wild cry Gilgamesh leapt to meet them, his swords a blur that cleaved their ranks. Cormac and the Britons rushed to his aid, and the battle was joined. There were no wounded or dead to encumber the fighting men. Mortal wounds saw the victim fall . . . and disappear. No blood, no screams of agony, no snaking entrails on which to slip and fall.

Victorinus fought, as ever, coolly and with his mind alert, missing nothing. He saw with wonderment the incredible skills of the warrior Gilgamesh, who seemed to float into action without apparent speed. This, Victorinus knew, was the mark of greatness in close combat: the ability to create space in which to think and move. Alongside him Cormac hacked and slashed in a frenzy, his passion and recklessness achieving the same result as the more graceful Gilgamesh, warriors falling before him like leaves before an autumn storm. Slowly the Loyals were pushed back along the narrow battlement.

Out on the plain the shadow horde had reached the gateway, and the teeth snapped shut. Once again Goroien sent up the shadow beasts, who harried the defenders on the battlements, swooping and diving, cold knives sweeping across unprotected throats.

Cormac dispatched an opponent, then leapt to the parapet and sprinted along the wall above the shadow horde a hundred feet below. A defender slashed at him, but he hurdled the blade, landing awkwardly and swaying out over the edge. Recovering his balance, he ran on, clambering up the outside wall of the gate tower and over the top to a second battlement. There were two warriors stationed there, both with bows. Cormac dived to one side as an arrow hissed by him. Dropping their bows, the archers drew short, curved swords, and together they rushed him. He parried the first lunge, his blade cleaving the man's neck, but the second man lashed out with his foot, spilling Cormac to the stone floor. His sword spun from his hand. Desperately he struggled to rise, but a curved sword touched his neck.

"Are you ready for death?" the man whispered.

A knife appeared in the warrior's throat, and he vanished from sight as Gilgamesh leapt lightly down to join Cormac. "Fool!" hissed Gilgamesh.

Cormac gathered his sword and looked around him. A stairwell led down to the gateway, and he moved onto it and began the descent. Below the battlement was a room, and—as Maedhlyn had said—it was filled with interlocking wheels and levers. Three men sat by the mechanism. Gilgamesh touched Cormac's shoulder and moved silently ahead. The men saw him, dragged their swords free . . .

. . . and died.

"You are very skilled," said Cormac.

"Just what I needed," responded Gilgamesh. "Praise from a peasant! How does this mechanism operate?"

Cormac gazed at the interlocking wheels, seeking the obvious and finding it. "I would say it was this," he said, pointing to the dark handle that jutted from the smallest wheel. Gripping it with both hands, he began to turn it from right to left.

"How do you know that is the right way?" asked Gilgamesh.

"It does not move the other way," said Cormac, smiling. "Does that not tell you something?"

Gilgamesh grunted and ran to a second door. "As soon as they see the fangs begin to rise, they will gather here more swiftly than flies on a wound."

Even as he spoke, the pounding of feet could be heard on the stairs. Cormac turned the handle as swiftly as he could, his muscles bunching and straining. The door burst open, and several men rushed in; Gilgamesh dispatched them swiftly, but others forced him back.

At last Cormac reached the point where the wheel would turn no more. Picking up a fallen sword, he rammed it into the mechanism and jammed it between the spokes of two larger wheels. Then he ran to aid the beleaguered Gilgamesh, and together they halted the advance.

From below them came the clash of sword on sword. The Loyals fought desperately, sensing that their doom was close. Shadow beasts appeared behind them on the stairs, and the battle ended.

Cormac pushed past the creatures and forced his way down to the gateway tunnel. Inside the walls all was chaos. He saw Goroien battling desperately against three warriors and raced to her side, his sword crushing the skull of the man to her left. Spinning on her heel, Goroien plunged one blade into an attacker's belly while blocking a slashing blow from the second man. Cormac killed him with a disemboweling thrust.

Everywhere the Loyals were falling back. Victorinus and the eight surviving Britons ran to join Cormac.

"The king!" said Victorinus. "We must find him."

Cormac had thoughts only for Anduine, but he nodded, and the group forced its way into the central tower, finding itself in a long hall. Men and women fled past them, desperate to find places to hide. One of them ran to

Cormac, grabbing his arm. He shook himself free but then recognized Rhiannon.

"What are you doing here?" he asked, pulling her clear of the melee. The Britons gathered around them in a sword circle.

"Wotan sent me here," she sobbed. "Please help me!"

"Have you seen Anduine?"

"No. One of the guards said Wotan has taken her back to the world."

"Back? I do not understand."

"It is a promise he makes to his Loyals. He has a way of returning them to life."

Cormac's heart sank, and a terrible rage began to grow. What more must he do? He had come beyond the borders of death only to find that fate had tricked him even there.

"The king!" Victorinus urged him.

"Lead us to the dungeons!" Cormac ordered Rhiannon, and the blond girl nodded and set off across the hall to a wide stairwell. They followed her down into a narrow torchlit, shadow-haunted tunnel.

Suddenly a taloned hand flashed out, encircling Rhiannon's neck. There was a hideous snap, and the girl disappeared. Cormac hurled himself forward, and a beast with the head of a wolf stepped into view, roaring with rage. Cormac rammed his sword deep into its belly, and it faded from sight.

Dungeon doors stood open through the length of the tunnel except one at the very end. Cormac lifted the locking bar and pulled open the door. Within was a shocking sight: a man covered in rats that tore at his flesh. Raising his sword, Cormac severed the chains of fire that bound him; the body fell, and the rats fled as the Britons came forward. The flesh of the man's body healed instantly, but his eyes were vacant and saliva drooled from the slack jaw.

"His mind has gone," said Cormac.

"Who could blame it?" Victorinus hissed as with great gentleness they lifted the man to his feet.

"Don't know," said Uther. "Don't know."

"You are with friends, sire," whispered Victorinus. "With friends."

"Don't know."

Slowly they led him from the tunnel and up into the throne hall, where Goroien sat with Gilgamesh standing alongside her. The hall was thronged with shadow beasts, which parted to make way for the small group of Britons and the naked man in their midst.

Goroien rose from the throne and walked slowly to stand before Uther, gazing into the empty eyes.

"There was a time when I would have been happy to see him this way," she said, "but not now. He was a mighty man and a fine enemy. When I was a child, my father used to say, 'May the gods give us strong enemies. For they alone will keep us powerful.' Uther was the strongest of enemies." She turned to Cormac, seeing the pain in his eyes. "And what of your lady?"

"Wotan . . . Molech . . . has taken her back to the world ith him."

"Then you must return there, Cormac."

He laughed, but there was no humor in the sound. He spread his hands. "And how shall I do that?" She looked down, and her eyes widened.

"However you do it, it must be done swiftly," she said, pointing to his right hand. A dark shadow nestled there, round and semitransparent.

"What is it?" he asked.

"It is the black coin, and once it is solid, there will be no return."

Maedhlyn waited in Molech's private chambers with a slender dagger in his hand. A light flared over the silver-crowned skull, and a man's shape formed in the air. As it became solid, Maedhlyn stepped behind it, his dagger plunging toward the back. With astonishing speed the man whirled, his powerful hand closing on Maedhlyn's wrist.

"Almost, Maedhlyn," hissed Wotan, twisting the dagger from his grasp and pushing the white-bearded Enchanter from him. Wotan moved to the doorway and stood in the corridor; then, stepping back, he shut the door.

"So," he said, "one empire falls. Well done, Lord Enchanter!"

"Kill me!" pleaded Maedhlyn. "I can stand this no longer."

Wotan laughed. "Give it time. You sent me here two thousand years ago, and now it is your turn to enjoy the unimaginable wonders of the Void: food with no flavor, women but no love, wine but no joy. And if you become so weary, you can always end your own life."

"Take me back. I will serve you."

"You have promised that already. You said that the boy Cormac might know the whereabouts of the sword. But he did not."

"I could still find it. They have rescued the king, and he trusts me."

"You will not find much left of your king unless I misjudge the many talents of the companions I left with him."

"Please, Molech . . ."

"Good-bye, Maedhlyn. I will pass on your kind regards to Pendarric."

Wotan shimmered and was gone. Maedhlyn stood for a while staring at the silver-ringed skull, then lifted it and made his way to the hall.

He knelt before Goroien. "Here, my queen, is a gift worth more than worlds. It is the spirit twin of the one Molech has in life. With it you can breach the world above and return yourself—and others—to the flesh."

Goroien accepted the skull, then tossed it to Gilgamesh. "Destroy it!" she ordered.

"But Mother!"

"Do it!"

"No!" screamed Maedhlyn as Gilgamesh dashed the skull to the stone floor, where it shattered into hundreds of tiny shards. The glowing silver band rolled across the floor, and Maedhlyn stumbled after it, but smoke began to issue from the circle and the band vanished. The Enchanter fell to his knees. "Why?" he shouted.

"Because it is over, Maedhlyn," she told him. "We had thousands of years of life, and what did we do? We set mankind on a road of madness. I do not want life. I desire no more titles. The Witch Queen is dead; she will remain so." She moved to Gilgamesh, placing her hands on his shoulders. "Now is the time for good-byes, my dear. I have decided to travel the road to see where it ends. I ask one thing more of you."

"Anything."

"See Cormac and the king across the dark river."

"I will."

"Good-bye, Gilgamesh."

"Farewell, Mother." Stooping, he kissed her brow,

then stepped from the dais and stood before Cormac. "Say good-bye to your friends. You are going home, peasant."

"We will journey with you," said Victorinus.

"No," Cormac told him, taking his hand in the warrior's grip. "You have your own journey ahead. May your gods accompany you."

Victorinus bowed and walked to Maedhlyn. "Come with us," he said. "Perhaps Albain was right . . . there *might* be a paradise."

"No!" said Maedhlyn, backing away. "I will return to the world. I will!" Turning, he stumbled from the hall and out into the Void.

Cormac bowed to Goroien. "I thank you, lady. There is nothing more I can say." She did not reply, and he took the king's hand and led Uther from the hall, following the tall armored figure of Gilgamesh.

Throughout the long journey Gilgamesh said nothing. His eyes were distant, his thoughts secret. Cormac's fears grew along with the coin that was now a dark and almost solid shape in his hand.

At last they reached the river and saw the barge waiting at the ruined jetty. The beast on it rose as it saw Cormac, its red eyes gleaming in dark triumph.

Gilgamesh stepped to the barge with his sword extended. The beast seemed to smile and spread its arms, offering its chest; the sword plunged home, and it disappeared. Cormac helped the king to the craft, then climbed in alongside Gilgamesh.

"Why did it not fight?"

Gilgamesh removed his helm and threw it out into the water. Then he stripped himself of his armor, hurling it from him. Taking the pole, he steered the barge to the far side of the river, holding it against the shore.

Once more Cormac aided Uther. Ahead of them was the cave mouth, and Cormac turned.

"Will you come with us?"

Gilgamesh laughed softly. "Come with you? The ferryman cannot leave his craft."

"I do not understand."

"You will one day, peasant. There must always be a ferryman. But we will meet again." Turning, he poled the craft away into the shadows.

Cormac took the king's hand and climbed to the cave. High above the light still twinkled, like a faraway campfire.

Slowly the two men walked toward it.

Cormac awoke to feel a gnawing pain in his back and an aching emptiness in his belly. He groaned and heard a woman's voice say "Praise be to God!" He was lying on something hard and tried to move, but his limbs were stiff and cramped. Above his head was a series of high rafters supporting a thatched roof. A woman's face appeared above him, an elderly woman with kind eyes who smiled.

"Lie still, young man."

He ignored the advice and forced himself to sit up. She supported his arm and rubbed at his back when he complained of pain. Beside him lay the Blood King in full armor; his red hair had grown, and white showed at the roots and the temples.

"Does he live?" asked Cormac, reaching for the king's hand.

"He lives," she told him. "Calm yourself."

"Calm? We have just walked from hell, woman."

The door opposite opened, and a figure in white entered. Cormac's eyes flared as he recognized her as the woman in the Cave of Sol Invictus, the mother who had left her child.

His mother.

Emotions surged over him, each battling for supremacy: anger, wonder, love, sorrow. Her face was still beautiful, and there were tears in her eyes. She reached for him, and he went to her, his arms pulling her to him.

"My son," she whispered. "My son."

"I brought him back," said Cormac, "but still he sleeps."

Gently she pulled away from his embrace, her hand rising to stroke his bearded cheek. "We will talk in a little while. There is so much to say . . . to explain."

"You have no need to explain to me. I know what happened in the cave—and before it. I am sorry your life has brought you such pain."

"Life brings us nothing," she told him. "Ultimately we choose our paths, and when they fail, the blame rests with us. And yet I have regrets, such terrible regrets. I did not see you grow; we did not share the wonders."

He smiled. "Yet still I saw them."

Uther moaned softly, and Laitha turned to him, but Cormac's hand took her arm. "There is something you should know," he said. "His mind has departed; they tortured him in ways I shall not speak of."

Laitha moved to the king's side as his eyes opened. Tears welled and ran back into his hair.

"Don't know," he said.

Her hands cupped his face. "There is no need to know, my love. I am here; Laitha is here." His eyes drifted closed, and he slept once more.

Cormac felt a cool breeze touch his back and heard the approach of several men. Glancing back, he saw a young knight with short-cropped blond hair and two old men. One was tall, his long white hair braided in the fashion of the southern tribes; the other was thin and slight and walked with a pronounced limp. The three stopped and bowed to Cormac.

"Welcome back," said the man with the braided hair. "I am Gwalchmai, and this is Prasamaccus and Ursus, who calls himself Galead."

"Cormac Daemonsson."

Prasamaccus shook his head. "You are the son of Uther, high king of Britain, and our hope for the future."

"Do not armor me with your hopes," he told them. "When this is done, I shall return to the Caledones mountains. There is nothing for me here."

"But you were born to be king," said Gwalchmai, "and there is no other heir."

Cormac smiled. "I was born in a cave and raised by a one-armed Saxon who knew more of nobility than any man I have met since. It seems to me that a king needs certain skills—and not just in war. I do not possess those skills, and more, I do not wish to possess them. I have no desire to rule the lives of others. I do not wish to be the Blood King's heir. I have killed men and slain demons; I have dispatched souls to the dark and walked across the Void. It is enough."

Gwalchmai was about to argue further, but Prasamaccus lifted his hand.

"You must always be your own man, Prince Cormac. You mentioned the Void. Tell us of the king."

"I brought him back—much good may it do you."

"What does that mean?" snapped Gwalchmai.

"His mind . . ."

"Enough!" said Laitha. "The king will return. You have seen him, Cormac, as he would wish no man to see him. But you do not know him as I do; he is a man of iron strength. The rest of you, leave us. Cormac, I have a hut prepared for you; there is food there, and Galead will show you to it. Do not overexert yourself; your wounds are healing well, yet still your body will be weak for a while. Now go, all of you."

For several hours Laitha sat beside the king, stroking his brow or holding his hand. Women came and lit candles, but she did not notice them, and as she gazed down on the careworn face and the graying hair, she saw again the boy Thuro who had fled to the mountains to escape the assassins who had killed his father. He was a sensitive boy who did not know how to start a fire or hold a sword. In those far-off days of innocence he had been gentle and kind and loving.

But the world had changed him, brought out the iron and the fire, giving birth to the Blood King of legend. It had taught him to fight and to kill and, worse, to hate.

What a fool she had been. This young man had loved her with all his passion, and she had spurned him for a child's dream. If there was one event in her life that she could reach back and change, it would be the night in Pinrae when the young Uther had come to her and they had made love beneath the two moons. Her feelings had soared, and her body had seemed more alive than at any other time in her youth. As the blood had pounded within her and her body had trembled in the ecstasy of the moment, she had whispered the name of Culain. The whisper flew into Uther's heart like an arrow of ice, lodging there forever. And yet—though she knew it not then—it was not the thought of Culain that had lifted her to such breathtaking heights but the love of Uther.

And she had destroyed it. No, she realized, not destroyed but altered . . . corrupted with the acid of jealousy.

Culain had once loosed the same arrow at her when they had been asleep together in a cabin near the queen's palace at Camulodunum. He had moved in his sleep, and she had kissed him.

"Are you there, my love?" he had whispered dreamily.

"I am here," she had told him.

"Never leave me, Goroien."

Oh, how that had hurt! How she had wanted in that moment to strike him, to tear at his handsome face. And was it not that one moment alone that had allowed her, later in Raetia, to spurn him, to send him from her? Was it not that whispered arrow that had caused her to be so cruel on the tor?

Uther stirred beside her. Once more his eyes opened, and he whispered the two words over and over.

"What are you trying to tell me?" she asked, but his eyes were without focus and she knew he could not hear her. Footsteps sounded behind her, and the shadow of Galead fell on the king's face.

"Cormac is asleep," said Galead. "May I join you?"

"Yes. Is Lekky well?"

"She is, my lady. She spent the afternoon with two of your women drawing unfathomable creatures on a flat stone, using up a great store of charcoal in the process. Now she is asleep beside Cormac. Is the king recovering?"

"He keeps saying 'Don't know.' What is it that he does not know?"

"They tortured him to find the sword, and I would

guess that he does not know where it lies. If he did, he would have told them."

"Yet he must know," she said, "for it was he who sent it."

"I saw his last fight in a dream. He hurled the blade high and screamed a name."

"What name?"

"Yours, my lady."

"Mine? Then where is the sword?"

"I have thought much on that," he said, "and I think I may have the answer. Uther could not have sent the sword to you, for he thought you dead. When Pendarric appeared to me, he spoke in what I took to be riddles, but in fact his words were plain enough. He talked of good and evil, and I thought he meant Wotan. He said that I should identify the real enemy, and then I would know how to fight it."

"And who is the real enemy?"

"Hatred is the enemy. When I saw the Goths destroy that Saxon village, I hated them. And it seemed such a small matter to find Lekky and take her with me. But bringing her here allowed her to meet you, and as you told me last night, it allowed you to see without bitterness. And now, as it should be, you are here with the man you love. And that is the key."

"Now you are speaking in Pendarric's riddles."

"No, my lady. Uther did not send the sword to a dead Laitha. He sent it to his love, thinking that it would never arrive and therefore no enemy would ever find it."

"What are you saying?"

"It is waiting, my lady. It could not come to Morgana of the Isle, only to the woman who has the king's love."

The queen took a deep breath and raised her arm, her

fingers open. A burning light grew around them, bathing the room in echoes of fire. Galead shielded his eyes as the brightness swelled, streaming from the windows and doorway and up through a hole in the thatched roof, a straight bar of golden light rising through the clouds.

In his hut Prasamaccus saw the glow outside the doorway and heard the shouts of the sisters who had gathered outside the round hall. Stumbling out into the night, he saw the hall pulsing with bars of flame. Fearing for the king's life, he limped toward the light, his arm before his eyes. Gwalchmai and Cormac joined him.

On the causeway the men of the Ninth stood in awed silence as the light spread, bathing the Isle of Crystal in gold.

Fifty miles away, in Vindocladia, the Goths also observed the phenomenon, and Wotan himself came from his tent to stand on a lonely hillside and stare at the burning light that smote the sky.

Back in the round hall, blinded by the brilliance, Laitha reached up and felt her fingers curling around the hilt of the great sword. Slowly she pulled it down, and the light faded. By the doorway Prasamaccus and Gwalchmai fell to their knees.

"He sent it to his love," Laitha whispered, tears flowing as she laid the sword beside the king, curling his hand around the hilt. "I have the sword, and now I must seek the man," she said. "Sit with me a while, Galead." Her head drooped, and her eyes closed, her spirit flying to a dreamscape of tall trees and proud mountains. Beside a lake sat a young boy with fair hair and a gentle face.

"Thuro," she said, and the boy looked up and smiled.

"I was hoping you would come," he said. "It is beautiful here; I shall never leave it."

She sat beside him and took his hand. "I love you," she said. "I always have."

"Nobody can come here. I won't let them."

"And what do you hope for?" she asked the boy.

"I never want to be king. I just want to be alone with you."

"Shall we swim?" she asked.

"Yes, I would like that," he said, standing and removing his tunic. As he ran naked into the water and dived below the surface, she rose and let slip the simple dress she wore. Her body was young, and she stared at her reflection in the water. No lines, no years of pain and disappointment had yet etched their tracks in her virgin beauty.

The water was cool, and she swam to where Thuro floated on his back, staring up at the impossibly blue sky.

"Will you stay here with me forever?" he asked, standing upright in the shallow water.

"If you want me to."

"I do. More than anything else."

"Then I will."

They waded back to the shoreline and sat in the hot sunlight. He reached out to touch the skin of her shoulder, and as she moved closer, his fingers slid down over the curve of her breast. His face flushed. Closer still she came, her arm slipping behind his neck and pulling his head toward her. Lifting her face, she kissed him gently, softly. Now his hand roamed free across her body. Pushing her back to the grass, he moved on top of her, entering her smoothly as her legs slid over his hips.

Laitha was floating on the rhythms of pleasure, and she felt those rhythms quicken and heighten.

"Thuro! Thuro! Thuro!" she moaned. She kissed his

mouth and his cheek, feeling the beard that grew there. Her hands stroked the broad back of the man above her, caressing the corded muscle and the many scars.

"Uther!"

"I am here, lady," he said, kissing her softly and moving to lie alongside her. "You have found me."

"Forgive me," she said.

"You shame me," he told her. "I treated you with disdain, and I forced you and Culain together. And for all your suffering I am sorry."

"Forgive me anyway?" she asked him.

"I do. You are my wife. And I love you now, as I have always loved you."

"Do you still wish to stay?"

He smiled sadly. "What is happening back there?"

"Wotan's army is approaching Sorviodunum, and the sword came to me."

"To you?" he said, astonished. "Then this is no dream? You are alive?"

"I am alive and waiting for you."

"Tell me all."

Simply and without embellishment she told him of Culain's saving of his body and Uther's son's journey across hell to rescue his soul. She spoke also of the terrible victories won by the Goths and lastly of the gathering of the Ninth.

"Then back there I have no army?"

"No."

"But I have the sword—and my wife and son."

"You do, my lord."

"It is more than enough. Take me home."

◊ 18 ◊

PRASAMACCUS, GWALCHMAI, CORMAC, and Galead waited at the foot of the tor, for the king had gone there soon after waking and had vanished from sight. Laitha told them to wait for his return, and for two hours now the men had sat in the bright sunshine, eating bread and wine. They were joined by Severinus Albinus, who sat apart from the group, staring to the southeast.

"Where is he?" said Gwalchmai suddenly, pushing himself to his feet.

"Be calm," Prasamaccus told him.

"He is back from the dead, but now he is lost to us once more. How can I be calm? I know him. Whatever he is doing entails great risk."

As the afternoon faded, Laitha approached them. "He wishes to see you," she told Cormac.

"Alone?"

"Yes. You and I will speak in a little while."

Cormac trudged the winding path, not knowing what to say when he reached the summit. This man was his father, yet he had never known him except as a mindless, wrecked creature rescued from the Void. Would the man embrace him? He hoped that he would not.

As he reached the crown of the tor, he saw Uther in

297

full armor sitting by the round tower with the great sword lying beside him. The king looked up and stood, and Cormac felt his heart beating faster, for this was no broken man—this was the Blood King, and he wore his power like a cloak on his broad shoulders. The eyes were blue and chilly as a winter wind, the stance that of a warrior born.

"What do you wish of me, Cormac?" he asked, his voice resonant and deep.

"Only what you have always given me," said Cormac. "Nothing."

"I did not know of you, boy."

"But you would have, had you not hounded my mother into fleeing to the cave."

"The past is dead," said Uther wearily. "Your mother and I are reunited."

"I am happy for you."

"Why did you risk your life to save me?"

Cormac chuckled. "It was not for you, Uther; I was seeking the woman I love. But you were there, and perhaps blood called me. I do not know. But I want nothing of you or your kingdom—what is left of it. I want only Anduine, and then you will hear from me no more."

"Harsh words, my son. But I will not argue with the judgment. I know the errors I have made, and no one can make the hurt less—or more. I would be glad if you would spend a little time with me so that I can know you and be proud. But if you choose another path, so be it. Will you shake hands, man to man, and accept my thanks?"

"That I will do," said Cormac.

Cormac walked back down the hill to the group, more

light of heart than he had been when he had climbed the tor.

Gwalchmai and Prasamaccus were the next to be summoned, and after them Severinus Albinus.

He bowed to the king. "I had thought to enjoy my retirement," he said accusingly.

"Then you should have refused the call," said the king.

Albinus shrugged. "Life was tedious without you," said the Roman.

Uther nodded, and the two men smiled and gripped hands. "Would that I could rely on other men as I can on you," said the king.

"What now, Uther? I have three hundred old men guarding the causeway. The latest arrivals tell me there are more than twelve thousand Goths. Do we attack them? Do we wait?"

"We go to them with sword and fire."

"Fine. It should earn us a splendid page in history."

"Will you come with me this last time?"

Albinus grinned. "Why not? There is nowhere else to run."

"Then prepare the men, for we will travel as we did once before."

"There were almost five thousand of us then, Lord King. And we were young and reckless."

"You think twelve thousand Goths are a match for the legendary Ninth?" Uther mocked, grinning.

"I think I should have stayed in Calcaria."

"We will not be alone, old friend. I have journeyed far, and I can promise you a day of surprises."

"I do not doubt that, sire. And I am no fool; I know where you had to go, and I am surprised they let you walk away alive."

Uther chuckled. "Life is a grand game, Albinus, and should be treated as such." His smile faded, and his eyes lost their humor. "But I have made promises other men may come to rue."

Albinus shrugged. "Whatever you have done, I am with you. But then, I am old and ready for a tranquil life. I have a crooked servant in Calcaria who is even now praying for my death. I would like to disappoint him."

"Perhaps you will."

Galead was the last to be called, and the sun was setting as he found the king.

"You have changed, Ursus. Would you like your old face returned to you?"

"No, my lord. It would confuse Lekky, and I am content as Galead."

"You found the sword. How can I repay you?"

Galead smiled. "I seek no payment."

"Speaking of swords, I see that you are no longer carrying a weapon," said Uther.

"No, I shall never bear arms again. I had hoped to find a small farm and breed horses. Lekky could have had a pony. But . . ." He spread his hands.

"Do not abandon that hope, Galead. We are not finished yet."

"Where will you raise an army?"

"Come with me and find out."

"I will be no use to you. I will never be a warrior again."

"Come anyway. The good sisters will look after Lekky."

"I have lost my appetite for blood and death. I do not hate the Goths, nor do I desire to see them slain."

"I need you, Galead. And leave your sword behind; another will take its place at the appointed time."

"You have spoken to Pendarric?"

"I do not need to. I am the king, and I know what is to come."

Lastly Laitha came to him on the hilltop, and they stood arm in arm, gazing out at the Sleeping Giants in the bright moonlight.

"Tell me you will come back," she said.

"I will come back."

"Have you used the sword to see Wotan's power?"

"Yes, and I have seen the future. It is not all bad, though there will be hardship ahead. Whatever may happen tomorrow, the realm is finished. We fought hard to keep it alive, like a candle in the storm. But no candle lasts forever."

"Are you sad?"

"A little, for I have given my life to Britain. But the men who will come after I am gone are strong men, good men, caring men. The land will receive them, for they will love the land. My realm will not be missed for long."

"And what of you, Uther? Where will you go?"

"I will be with you. Always."

"Oh, dear God! You are going . . ."

"Do not say it," he whispered, touching his finger to her lips. "I will come back to the isle tomorrow. You will stand on this hillside and will see my boat. And from that moment we will never be parted, though the world ends in fire and the stars vanish from memory."

"I will wait for you," she said, and tried to smile . . .

But the tears came anyway.

* * *

Wotan rode at the head of his army, ten thousand fighting men who had tasted only victory since he had first walked among them. The Saxons had deserted during the night, but they were not needed now. Ahead lay the Great Circle of Sorviodunum, and Wotan could remember the days of its construction and the mystery contained in its measurements.

"I am coming for you, Pendarric," he whispered into the breeze, and joy swept through him.

Slowly the army moved across the plain.

Suddenly there was a blaze of light from the circle, and Wotan reined in his horse. Sunlight gleamed from armor, and he saw several hundred Roman soldiers ringing the stones. Then a tall man strode from the circle to stand before the Goths. On his head was a great winged helm, and in his hands was the Sword of Cunobelin.

Wotan touched his heels to his mount and cantered forward.

"You are a stronger man than I thought," he said. "My compliments on your escape." His pale eyes scanned the warriors. "I have always believed you cannot beat a veteran for experience and strength under siege. But this . . . ? This is almost comical."

"Look to your right, you arrogant son of a whore," said Uther, raising the Sword of Cunobelin and pointing it to the north. White lightning leapt from the highest hill, the air around it shimmering. From out of nowhere came Geminus Cato, leading his legion. Behind the disciplined British ranks streamed thousands of Brigantes riding war chariots of bronze and iron.

"And to your left," hissed the king, and Wotan swung in the saddle.

Once more the air shimmered and parted, and thirty

thousand Saxon warriors, led by the forked-bearded Asta, marched to form a battle line. Grim-eyed men bearing long-handled axes, they stood silently awaiting the order to take their revenge on the Goths.

"Where is your smile now?" asked the Blood King.

The Goths, outnumbered six to one, fell back into a huge shield ring, and Wotan shrugged.

"You think you have won? You believe those men are all I can call on?"

He removed his helm, and Uther saw a glow begin beneath the skin of his brow, a pulsing red light that shone like a hidden crown.

The skies above darkened, and in the clouds the king could see a demonic army of taloned creatures wheeling and diving, tearing at some unseen barrier.

Without warning Wotan's horse shied before the king, scales appearing on its flanks, its head becoming long and wedge-shaped, fire exploding from its mouth. Even as the beast reared, Uther raised his sword, deflecting the fire to scorch the grass at his feet. The blade hissed down through the scaled neck, and the creature fell writhing to the grass. Wotan leapt clear, his sword snaking into his hands.

"As it should be," he said. "Two kings deciding the fate of a world!"

Their swords clashed together. Wotan was a warrior of immense power and confidence, unbeaten in combat since his resurrection. But Uther was also a man of great strength, and he had been trained by Culain lach Feragh, the greatest warrior of the age. The battle was evenly balanced; their swords hissed and sang, and the watching men marveled at the skill of the fighters. Time had no meaning, for neither man tired. Nor was there any evidence of supremacy as the battle continued. Only the demons moved, striving to break through the invisible barrier, while the warriors of all the armies stood silently awaiting the outcome.

Uther's blade cut into Wotan's side, but a savage riposte sliced the flesh of the king's thigh. Now both men were bleeding from many cuts, and the battle slowed. Uther staggered as Wotan's blade lanced beneath his ribs. For a moment only Wotan's eyes gleamed with triumph, but the king fell back and the Great Sword of Cunobelin swung in a high, vicious arc. Wotan, his blade trapped in Uther's body, could only scream as the blade smashed into his skull, slicing under the Sipstrassi crown and smashing the bone to crimson-streaked shards.

The Gothic king staggered back, calling on the power of Sipstrassi, but Uther rolled to his knees and hurled himself at the enemy, his sword ripping up through Wotan's belly and splitting his heart in two. Wotan fell, his body twitching, and with one stroke Uther cut the head from the torso. But the Sipstrassi still glowed on the skull, and above the heads of the army the barrier was giving way. Uther tried to raise the sword, but his strength was failing.

A shadow fell across him as he knelt in the grass.

"Give me your sword, my king," said Galead.

Uther surrendered it and toppled forward to lie beside his enemy as Galead raised the blade over his head.

"Begone!" he called, and a great wind grew, the clouds bunching in on themselves as lightning forked the sky. A beam of light shone from the sword, cleaving the clouds.

The demons vanished.

High in the heavens a shining light appeared like a silver coin trailing fire. Galead saw the stone set in the sword shimmer and pale. This was the comet spoken of by Pendarric, the moving star that could draw Sipstrassi magic . . . and Galead knew then what to wish for.

"Take it all!" he screamed. *"All."*

The sky overhead tore like a curtain, and the comet seemed to swell. Closer and closer it came, huge and round like the hammer of the gods descending to destroy the earth. Men flung themselves to the ground, covering their heads. Galead could feel the pull of the comet dragging the power from the sword, drawing the magic from the stone, and pulling the life from his frame. His strength wilted, his arms becoming thin and scrawny; his knees gave way, and he fell, but still he held the blade high above his head.

As suddenly as it had come, the comet was gone, and a great silence settled on the field. Cormac and Prasamaccus ran to the king, ignoring the broken, ancient man who lay on the grass with his bony hand still clutching the Sword of Cunobelin.

From the Great Circle there was a blaze of light, and Pendarric stepped into sight. Kneeling beside Galead, he touched a stone to his brow, and youth flowed once more into his veins.

"You found the words of power," said Pendarric.

"Has the evil gone?"

"There is no more Sipstrassi on the face of your planet. Far below the sea perhaps, but none where men will find it for a thousand years. You achieved it, Galead. You have ended the reign of magic."

"But you still have a stone."

"I have come from the Feragh, my friend. The comet was not seen there."

"The king!" said Galead, struggling to rise.

"Wait. Gather your strength."

Pendarric moved to where Uther lay. The king's wounds were grievous, and blood was streaming from the injured side. Prasamaccus was doing his best to stanch the flow while Gwalchmai and Severinus Albinus supported the body and Cormac stood close by.

Pendarric knelt beside the king and made to press the stone to his side.

"No!" whispered Uther. "It ends here. Bring the leaders of the Goths and the Saxons to me, Prasamaccus. Do it swiftly!"

"I can save you, Uther," said Pendarric.

"To what end?" Blood stained the king's beard, and his flesh was deathly pale. "I could not be anything less than I am. I could not live on a farm. I love her, Pendarric; I always did. But I could never be just a man. You understand? If I stay, it will be to fight the Saxons and the Brigantes and the Jutes—trying to keep the candle aflame just a little longer."

"I know that," Pendarric said sadly.

Prasamaccus returned with a tall, fair-haired Goth, who knelt before the king.

"Your name?"

"Alaric," answered the man.

"You want to live, Alaric?"

"Of course," the warrior replied smoothly.

"Then you will lay down your weapons, and I promise you that you will be allowed to return to your ships."

"Why would you do this?"

"I am tired of blood and death. Your choice, Alaric: live or die. Make it now."

"We will live."

"A good choice. Severinus, see that my orders are obeyed. There is to be no more killing. Where is Asta?"

"I am here, Blood King," said Asta, crouching before the dying monarch.

"And I will be true to the promise I made to you yesterday. I give you the land of South Saxon to rule and to govern. This I say before witnesses."

"Not as a vassal?"

"No, as a king, answerable only to your own people."

"I accept. But this may not end the wars between my people and your own."

"Not a man alive can end war," said Uther. "See that the Goths reach their ships."

"Is that an order, Blood King?"

"It is a request such that one king might make to another."

"Then I agree. But you should have those wounds treated."

Uther raised his blood-covered hand, and Asta took it in the warrior's grip, wrist to wrist. Then he rose and walked back to his host.

"Get me to the isle," said Uther. "There is someone waiting for me."

With great care the men around him lifted the king and carried him back into the Great Circle, where they laid him on the altar. Pendarric stood by, and the king called Cormac forward. "We did not have time to know one another, my son. But do not think of me with bitterness. All men make mistakes, and most suffer for them."

"No bitterness, Uther. Just pride . . . and regret."

The king smiled. "Galead," he whispered, his voice fading.

"I am here, my lord."

"When we come through the gateway, you will see a boat. Carry me to it and sail to the isle. A woman will be waiting there who knows that I lied. Tell her my last thoughts were of her." Uther sagged back on the stone.

Pendarric moved forward swiftly, raising his arm, and the king and Galead disappeared.

Prasamaccus cried out in his anguish and stumbled away. Gwalchmai stood dry-eyed, his face set.

"He will return. I know that he will . . . when our need is great."

No one spoke. Then Severinus Albinus placed his hand on Gwalchmai's shoulder.

"I do not know all your Celtic beliefs," he said, "but I believe also that there is a place for men like Uther and that he will not die."

Gwalchmai turned to speak, but the tears could not be held back. He nodded stiffly and walked away to stand alone at the altar, staring up at the sky.

Cormac stood by, his heart heavy. He had not really known Uther, but he was blood of his blood and he was proud. Turning, he saw a young woman running across the field, her hair flowing behind her.

"Anduine!" he cried. "Anduine!"

And she heard him.

Epilogue

GOROIEN LIFTED HER silver helm and laid it on the throne, her gauntlets and breastplate beside it. Her swords she kept. Then she walked down to the hall, through the silent ranks of the shadow beasts, and out onto the plain before the keep.

She could see the gray ribbon of the road wending its way into the distance, and upon it stood a shrouded figure. Slowly she walked to the hooded man, her hand on the hilt of a silver sword.

"Are you a servant of Molech?" she asked.

"I am no one's servant, Goroien, save maybe yours." He pushed back the hood, and she gasped, hiding her face in her hands.

"Do not look at me, Culain. You will see only decay."

Gently he took her hands and stared down at her unsullied beauty.

"There is no decay. You are as beautiful now as the day I first saw you."

She looked at her hands and saw that he spoke the truth.

"Can you still love me after all I have done to you?" she asked him. He smiled and lifted her hand to his lips.

"No man knows where the road leads," she said. "You think there is a paradise?"

"I think we have already found it."

Epic fantasy invades the era of Alexander the Great in tales that unite heroes of history with those of legend . . .

LION OF MACEDON: In every possible future, a dark god was poised to reenter Greece. Only the half-Spartan Parmenion could hope to defeat its evil. And so it had been foretold—Parmenion's destiny was tied to the dark god, and to Philip of Macedon and the as-yet-unborn Alexander the Great.

DARK PRINCE: The Chaos Spirit had been born into Alexander, but the intervention of Parmenion had prevented it from taking the boy's soul completely. But in another Greece where the creatures of legend flourished, a demon king sought the power of the Chaos Spirit. The demon called to the boy who would be king, and only Parmenion could hope to intervene.

"Gemmell works the reader's emotions adroitly. . . . It's a satisfying, often exciting fantasy that will thrill many readers." —Locus

KNIGHTS OF DARK RENOWN
The legendary knights of the Gabala had been greater than princes, more than men. But they were gone; they had disappeared through a demon-haunted gateway between worlds. Only one tormented knight had held back—Manannan, whose every instinct had told him to stay. But as murder and black magic beset the land, Manannan realized he would have to face his darkest fears, ride through that dreaded gate, and find his lost companions.

"A sharp distinctive medieval fantasy. Dramatic, colorful, taut." —Locus

MORNINGSTAR
Jarek Mace was an outlaw, a bandit, a heartless thief. He needed nothing and no one. But Angostin hordes raged over the borders, evil sorcery ruled, and the Vampyre kings lived once again. The Highland people needed a hero, and Mace inadvertently became that hero, a legend—the great Morningstar returned. But Mace was an outlaw, not a savior. Or was he?

"It seems that every time I read a new David Gemmell novel it is better than the last—and MORNINGSTAR is no exception." —Starburst

THE WORLDS OF DAVID GEMMELL

Author David Gemmell is hailed as Britain's king of heroic fantasy, and through sixteen of his most famous battle-charged adventures, Del Rey brings the action to American shores.

THE DRENAI SAGA: Experience the Drenai cycle that was launched with the international bestseller LEGEND. Meet the heroes of the Drenai people . . .

LEGEND: Druss was a legend even in old age, and he would be called to fight once more, to defend the mighty fortress Dros Delnoch, the last possible stronghold against the Nadir hordes.

THE KING BEYOND THE GATE: Tenaka Khan was an outsider, a half-breed, despised by both the Drenai and the Nadir, but he would be one man against the armies of Chaos.

QUEST FOR LOST HEROES: Among the travelers—the boy Kiall, the legendary heroes Chareos the Blademaster and Beltzer the Axman, and the bowmen Finn and Maggrig—lurked a secret that could free the world of Nadir, once and for all.

WAYLANDER: He was charged with protecting the innocents and journeying into the shadow-haunted lands of the Nadir to find the legendary Armor of Bronze. But Waylander was an assassin, a slayer, the killer of the king.

And don't miss these *new* Drenai adventures, coming soon:
WAYLANDER 2: IN THE REALM OF THE WOLF
DRUSS THE LEGEND
LEGEND OF DEATHWALKER

"Gemmell's great reading; the action never lets up; he's several rungs above the good—right into the fabulous." —Anne McCaffrey

THE STONES OF POWER: Tales of dark magic, sorcery, and conquest stemming from the Sipstrassi Stones of Power . . . a new dark age, a witch queen, a Hellborn army, and a man seeking the child born of a demon. Evil times call for bold heroes, including Uther Pendragon, Culain, and the famed Jon Shannow, the tragic figure known as the Jerusalem Man.

The Stones of Power Cycle
GHOST KING
LAST SWORD OF POWER
WOLF IN SHADOW
THE LAST GUARDIAN
BLOODSTONE

"David Gemmell tells a tale of very real adventure, the stuff of true epic fantasy." —R. A. Salvatore

"Gemmell . . . keeps the mythic currents crackling." —Publishers Weekly